# Freezeout

A JAKE MORGAN MYSTERY

# Freezeout

## Rick Gadziola

ECW Press

Published by ECW PRESS
2120 Queen Street East, Suite 200, Toronto, Ontario, Canada M4E 1E2

NATIONAL LIBRARY OF CANADA CATALOGUING IN PUBLICATION

Gadziola, Rick
Freezeout : Rick Gadziola.

(A Jake Morgan mystery)
ISBN 1-55022-689-4

I. Title. II. Series: Gadziola, Rick. Jake Morgan mystery series.

PS8613.A398F74 2005    C813'.6    C2004-907046-0

Editor: Michael Holmes
Cover and Text Design: Tania Craan
Production & Typesetting: Mary Bowness
Printing: AGMV

This book is set in Serif and Minion.

The publication of *Freezeout* has been generously supported by the Canada Council,
the Ontario Arts Council, the Ontario Media Development Corporation, and the
Government of Canada through the Book Publishing Industry
Development Program. Canada

DISTRIBUTION
CANADA: Jaguar Book Group, 100 Armstrong Avenue, Georgetown, ON, L7G 5S4
UNITED STATES: Independent Publishers Group, 814 North Franklin Street,
Chicago, Illinois 60610

PRINTED AND BOUND IN CANADA

ECW PRESS
ecwpress.com

*For Susan, Paul, and Marie.*

The greatest rush a gambler experiences
is betting and winning.
The second is betting and losing.
— Anonymous Gambler

*8:27 p.m., October 2, 1959,*
*58 miles northwest of Las Vegas*

The armor-reinforced Bugatti lumbered through the soft, shifting sand. Its long, bulbous nose climbed, pointing to the apex of some distant mountain in the darkening sky; it sank just as abruptly, while finely tuned cylinders fought desperately to drive the rear axle. A low, howling wind buffeted the vehicle as it skimmed over a dune and set down on the other side.

The driver muttered in Sicilian, "Questo deserto maledetto."

The passenger in the rear grinned at his trusted aide and countryman, then put a match to his thick cigar. "Relax, Mass." He puffed until the end glowed to his satisfaction. "You have driven this desert successfully many times, no?"

"Sicuro, Mr. Bonello. But not at such a late hour." And you never get used to the ridiculous whims of an old fool who claims he needs the quiet and solitude to practice his stupid cello, he wanted to add.

The times they had ventured out in the dark, from the neon-lit hotel to the starlit desert, almost always meant some other occupant wasn't returning. Those excursions, at least, were capped with a sizable bonus, while bullshit assignments like this fell under his regular duties. But not for long.

A moment later they reached a familiar landmark: a broken-down wooden tower surrounded by scrub cacti. The driver brought the Bugatti to a stop and engaged the handbrake. Carmine Bonello didn't need to order Massimo to stay in the car; he knew better. This was a weekly ritual.

Bonello pushed the rear door open and stepped out. Sand whipped at his face, and he forced his hat down harder on his head.

"Not so bad," he said to himself, pulling out a bronze-colored key on a finely linked silver chain from his vest pocket. He opened the trunk and took out a large black cello case. The weight caused the bottom end to drag slightly as he trudged around an eastern dune with a backhand wave to the driver watching through the side-view mirror.

Massimo cracked the window open a few inches and took a cigarette from a pack inside his jacket. He struck a match, and it shook, badly. Looking at his right hand in the glow, he remembered the woman from only a few days ago. His knuckles were still raw from causing so much damage, hitting her far too many times. He took in a lungful of smoke and held it for a moment before exhaling toward the window. He hadn't meant for that much violence.

"Steady, Mass," he whispered, once again unwilling to acknowledge that his troubles were his own damn fault. He had gone over and over the plan for the past three days and now had no choice. If he did nothing, he was a dead man. If he failed at what he had to do, he was a dead man. If he made it to the airport and out, he might make it to his twenty-sixth birthday before they found him. And then, of course, he would be a dead man.

Massimo shot the cigarette out the window and swung open the door. He was downwind, and knew the sound wouldn't carry, but he still eased the door shut as a precaution. Out of habit, he surveyed for signs of an ambush or witnesses.

Nothing but broken rock, one-story dunes, stumpy Joshua trees, and rolling sage. He would not miss this God-forsaken place.

Massimo reached inside his jacket and pulled free his Ruger Blackhawk. He had taken friendly teasing from some of his *compagni* because of his cherished weapon's long-barrel styling, so unlike their stubby-nosed S&Ws and compact Remingtons. He didn't care. He was in the old west, he reasoned. And besides, no one who had looked down the wrong end of the .44 Magnum had ever laughed.

Massimo checked the cylinder and cocked the hammer. He kept the pistol behind his thigh, pointed down, and made his way along the trail of footprints, staying close to the edge of each dune as he walked.

Although he knew his boss was doing more than playing his cello, Massimo had never chanced following Bonello before. If he had, and had been caught, he would have been buried right where he would have been shot. And up until now, he had valued his life. Still, he had a good idea of what Bonello was hiding, and it wasn't musical talent.

Massimo knew this area had been used for the American military's weapons tests, including the ones that produced the mushroom clouds, and the area was scattered with the occasional intact watchtower and bunker. It was the perfect place to hide what needed to be hidden — temporarily — from suspicious minds and prying eyes.

After a few minutes, Massimo heard the faint trill of whistling carried on the swelling wind. He hugged the side of the hill with his left shoulder and peered slowly around a piece of broken rock. Forty feet ahead Bonello knelt on one knee, fidgeting with a bronze clasp on the open case. Massimo was going to wait until his boss revealed the exact location of his secret hiding place. But then he noticed two things: a three-foot by three-foot wooden door against the side of the hill nearest Bonello, and the small mountain of cashier bags and elastic-bound packages of currency.

He bit softly at his bottom lip and after a moment decided not to wait. It was all there for the taking.

Massimo stepped around the dune and walked briskly toward the bent-over man.

"Ciao, bella," he called out from 10 feet away.

Bonello turned on his knee. "Mass?" An astonished look filled his face. "Ciao, bella?" he asked incredulously.

"I was talking to the money."

Bonello noticed the gun. "Are you fuckin' nuts?"

"Yeah, probably."

"I'm going to stand up. Relax." Bonello slowly stood, wiping sand from his pants and then his hands. "Look, Mass, whatever it is, we can solve it. We'll be partners in this load. You and me."

"Mr. Bonello, don't treat me like a fool. We cannot go back. I can never go back."

The wind was picking up, and both men used a hand to shield their eyes from the biting sand.

"If it's the money, no big deal," he reasoned. "I've heard. I know you're on the sheet for a few bad bets. We'll take care of it. I promise you, Mass."

Massimo forced a laugh. "Sure. Whatever you believe I owe, I probably owe 10 times." His face went solemn. "And Clarista is dead."

"What are you talking about? She went to L.A. to visit her sister."

The gun barrel rose. The time had come.

"No, I passed that story around the hotel. It gave me a few days to clear this mess up."

Bonello spoke slowly and distinctly. "You hurt Clarista?"

Massimo laughed out loud this time. "You think you were the only one sleeping with her? She was a fucking dancer! A dancer with a big mouth I had to shut. I didn't know it was going to be permanently."

"You piece of shit!" Bonello shouted over the wind. "After everything we have done for you. Do you know how far back our families go? Your uncles and me? You lousy piece of shit!" Sagebrush tumbled against his right leg, and he kicked it free. "I'll give you one more chance to put that gun down. Think about it."

Massimo wasn't going to think about it, and Bonello never meant to let him. In an instant, Bonello reached behind him and came out with his own weapon.

As he leveled the sight, a shot rang out. The white of his shirt went crimson; he was thrown three feet and fell on his back.

Massimo Turito walked toward the fallen body of Carmine Bonello. Once again he pulled back on the hammer of his pistol. Bonello had a gaping wound in his chest, and blood was gurgling from his mouth. The shooter held out the .44 at arm's length and then fired two more bullets into the dying man's head, just like he'd been trained to do.

Massimo bent over the cello case and surveyed the contents. There were three casino cashier bags, which regularly held $1,000 in coins. Wrapped in individual denominations, and mostly $20 and $100, were 25 to 30 bundles of bills. A quick count put the cello case's contents at somewhere between $60,000 and $70,000 dollars. Massimo let out a low whistle and closed the case. He was no accountant, but he knew that they had been driving out here almost every week for over a year and that the combined amount of what Bonello had buried had to be at least three or four million. And Bonello had a driver or two before him.

Massimo stood and again looked around nervously. The wind was picking up, and already sand was beginning to drift on one side of Bonello's lifeless form. He would have to hurry before the trail back to the main road was lost. He had planned to bring the Bugatti closer to the bunker to make the transfer easier, but his emotions got the better of him.

He had to see how much was really in there. He walked to the wooden door at the side of the nearest dune, reached out, held his breath, and pulled firmly at the rope handle.

The door lifted entirely from the earth and dangled in the air. Behind, there was only sand. What Massimo had thought to be the door to great wealth was just a piece of wood lying against a dune.

So it had to be around here somewhere. He circled where he stood and counted at least twenty to thirty mounds over a couple of acres of land that were high enough to have been bunkers covered up by sand and time. As if laughing at him, the wind picked up its low howl as it raced across the desert floor and channeled through the dunes. The sand began to sting as it whipped at his exposed skin.

Massimo dug his hands furiously into the side of the hill where the wooden door had been, but nothing gave way. He moved down 10 feet and did the same with the same results. He shouted something unintelligible and raced to another hill.

He located a broken piece of lumber and used it as a pick and shovel. He speared as hard as he could into the sand from one dune to another with no luck, and after 10 minutes he fell back sweat-drenched against the seventh mound attempted, out of breath and out of time.

"You stupid ass!" he howled against the wind.

Glancing at his watch and knowing the sky would soon be dark, he was forced to abandon his search. If he should escape from those who would come after him, he might return at a later date. For now, he would settle for what he had. He was still a rich man. He looked around wistfully one last time and thought, "But I could be so much richer. . . ."

At the Las Vegas Airport, Massimo turned the Bugatti into the darkest corner of the parking lot. He had discarded the bags of coins where he had found them, deciding their conspicuousness was more dangerous than their worth. The wads of bills were transferred into a suitcase he had brought in his own vehicle, which he had driven to the airport earlier that day. Leaving the Bugatti there would make it look like Bonello and Clarista had taken off to some secret locale.

Massimo started his car and made his way onto I-95, heading north-east toward Utah. He had second cousins who operated a funeral home in Buffalo and a brother-in-law with a small construction company in Niagara Falls, on the Canadian side. If he was lucky, stayed on the lesser-traveled routes, drove at night, and wasn't recognized, he might make it in a week.

If he was lucky. . . .

"Where the hell did you learn to deal? In jail?"

A wave of laughter came from the rest of the players as the loser fired his cards along the table in my direction. The cards skipped once, like a flat stone on water, and caught me on the chest. The winner gently tossed three red, five-dollar chips my way.

I was dealing a lively $10-$20 Texas Hold 'Em game to a bunch of big equipment conventioneers from the Midwest. It was just after 11, Tuesday night, and all 10 players were well lubricated and loud after touring the Vegas strip. The entire table wore Caterpillar or John Deere baseball caps in varying degrees of disarray. Some couldn't see their cards clearly, others belched and nodded off now and again, but they all tipped heavily. My shirt pocket was overflowing with red and green $25 chips.

I was probably more tired than they were, but the money was keeping me awake. I'd started my shift at four, after playing in an all-night-and-into-the-afternoon game myself. I'd had just enough time for a shower and shave before leaving for work. It was also the reason I stayed: the gratuities would help make up for the two weeks of paychecks I'd just lost. I had turned off my usual hostile responses to cards being thrown at my head and settled on a big smile.

They had slipped the manager a few greenies, too, and convinced him to let me stay on as their dealer for the night. Life was good. I was making $250 an hour, and they gave me a five-minute pee break every now and again. At this rate, and if they could stay awake until dawn, I'd have enough to get the exhaust fixed on my dying Chevy and get my ass out of debt. Well, at least one cheek.

"What can I say? I make one friend and nine enemies every hand," I apologized amiably, riffling the deck quickly. Time is money. Even more so in Vegas. "Now stop your whining, or I'm going to go deal for the Komatsu guys!"

This was met with a round of boos, and then I got pelted with peanuts, straws, gum wrappers, and a bunch of white one-dollar chips, which I happily changed into reds and dropped into my bulging shirt pocket.

"Okay, gents. Here we go." I fired two cards to each of the 10 players with the precision of a Lockheed Martin guided missile. "You can't win if you don't play."

During the hand, I felt a finger tap me twice on the left shoulder. It was McClusky.

"Come on, Morgan, finish the hand. I got a replacement comin' in."

McClusky was the gaming floor manager of the Oasis Hotel and Casino, a bit of a throwback to the "good old" days of Las Vegas. Back when the pit bosses were thick, ugly bastards, with leathery faces, broken noses, pinkie rings, and suit jackets that wouldn't do up. McClusky didn't wear a ring.

"Not tonight. Jimmy's letting me deal to our out-of-town friends here." I waved my arm from one side to the other. There was a noticeable air of discontent from the players at the table. "We have an arrangement," I tried to explain, puffing my chest out for him to see the small fortune accumulating in my shirt pocket.

"Piss on your arrangement. Mr. Contini wants to see you, up in his office. Pronto."

Contini was the "owner" of the Oasis. At least it was his name on all the official paperwork. He, too, was a bit of a throwback, but in an owner-like way.

"Hey, buddy," somebody slurred. "Leave our boy, Jake, alone. We want him dealin' for us, and we ain't gonna take no for an answer!"

A loyal round of "yeahs" and "screw yous" rang out in support.

"Stop it, you guys," I told them. "You're gonna make me all misty-eyed." I gathered the slush from the last hand and prepared to shuffle.

"Look, gentlemen," McClusky began in a soft voice, but loud enough to be heard around the table. "Have any of you met our Hold 'Em dealer Katrina?"

The table quieted to a few mumbles. "Katrina?"

"It's hard to miss her. She's about five-eight, platinum blond. Tiny little waist, a little junk in the trunk, and a set of ta-tas out to here."

Somebody croaked, "Out to where?"

"Out to here," explained McClusky, jiggling his cupped hands in front of him.

"Holy shit," somebody else cracked. "Really?"

"Yep, I heard she used to be a dancer or somethin'." He gave the table a big wink. "Up in Tahoe."

The players looked around at each other for a moment. Some tried to straighten themselves up a bit. Some squared their hats and wiped the sleep away from their eyes. Others practiced sucking in their guts.

"Well, we'll see ya, Jake!"

"If you gotta go, you gotta go. . . ."

"Duty calls."

I laughed out loud, split the deck, and left the cut card for the dealer coming in. "It's been real. I'll always hold a special place in my heart for you boys." I placed my hand over my chest, but it was closer to my pocket than my heart.

"Hey, Jake." A friendly player at the end flicked a business card down the table. "If you're ever in Peoria, or need to rent a skid steer or knuckle-boom loader, you look me up, okay?"

I picked up the Caterpillar business card and read it. "Thanks, Larry. I'll do that. Especially if I'm invited to your weekly game. I'd love to pick your pockets clean from the other side of the table."

A few of them laughed along with me.

"Yeah, fresh meat," one of them said. "Yum, yum."

McClusky grabbed me by the elbow and guided me through the busy card room. In the hallway, he let go but signaled for me to follow him.

"So what's up with Big Julie?" I asked, still slightly pissed at being pulled from my table.

"Dunno. He just called down and asked if you were on tonight. I was in the BJ pit and told him I'd find out. He asks. I answer. You go. End of story as far as I'm concerned."

Julius Contini was not a bad guy as far as owners of upscale Las Vegas hotels go. He was in his mid-sixties, having worked his way from some shady-type properties in the Catskills and Jersey in the late '50s to Vegas and "the boys" in the '60s and '70s. We'd become acquainted a while back when I'd saved his ass and the hotel's reputation in one of the biggest murder investigations to rock this town — outside of a Binion's.

We passed the high-roller $25 slot carousel that was usually located at a dead-end space of a casino because it didn't attract a lot of play. Tonight, however, a mini-mob surrounded some guy who lifted a bottle of champagne high in the air with his left arm while he "woo-hooed" a kind of train sound and pulled the handle with his right.

"Son of a bitch," McClusky growled. "The guy's been popping a buck and a quarter a yank, jumping boxes, and jerkin' us off for 72 large in just over 60." That was Vegan for "That lucky fellow is wagering $125 on each pull of the slot machine handle, selecting a different machine each time, and he's beaten the establishment to the tune of $72,000 in the past hour." McClusky didn't mind the players winning; he just didn't want them leaving. . . .

We finally came to an inconspicuous door behind one of the thick white pillars — Contini's private elevator to his penthouse/office. McClusky pulled out a key card and swiped it across a black panel on the wall. The door opened immediately.

"Okay, Morgan, you know the drill. Mr. C has a lot on his mind right now, and I don't want you pissin' him off and addin' to it. Understand?"

I gave him a big wink with my left eye.

"I mean it, Morgan, I really —"

The elevator door closed, and the ride up was quick and quiet. I barely had time to check the bags under my eyes in the copper-colored mirrored panels, rearrange my pocketful of chips, and pop a breath mint.

The door opened into the living room of Contini's quaint little home away from home: three thousand square feet of imported Italian marble checkered with elaborate Persian rugs, classic British colonial furniture, and irreplaceable artifacts from the Orient.

Contini sat in a tall leather chair behind a massive, mahogany desk, tapping a pen against a unique, antique telephone. The chair had been custom made to fit his body, and despite its modifications I was pretty sure his feet weren't touching the floor. He was about 320 packed into a five-foot-six frame, lavishly displayed in what looked to be Armani. His hairpiece-for-today was also by Giorgio, but not Armani. Giorgio Roma ran the trendy Hair to the Throne men's salon in the hotel's mall, and he and Contini went back to the days when Big Julie was Little Julie, and a dab of Brylcream just wasn't enough.

"Hey, Ace. Take a seat. How they hangin'?"

He was referring to the little adjustment made to my anatomy while working for him on the Valentine murder the past summer. I sat as instructed and crossed my legs to show him I could.

"The boys are doing fine, sir. Thanks for asking."

"Doc did a pretty good job on the schnozze, too. Straightened it out nicely. Working okay?"

"I can still smell a fresh C note from 10 feet."

"That's great." Contini stopped tapping and placed the pen in its holder. "Let's have ourselves a drink." He slipped out of his chair and made his way to an elaborate, miniature replica of an English pub bar. "What'll it be?"

I was pretty sure he hadn't asked me up to be a new drinking buddy, and I was still a couple of months away from my second anniversary working at the Oasis, but I went along with it anyway. "I really should be getting back soon, Mr. Contini. Just make it two of whatever you're having."

"With or without the nitroglycerin, Ace?" He laughed and pulled out two pink tablets from a yellow plastic case and washed them down with a glass of water. "Beer okay?"

"Sure."

Contini rummaged around in the built-in refrigerator and came out with two bottles. He opened both, brought them over, and placed one in front of me on a square coaster made of dark cork. He pointed the business end of his bottle at me. "*Salute.*"

I picked up mine and pointed it right back at him. "*Cin cin.*"

Contini reached into a wooden case on his desk, pulled out one of his trademark Cuban cigars, clipped off the end, and fired it up with a butane flame about six inches long. He puffed hungrily, until he got it going to his satisfaction. I had a terrifying vision of his toupee catching fire. And there I was with only a bottle of Corona.

Clouds of thick gray smoke dissipated quickly into the built-in ventilation above.

"Look, Ace," he finally said. "I need another favor."

This couldn't be good. "A favor?"

"Just a small one."

Why was I getting the feeling I'd rather grab a bite to eat at a roadside sushi stand in the Mojave?

"It'll only take a couple of days." He opened a small drawer in the desk and pulled out a piece of hotel stationery. "I believe you still owe me for your night of extravagance with that showgirl, what's her name?"

"Rachel."

"Yeah. Remember, I gave you a $5,000-a-night room so you could play hide-the-salami with the most beautiful broad that ever danced here?"

I sipped my beer and didn't say anything. It *had* been a good night.

"You still seein' her?"

"Uh, no. . . ." I put the bottle down on the coaster. "What kind of favor, exactly?"

Contini seemed pleased to have my attention. "Hardly even a favor, really. More like a paid vacation. With an expense account."

"A vacation, with expenses?"

"Yeah, you can look at it that way. See, I've got this distant relative of my wife's — a second or third cousin, niece, who the hell knows. Anyway, she's coming into town for a few days to visit family, and, well, you know what this town is like, my wife would feel so much better if there was somebody around to look after her, take her out, keep the scumballs away."

"You want me to escort some woman around town? I know my social life may be lousy, Mr. Contini, but I don't need to be fixed up." I could just imagine: some wrinkled spinster from the old country, dressed in black with knee-high stockings, and sporting a mustache thicker than my uncle Louie's.

"Listen up, Jake. You're not being fixed up. It's not a date. It's a favor!"

"If you're worried about her, why not use somebody from Security?"

"This isn't a goddamn work project. It's off-the-record. Personal."

"But why me?"

"Let's just say I liked the way you handled yourself with that little matter last year."

"That little *murder* matter?"

"You know what I mean. Security does a good job here, but that's mostly to watch the cheaters and scammers."

"And the staff."

"Yeah, well, that too. But it's what they're trained for. I want you because you've got the background with the cops, and you've got the street sense for something like this. And you've got a gift for bullshit, which can always come in handy."

"Thanks, Mr. Contini, but I don't know. . . ."

Contini rattled the stationery at me. "Oh, and apparently there was the small matter of a room service charge on the suite I loaned you. Twenty-three hundred dollars for lobster and champagne?"

I cleared my throat. "There was chateaubriand in there somewhere, too. Excellent, by the way. . . ."

The two of us played eyeball tag through the fine gray smoke of his cigar for a minute or so. Then I gave in. "Okay, give me the rundown."

Contini prattled on for a while, informing me that her name was Angelica Bonello and that she was from back east. Jersey, actually. There was a suite booked here at the Oasis in her name. He assured me that, based on the family lines explained to him by his wife, Angelica couldn't be over 30. She worked at some trendy New York City fashion outlet, so we decided she couldn't be a total eyesore. As far as the mustache went, Big Julie wasn't sure.

"You got vacation time coming up anyway, Ace. I'm going to give you triple time for this."

"I guess. . . . But how about a comp card for any hotel expenses or meals that may come up?"

Contini weighed his decision. "Okay, but no two-grand dinners. See Carl for that."

We chatted for a few more minutes while he laid out the instructions. "Just take her around to where she has to go when she wants to go. Big deal. You're a gambler, Jake. I'm paying you three times what you make whether you're needed or not. What are the odds she's going to take up that much time? If she decides to stay in her room for twenty-two hours a day, then you're laughing. If she wants to go see some sights, or go to a show, big deal, you're getting paid for it and probably still laughing." He raised his beer. "*Salute?*"

"I guess so."

Contini gave me a grateful smile, as if I'd just saved his ass back home. "Atta boy, Ace."

"So what day does this Angelica get in? I've got a few things to take care of."

His smile slipping, Contini looked at his shiny Rolex. "Well, that's the thing. She lands in about 40 minutes. . . ."

"*Forty* minutes! *Tonight?*"

"It was last-minute." He cleared his throat. "I told you it was some kind of family thing. . . ."

"Ah, come on, Mr. C. Not tonight." I couldn't tell him I hadn't slept in 36 hours. He would have had my nuts for coming into work ill-prepared. "My car needs a little work. Let me get it fixed tomorrow, and we'll start fresh."

Contini stubbed out his stogie. "I saw that piece of crap in the parking lot one day and told Security somebody had dumped a junker in our lot and to have it towed. They said it was yours. If my wife ever saw one of her family in that, she'd have my ass. Talk to Carl about getting a real set of wheels."

I wanted to bitch but didn't.

Contini glanced at his watch again and tapped its face with a shiny, manicured nail. "We don't want to be late for our first day on the job now, do we?"

*We* didn't want to be on the job at all, to be honest.

I lifted myself out of the chair, thanked him for the beer, and headed for the elevator.

Contini wiggled his way out of his chair and pulled out his wallet. He slapped a couple of $100 bills into my hand as we shook.

"This'll tide you over for a while. Remember, I don't want you turning down something she wants to do because you're too cheap. What the comp card and cash won't cover, use your own money. Keep track of everything, and we'll settle up later."

The elevator arrived, I stepped in, and Contini and I waved each other little tootle-loos as the door closed. This night was nothing but extraordinary. Damn right we'd be settling later.

Except for the pocketful of chips, and the money Contini had just given me, I was flat broke. Actually, that was a lie. I'd forgotten I was two paychecks in the hole from last night. Damn, the only thing I hated more than being broke was being *minus* broke.

# Chapter

The lobby was hopping. At check-in, a long line of impatient couples snaked between velvet ropes and chrome stands, fidgeting for action, to see either how hot they could get on the tables or how hot they looked in the mirrors over the beds in their rooms.

On my way through the casino, I took a few minutes to cash in my tips. With $340 burning a hole in my pocket, I did one of the most difficult things a gambler could do. I went by the work stations of three people I owed money to and paid them back. I also stopped by the Sports Book and dropped the $185 I had left over on the Mighty Ducks.

A quick check for Carl at the casino host office and I found out that he was fishing. Not in the literal sense. Although you probably could, in the middle of the night, somewhere in or around Las Vegas. No, if Carl was fishing, he was taking care of some whale with a minimum $1 million line of credit here at the Oasis. No one else around could authorize a corporate vehicle, so I quickly made my way to the valet booth to find myself a limo I could borrow.

The driveway beneath the brightly lit portico was teeming with taxis and customer vehicles arriving and departing. Octane and propane fumes fought for the attention of olfactory nerves, while car doors slammed, horns tooted, and whistles sung, as a platoon of attendants in floral shirts and khaki shorts shuttled vehicles in and out.

And if the truth be known, most of the valet parking personnel were in a high tax bracket. Well, they would be if they owned up to what they made in the cash-only occupation. Try getting the job. The money for opening and closing car doors and running up and down hot pavement could be so lucrative at some of the better hotels that you not only had to know somebody to get in but also had to pay that somebody to work there. And like the higher-end strip clubs, where the lap dancers had to pay the house a couple of hundred a day to shimmy and shake their goodies, so too did the valets. A couple of bucks or five from every car, in and out, back and forth, every few minutes, over a 10- or 12-hour shift added up. Not only that, but all that running also kept them in great shape for the single ladies arriving from California. The most enviable perk.

"Hey, Gary," I called out to the head valet, who was standing behind a small counter rearranging a wad of currency by denomination. "I need a stretch. Right away."

"Yo, Jake," he answered, sliding the money away as if I was the taxman. "Sorry, pardner, no can do."

"But Contini wants me to pick somebody up."

"Ain't got no wheels, my man. Give me an hour, and I'll fix you up."

"I haven't got an hour. They're arriving at McCarran in 30 minutes."

Gary gave me a big shrug of his shoulders. "There's always the company chopper."

"Yeah, right. With my luck, the airport pickup is some old biddy who has a stroke on the way in, and Contini blames me. Nah, as much as I'd like to take a ride in the hotel's whirlybird, I guess I'd better go get my car."

"Jesus, Jake, now you're making me feel real bad. That piece of crap is more dangerous than a 'copter."

I thanked Gary and began the trek to the employee parking lot situated around the back of the hotel. The smells of barbequed meats and poultry coming from the pool area reminded me I hadn't eaten dinner, and my stomach let me know with a couple of sharp pangs. Tuesday night was Calypso Night at the Oasis, and the sounds of people laughing and splashing in the swimming pool mixed with the beat of steel drums and the light chords of electric guitar. The thought of catching a quick nap on one of the pool lounges crossed my mind, and I couldn't decide if I was more hungry than tired. I fought off both urges and continued to the car.

The drive to McCarran was uneventful. Just outside the terminal, I gave the kid at the Hertz booth $20 and asked him to keep an eye on my car. He put his fingertips to his temples. "But it's starting to hurt my head, looking at it," he joked good naturedly. This town is filled with wannabe comedians.

The terminal was packed with people arriving fresh-faced and eager and those leaving with bloodshot eyes on red-eye flights home. The clocks all flashed 1:03 a.m., and the ETA on the flight board had a LaGuardia flight landing in two minutes. I hit the men's room and splashed my face with handfuls of cold water. I dried with another handful of paper towels and studied my mug in the mirror.

The guy looking back at me was on the wrong end of 39 and felt like 59. But in a city like Vegas, that was hardly unusual. If the desert sun didn't get your face, the hard living would. I'd been out here only a couple of years, but it felt like 10. Not that I couldn't have done something about it, I just hadn't bothered. I'd fallen in love with the place and a few of the people, and I still indulged the dream of making it big. I slapped myself hard on the cheek a couple of times, not sure if it was just to help me stay alert or remind myself what an idiot I was for having moved my ass out here.

I looked around the carousel area for the LaGuardia flight, but it was void of people and bags. There was a coffee stand nearby, so I headed that way. The girl behind the cart took my order for a double-double and laughed when I changed the order to a double-quadruple for the sugar rush. While sipping my sweet brew, I borrowed a black marker, tore off the bottom of a carry-out carton, and made an arrival sign in the name of A. BONELLO.

Another herd of disembarking passengers was making its way to the row of baggage carousels, so I dragged my sign, my coffee, and my sorry ass off in that direction. I took up a position between them and the exit doors, leaning back against a white tile column. I tasted the coffee and placed the hot cup on top of a stand holding a large plastic plant. The bags hadn't started down the chutes, so I crossed my arms with my sign facing out and rested my eyes.

♣

"Hey, mister! You waiting for me?"

The tugging on my shirtsleeve slowly brought me out of my reverie. "Huh?"

"The sign." She poked at the cardboard resting across my forearms. "That's me."

She was a girl/woman, somewhere between 16 and 25. Who could tell these days? At first, as my eyes focused, I thought I was looking at Britney Spears.

"Oh, yeah, right," I mumbled, looking around at the crowded terminal, fitting together the pieces of what I was doing out here. I picked up the sign and looked at it for a reminder but couldn't for the life of me remember what the A stood for. "Yeah, okay. You, um. . . . Yeah, A."

"You're so eloquent," she replied, rolling her eyes, and then looked around as if she was hoping to see another sign with her name on it being held by someone a little brighter. After a moment, she said, "It's Angelica."

"Right." The cloud in my head finally cleared. I reached over, found my coffee cup, and took a long drink. "Angelica Bonello."

A big smile filled her face. "Faboo!" she exclaimed, bouncing on the balls of her feet.

She was wearing a white cotton belly shirt, cut low, with a light pink satin jacket, and when she bounced all kinds of things bounced along with her. I suppose it could have been baby fat, but she seemed far too well endowed for someone so young. Her outfit was topped off with a deep red fedora and a matching pair of satin harem pants barely hanging on her hips. I caught all this in a split second since I was damned if I was going to be caught staring. At least not until I determined how old she was.

"Faboo?" I asked, keeping my feet planted firmly on the floor. After all, I had parts that lately were starting to jiggle, too.

"Yes," she squealed, flinging her arms out. "Faboo, like Las Vegas. *Fabulous!*"

"Ah, fabulous. . . . Okay, I get it."

Angelica crossed her arms and gave me a reproachful look. "Are you sure you're a limo driver? I hope Uncle Julius isn't playing one of his practical jokes on me. Aunt Sophia says he's a real joker."

"*Uncle* Julie?"

"Yes. Julius Contini. He still owns the Oasis Hotel, doesn't he?"

"Oh, sure." I was nodding my head, but *Uncle* Julie sure had some explaining to do. "Big Julie still runs the Oasis. And he's such a joker."

"I can't wait to meet him. Let's get my bags."

At the baggage carousel, I spent some time explaining who I was, my connection with the Oasis, and my responsibilities to her while she was visiting. I learned she was here to see an ailing grandmother and would probably be staying with her most of the week. It didn't sound too bad.

After a while, we located her luggage, and I carried the set of Gucci bags toward the exit. Angelica marched alongside with a matching shoulder bag.

The last few minutes had allowed me to get a better look at my newfound companion. Her youthful exuberance was only outshone by her extraordinary beauty. She was about five-eight, 130 pounds, with shoulder-length blond hair tied back in a ponytail. Her skin was light and flawless, and she was unafraid of showing as much as legally possible. She had a medium build carved with curves that were probably natural, not marbled in a gym. What little makeup she used was applied to bring the entire package together seamlessly. It was still impossible to determine her age with any accuracy, but she wasn't the 30 Contini thought she might be, and thankfully she wasn't sporting a hereditary mustache.

I couldn't help noticing the attention we were attracting from the people around us. Although I was still wearing my palm-tree-patterned corporate shirt, I could tell I was being mistaken by many for a sugar daddy just arrived in Sin City. Some of the looks from the women were that of disgust, while most of the looks from the men were filled with admiration, respect, and more than a touch of jealousy.

Angelica stepped out into the warm evening air and looked up and down the empty curb. "So where's the limo?"

"I'm parked over in the rental lot."

"How come?"

"For security reasons."

"Cool." She popped a piece of gum into her mouth. "Let's go."

♣

"You have *got* to be kidding! It's fugly." Angelica walked around the Chevy. "It's called a *what?*"

"A Vega. . . ."

"I was hoping an s had fallen off."

The rental car kid had come out to see what all the commotion was about. His big, goofy smile turned into an open-mouth gape when she came around the car and gave him a full frontal view.

She gave the tire a little test kick, and I cringed. If the axle broke and it fell to one knee right here in the parking lot, I would have been extremely embarrassed. "Okay," she announced. "What the hell. We're in Sin City. Let's gamble."

The rental kid shuffled over nervously. "H-h-hi. M-m-my name is M-m-m-marty. And m-maybe I could loan you somethin', you know, f-f-from here on the lot."

Angelica gave him the kind of smile a dental hygienist would have applauded.

"Okay, down boy." I turned the kid around, grabbed him by the back of his waistband, lifted him off the ground in what had to be an agonizing wedgie, and walked him to his little office.

When I came back to the car, Angelica was bent over, cursing, banging on the trunk.

"It doesn't work," I told her.

"No shit. I think I broke a nail."

I picked up her bags, opened the rear door, and piled the luggage inside. She laughed and shook her head, turned, and walked to the passenger side of the car.

"Uh, that door doesn't work either. You'll have to crawl over from the driver's side or sit in the back."

Angelica cupped her palms around her eyes and peered in through the rear window. "Is that the pavement I can see down there?"

"Some of the floorboard is missing."

She marched around the front of the car. "I'll take the front."

I held the door for her, and she smiled, leaned over, and began to crawl on her hands and knees. As difficult as it was, I averted my eyes from her bucket seat as she worked her way across mine. I noticed the Hertz kid peeking from around a curtain, transfixed at the sight of her expedition.

"Well," she said when she had wiggled herself into a comfortable position, "that was fun."

"More for some than for others."

She pretended not to hear me but afforded herself a knowing smile. "This thing have air-conditioning?" she asked, looking around the dash and playing with the vents.

"Yeah," I said, "see that handle on the door? Grab the knob on the end and turn it counterclockwise, like this." I rolled my window down four or five inches.

She did the same to her side. "Cool," she said, reaching into the back and pulling a soft pack of Marlboro Lights out of a small suitcase. She offered me one, and although I was dead-ass tired, mentally weak, and pissed off at Contini I declined. It had been too hard to quit for me to break down now. She slid one out for herself, lit it with a pink Barbie butane lighter, and tossed the pack onto the dashboard. I could tell by the big cloud of white she blew at the window that she wasn't used to inhaling.

I worked the key into the ignition, prayed she would start, and gave it a turn. All four powerful cylinders decided to fire, albeit a little out of unison. The tranny clunked into submission, the exhaust experienced a bout of flatulence, and the vehicle surprised everyone and began to roll out of the parking lot. I turned to my passenger. "Faboo."

# Chapter

"Been smoking long?"

We had turned out of the main terminal and were going west along Tropicana. The night air was warm for mid-October, and, not to be outdone by the hundreds of thousands of flashing neon lights, the evening sky was flashing a few million twinkling stars.

"Sure," she said, holding the cigarette uneasily between her thumb and forefinger. "Ever since I was a kid."

"And no one ever told you how bad those things are for you? If you don't mind me asking, exactly how old are you?"

She was looking out the window and answered, "Old enough." Then she turned her head toward me, smiled, and said, "And people have been telling me I do a lot of bad things, but I think I turned out okay, no?"

I wasn't about to give her the satisfaction of knowing how well I thought she had turned out and instead stared ahead with my hands in the ten-and-two position.

"This rust bucket got any music?" she asked, leaning toward the dash.

"Just AM."

"That sucks," she said, falling back into her seat. "What do you listen to at night?"

Poor kids, growing up with their expensive CD and MP3 players, downloading file after file as they slept, never giving themselves a chance to even learn how that crap they called music made it from the station to the little earplugs stuck in their empty heads.

"Hey, I almost forgot," I said, slapping my forehead and pointing at the face of my watch. "It's after two o'clock in the *morning*. It *is* a.m."

Angelica looked at me for a second, and then a great big smile filled her adorable, naïve face. "You're right!" She turned the radio on with a loud crackle and played around until she found some spastic sounds generated from a computer instead of musical instruments; the words were unintelligible, and the bass beat looped over and over.

I reached over and adjusted it down by half in decibels.

"What's that?" she asked, pointing below the radio, under the dash.

"Ah, that," I observed, "is a true piece of musical genius. Never fully appreciated by the discerning listening public. A true loss to audiophiles worldwide."

She cocked her head like the terrier I had as a kid did when it didn't comprehend what I was saying. "So what is it?" she asked, unable to hide her anticipation.

"That, my dear, is an eight-track player."

"Wow, can we play something?"

"I'm afraid not," I sighed. "I was down to Steppenwolf and The Doors, and both broke. I've got a pile back home that I have to splice."

"Who?"

"Nah, I wasn't much into The Who."

"No, I mean who were Steppenwolf and The Doors? Were they like big-band music, from the old days?"

I took my eyes off the road to look at her to make sure she wasn't kidding. She wasn't.

I was a child of the '60s, and, although my formative teenage years were in the late '70s and early '80s and I grew up on ABBA, DEVO, and the whole disco scene, I couldn't get into it. I think it had something to do with the wild weekend parties my parents used to throw when I was a kid — with the stereo cranked up to Led Zep, Cream, and Grand Funk and the funny-smelling cigarette smoke all through the house.

The street ahead was busier than the rest. I made a sharp right at the next lights.

"This here is Las Vegas Boulevard," I announced. "The famous *Strip*. Home of the most prestigious hotels in town, if not the world. The Oasis is about halfway down and just off the main drag. You can't miss it. There's neon palm trees splattered everywhere. We should be there in 15 minutes if the traffic stays light."

And then I could hurry home to the comfort of my bed.

"Forget the hotel," she said. "I just got here, and I want to party."

"I'm supposed to pick you up and take you to the Oasis. That's it."

Angelica flicked her smoke out the window. "I don't think so, dude. If memory serves me correct, you said Uncle Julie instructed you to tag along wherever I wanted to go and keep me company. No?"

I counted to 10 by twos. "But it's after 2 a.m., on a Tuesday night, for God's sake. What's wrong with starting that in the *morning?*" I put on my best puppy-eyed look and gave her a big smile. "You know, bright-eyed and bushy-tailed. Then I can take you to all the sights you want to see."

She crossed her arms over her chest. "Hmmph. What an old fart. Where's your sense of adventure? Look at me." She gestured her hands from head to toe. "Does this look like it should be locked up, alone, in some hotel room while this town gets down to party? Exactly how old are you, old man?"

My eyes were so heavy I almost didn't see the bag lady start to push her cart off the curb and wander across the 10 lanes. I slammed on the brakes, and the Chevy slowly rolled to a stop.

"I'm not that old," I explained. "And I can still party with the best of them. Probably. But listen, it's been a real long day, and I have to get some zees soon or I am going to be a mess tomorrow. You understand, right?"

I stomped on the gas, and we started to roll gradually down the Strip again.

"Nope. What I understand is that the club scene here is hot, and I want to see it. I want to live it, breathe it."

"But that's the thing about Vegas. It's not going anywhere. This town rocks 24/7 because most of the people are only here for three or four days. Believe me, it'll still be rockin' tomorrow. I guarantee it."

Angelica wasn't buying it. "Wait till my uncle finds out you didn't follow his instructions. I want to go out, and I want to go out *now!* If you take me to the hotel, I'll go out after you leave. And believe me, I'll make sure I get into trouble. . . . Las Vegas, here I come."

We had come to a red light, and I sat there drumming my fingers on the steering wheel and wondering what I had done to deserve this. I thought about kicking her ass out on the sidewalk right where we were, but it would have looked silly trying because her door was stuck closed, and I would have had a hard time dragging her through the window.

"Do you always get your way?" I asked.

"I do when I want something badly enough."

"And this is one of those times, right?"

"Uh-huh."

The light flashed green, and I curled my lip, pulled a U-turn, went down a block, and made a right.

"Okay, we'll drop into a club for a look-see. But I've gotta stop at my place first for a quick shower and a change of clothes."

"Sweet." She rifled through a backpack. "I had a visitor guide somewhere." She flipped through a booklet. "We can stop in at the Hard Rock first; then I'd like to see Studio 54, the Voodoo Lounge —"

"Uh, Angelica, I hate to rain on your parade, but we are *not* going to be doing the entire city tonight. We'll hit a couple of places. Check 'em out. And leave the rest for later this week if we have to. You can bitch and complain all you like, little lady, or threaten to tell Big Julie, but that's the way it's going to be."

She gave me an exaggerated pout. "Okay, Mr. Meanie," she delivered in Shirley Temple fashion. She pulled another cigarette from the pack on the dash and fired it up. This time she sounded like Mae West when she said, "I like a man who's not afraid to try to put me in my place."

I started hacking from the cloud of smoke and rolled my air conditioner all the way down. "You do a good Shirley Temple and Mae West."

Angelica gave me a puzzled look and asked, "Shirley and Mae who?" Then she went back to her page turning. "And we gotta see Coyote Ugly, C2K, Rumjungle, and, ohmygawd," she exclaimed, "I almost forgot about Seven and The Red Dragon!" She gave me a playful punch on my arm. "Come on, dawg, go get yo' self some bling-bling, and let's bounce this scene."

I kept both hands gripped on the wheel and stared fuzzily ahead. "Groovy."

# Chapter

I had a large, one-bedroom condo on the top floor of a three-story building. The parking lot was around back, behind the community swimming pool. Not wanting any nosy neighbors seeing me bringing in something this young when the night was so old, I pulled up in front of the now quiet complex and stopped in the no-parking zone.

I really must have been half asleep, because when I went to get out of the Chevy a big black Caddy, or Lincoln, swerved around my open door without even touching the brakes. The guy fish-tailed for a second or two, stopped, put on his back-up lights, stopped again, then took off slowly down the street before I could give him the finger or a piece of my mind.

"Where did he learn to drive?" Angelica said, wiggling her way out the door. "That was wicked! Maybe you *do* have a sense of adventure."

"Okay, fun's over. Grab a bag or two, and let's get going." As safe a neighborhood as this was, only one of the car doors locked, and I didn't feel lucky enough that a thief would choose the one that did and not take the suitcases if I left them behind.

Without wanting to, we unknowingly discovered the origin of the word *luggage* as we "lugged" the suitcases and carry-on up the three flights of stairs. We caught our breath and looked out over the adjoining roofs, through the tall palm trees, toward the bright glow coming from the Strip.

"I am so down with this place," Angelica said excitedly.

"Let's go." I walked over and opened the door to my unit, holding it open while she slipped inside. I went back and grabbed the suitcases, turned, and looked back down the darkened street. I didn't feel anywhere near as "down" as Angelica: I had noticed that the headlights had not been turned on when the black car had shot by, missing me by inches.

"You keep this place pretty clean, for a guy."

"Thanks," I said, after closing the door and slipping the bolt. "Cleaning lady comes in every other Monday. I haven't had time to mess it up yet."

I let Angelica use the facilities first; then I gave her instructions to sit there and wait for me while I showered and changed.

"There's soda and water in the fridge," I told her. "The remote is on the coffee table. MTV must be on there somewhere."

"I'll be fine."

"And don't open the door." I pointed a finger at her and wagged it so she'd know I was serious. "Not for anyone."

After running the shower on hot for five minutes, I found myself starting to nod off, standing up with my forehead against the tile. I switched the water to cold and let it run over my upturned face for another five as I tried to figure out what the best plan was to get Angelica out on the town for an hour or two. My Vega wasn't going to get us in any VIP line, so the first thing I thought we'd do when we left would be to go to the Oasis, have her bags taken to her room, and then have Gary get us a new set of wheels. A nice white limo with a moon roof would do just fine.

All in all, she wasn't a bad kid. And it wasn't her fault I hadn't slept in two days. She was right: she had just arrived in one of the most exciting cities in the world, and I really couldn't expect her to just lock herself up the minute she hit town. What the hell, I'd take her to a couple of places, try to pick up on her lingo, and stay in the background while she checked things out. Besides me getting up on the dance floor, how bad could it get?

I finished up in the bathroom, went to the bedroom, and started to go through my closet for something to wear. My *Saturday Night Fever* white suit was a couple of sizes too small, so I settled on a pair of black slacks and gray-checked shirt, no tie. I rounded off my ensemble with a shiny pair of loafers and a light gray jacket.

I checked myself out in the full-length mirror behind the door. I was no Travolta, but I wasn't a candidate for *Queer Eye for the Straight Guy* either. I spritzed the inside of my jacket with my two favorite colognes, Spark and Ignition, because they sounded like they were made to go together. I slapped in an Altoid wintergreen strip and left the room.

"Okay, let's boogie," I called out good naturedly, entering the living room.

There was nobody there.

I stepped into the room two or three paces, turned, and looked in the kitchen. "Angelica?"

No answer.

What the hell?

I went and checked to see if she had gone back to the bathroom, but it too was empty. I turned back to the living room.

"Angelica," I yelled, surprised at the tone of desperation that had crept into my voice.

I noticed the front door was ajar, three or four inches, and I hurried over, flung it open, and stepped onto the balcony. "Angelica?" I called out, hoping she had stepped out for a smoke, but she was nowhere to be seen, and the air was free of the scent of burning tobacco.

I looked up and down the street, but nothing moved. Then I noticed the driver-side door open on the Chevy, but from that angle I could tell there was nobody inside. I turned and looked back in my apartment, to the counter where I always left my keys.

Gone.

I wheeled around and took the stairs two at a time, amazed at how awake I was. At the bottom, I sprinted across the grass, up to the passenger side, and looked in. Everything looked as bad as it had before, but I noticed Angelica's cigarette pack had left the dash and was now occupying the driver's seat. Three or four of the coffin nails lay across the seat where they had fallen.

"Uhhh."

I turned at the faint noise, trying to trace its source.

"Angelica?"

"Uhhh."

I stood up, realizing the noise was coming from the garden area to the side of the complex, and started in that direction. I ran around the corner of a six-foot brick wall and face first into another. This six-foot wall wasn't brick but damn close. It had arms and legs and a big, thick head, and it was covered in a black silk suit. Another one just like it crouched on the ground, holding what I figured must be Angelica because the shape was moaning as it twisted left and right.

The arms spun me around and wrapped across my chest, and the legs drove me hard and fast toward a cast-iron fence that surrounded the swimming pool. I tried to lift my hands to protect my face but only managed to turn my head aside at the last second. I seemed to rattle a little longer than the metal did, and, when the thing with arms and legs felt me subside, he hugged me harder, ran back to the path, turned, and charged once again with me out front.

Once, shame on you. Twice, shame on me. This time I helped him pick up speed by running with him as the two of us rushed forward. About six feet before facial impact, I jumped and lifted my legs, bending them at the knees. I brought my head forward to my chest, and, when the bottom of my shoes hit the iron of the fence, I shot my head back. My skull crushed his nose as my legs sprang both our bodies back, staggering for about 12 feet as we tried to catch our balance. We fell to the ground, and he threw me aside, clutching his hands to his face while I lay watching on my back, stunned.

"You bro' mah fuggin' node," he sputtered, squeezing and trying to realign the bone. "I'll fuggin' kill you!"

With fire in his eyes, he stomped toward me, arms stretched out like Frankenstein's monster. He was at my feet, and starting to lean over to pick me up, when I shot my right leg up and out and caught him square in the sac. His eyes bulged out like a cartoon character as he tried to gasp for air that wasn't there. I got up as fast as I could and, not wanting to break any bones in my dealing hands if I didn't absolutely have to, drove the heel of my hand hard into his already smashed nose.

He fell to the ground in one big heap, and I turned my attention to his partner. "You want some of this, motherfucker!" I shouted with all the testosterone I could muster, trying to scare this one off without enduring another physical confrontation.

"Sure," he answered enthusiastically.

It had really been a rhetorical question.

In one motion, he flung Angelica into a bush and sprang to his feet. Now I'm not a little guy, but this one was well over six-foot-three and probably weighed in around 240. A good size if you were picking tight ends for your football team but not as a sparring partner at three in the morning.

Although it was dark in this corner of the property, there was enough light to see him smile. He flicked his arm, and I heard a click; then a three-foot metal rod telescoped out. He swung it, and before I could react the baton caught me flush on the temple. I walked around like a drunken sailor for what was probably only a few seconds, and then I felt myself being pushed along until I could see a big blue light coming up in front of me. The hands let go, and I stood there tottering until I felt the metal rod smack me in the back.

I fell forward and hit the water, disappointed to find it wasn't the kiddie end of the pool. Apartment management kept it lightly heated until the end of October, but the water was cool enough to bring me almost fully conscious. I tried to decipher which way was up and eventually found the surface. I made my way to the plastic rungs of a white ladder and dragged my sorry ass out.

"Angelica?"

I was relieved to hear her answer, although meekly, "Over here."

"Over here" was a juniper bush beside the corner brick wall. I sloshed toward her in my sopping shoes and helped her out.

"You okay?" I asked her.

She held onto my arm for support. "Yeah. I think so."

A car door slammed somewhere off in the distance, then another. A dog barked sharply twice, and then an engine gunned, followed by the chirp of burning rubber.

"What about you?" she asked. "It looks like you're wearing a golf ball on the side of your head."

I remember seeing what could have been flashlights and hearing voices asking if everything was all right before I slipped to my knees and blacked out.

# Chapter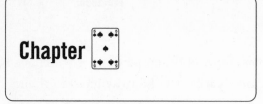

"I don't friggin' believe it, Morgan."

I tried three or four times but managed to convince only my left eye to open, partially. Waking to the pissed-off puss of Julius Contini did nothing for the pounding of the construction crew in my head. I propped myself on an elbow, tried to pry open my right eye, and stopped when I found that side of my face and head swathed in gauze. There was no light coming in through the room's small window. I turned my wrist around so I could read the time and discovered it was just after 4 a.m.

"Christ, I leave her with you for an hour, and what happens? You get yourself beat to hell and tossed in a pool, and poor Angelica gets herself slapped around. You were supposed to protect her, for cryin' out loud!"

"Well, I —" My throat was drier than week-old Death Valley road kill. "Is there any water or juice around?"

"That's not the way it was, Uncle Julie." I turned my head farther and saw Angelica sitting in a red leather chair with an ice pack on her cheek. While I was out she'd become acquainted with her uncle. "Jake was totally awesome. If it was anybody's fault, it was mine. He told me to wait inside, but I took a walk. I didn't even see those creeps until they were already on top of me." She got up from her seat and brought over a white Styrofoam cup with one of those clear plastic straws that bend. "Here, take a sip."

It was a little warm for the way I liked my orange juice, but I wasn't about to complain. "Thanks."

Big Julie sighed. "Okay, so what the hell happened?"

I gave him a rundown of the evening after I'd left him, and Angelica filled in what I missed. She gave her side while sitting in her chair, occasionally dabbing at her cheek with the ice pack. All in all, she didn't look the worse for wear. She'd found a UNLV sweatshirt a couple of sizes too large, possibly wearing it as a cover-up for the slightly risqué outfit she had on underneath. Besides her hair being a little tousled and some dirt on her clothes, she still looked good in a sexy, disheveled way. There was a slight discoloration on her upper left cheek but nothing a little makeup wouldn't fix.

"So neither one of you had seen these two guys before?" Contini asked. We both shook our heads.

"Well, what the hell. Were they just trying to rob you?"

"No, nothing like that," Angelica said.

"And they were too well dressed," I said, describing their imported suits. "Plus I think they were driving a Cadillac. A big black classic one."

Big Julie thought about that for a moment.

Then Angelica chirped in, "Uncle Julie, these men kept asking me about *nonna*."

Contini's forehead scrunched up into little wave patterns. "They asked you about your grandmother?"

She nodded her head. "They kept asking me why I was here and why I was going to see *nonna*."

"They *what?*" The wave patterns on his forehead grew bigger. "How the hell did they know you were coming out here to see her? Christ, I didn't know until a few hours before you were getting on the plane."

"It freaked me out totally," Angelica admitted. "But what was really whacked was that they kept asking me about the money."

"The money?" Contini and I asked in unison.

"Yeah. They wanted to know what I knew about *nonno*'s money."

"Your grandfather's money?" Big Julie pondered. "He hasn't been in the picture for more than 40 years. Are you sure, sweetheart?"

She nodded her head. "That's what they said. It didn't make any sense to me. It was just about then that I heard Jake calling my name from his balcony. I would hate to think what might have happened if he hadn't been there."

Big Julie didn't look convinced. "This doesn't make sense. And they never even mentioned any real names. *Nonna* and *nonno* and that's it? That's so crazy I'm starting to wonder if maybe they got you, or even Jake, mixed up with somebody else."

The three of us discussed it a bit more but with no further results or conclusions. Eventually, a middle-aged nurse dressed in a pale blue uniform came into the small waiting room, introduced herself as Wanda, and proceeded to take our temperatures. She told us to roll up our sleeves so she could take our blood pressures. She took one look at Big Julie's sweating red head and demanded to take his as well.

We passed her tests, and, after taking off my bandage and checking my eye for damage, she explained that we were free to check out. As we were leaving, she gave me a prescription for something she promised would convince the guy working the jackhammer in my head to take the rest of the day off. She instructed me to take the rest of the day off, too, in case I'd suffered a minor concussion, but Big Julie took her aside, and eventually she came back and told me to rest when I could.

Contini told Angelica he needed to speak with her in the hall, and the two of them left to discuss whatever it was that was so private. I tried to tidy myself up as best I could in an outfit that had been tossed into a metal fence, rolled around in a patch of grass, and gone a few laps in the wash. I felt silly making sloshing noises in my shoes, so I took them off, tucked my wet socks inside, and carried them.

The three of us made our way to the parking lot, where Contini quickly fired up a custom Cuban cigar. When he got it going to his satisfaction, he pointed it back and forth at the two of us. "Now look," he said, "I don't know what the hell is going on here, but it's not making any sense. Here's what I want you two to do: Jake, you go home and catch a few zees, and Angelica, you take the room we have for you at the Oasis. You'll be safe there. Later in the morning, I want Jake to take you out to your grandmother's place."

"So you still want me on the job?" I asked, hoping he didn't so I could sleep for a week or maybe even two. "I mean, after the screwup and all?"

Contini shook his head and blew a stream of smoke at the moon. "Apparently, Princess Angelica here thinks you're Sir Galahad or somethin'. I told her a bit about your past, and if she still thinks you know what the hell you're doin' then, hey, I'll give you another chance. But listen here, Prince Charmin'," he said, putting a fatherly arm around my shoulder. "Let's just hope you can take better care of her." He tapped a thick sausage finger against the soft-boiled egg on my head, and for a second it was so bright I thought the sun had come out. "She's out here for a nice visit with her *nonna*, so let's keep it that way. We wouldn't want any bad impressions from this little part-time job to affect one's full-time job now, would we? *Capice?*"

When the pain upstairs subsided, I said, "Yes, sir."

Angelica bent down slightly and whispered something into his ear.

"Oh, and Morgan," he said. "Don't forget to see Carl about a new set of wheels later. That piece of crap you drive really is fugly."

# Chapter

Angelica's grandmother lived in Boulder City, about 45 minutes southwest of the Oasis. The town was originally built to house Hoover Dam workers. Today it is known as a beautiful, idyllic hideaway from Vegas and the only city in Nevada where gambling is illegal. We were heading down Boulder Highway doing a leisurely 65 with the help of the electronic cruise control. It was a luxury I would never experience in my Vega. Not only would my car's speedometer never see 65 again, but her cruise control was a broken baseball bat and a brick. The car we were in now also had a GPS system, but neither one of us had the time or patience to figure it out.

As Contini had suggested, I'd spoken with Carl, who'd arranged for me to have a new, hemi-powered Chrysler 300 for as long as I liked. After a couple of unanswered calls to her room, I'd found Angelica in the Ali Baba Deli eating a bowl of Rice Krispies doused with chocolate milk, capped off with a latte and a Virginia Slim.

I'd managed to grab about four hours of restless shut eye before one of Big Julie's secretaries had called to make sure I hadn't forgotten his chore. How *could* I have forgotten? The pain from the bump on my head had reminded me every time I rolled over in my sleep.

I'd made it through a gentle, warm shower, chosen a dull blade for my shave just in case I was too jittery, and brushed my hair with a bit of a comb-over to hide the bluish lump. I'd checked myself in the mirror after about 15 minutes of meticulous grooming, and I'd still looked like shit.

My hair wouldn't sit flat on the side that throbbed, there was a scratch and a purplish bruise on my right cheek, and my eyes were so red I could've been a model in a Visine commercial. On the bright side, my upper lip had just enough swelling to give me a quality Elvis sneer. I'd donned my pair of Ray Bans, not sure that they would be enough to hide the damage.

Screw it, if anybody asked, I'd tell them I was a hockey player.

◆

Boulder Highway was really an extension of downtown Las Vegas's famous Fremont Street. It ran straight as an arrow, first through Henderson, then to Boulder, where it changed its name back to I-93, and headed east toward Lake Mead, the Hoover Dam, and the even more arid Arizona.

At this time of day, the traffic was light, most of which was going the same way we were. Also light was the conversation as the two of us skirted the seriousness of last night's encounter.

"I swear, you looked like a swamp monster when you climbed out of that swimming pool," Angelica said. "Water squirting up out of your loafers just like those fountains we saw this morning when we drove by Caesar's Palace. That was way dope."

"Yeah, well," I countered, checking my battle scars in the rearview mirror. "Who looks cooler now?"

Angelica was sitting with her feet underneath her, wearing an oversized knitted sweater and a pair of stone-washed jeans, dressed down about three categories from the night before but unable to hide the natural beauty she was blessed with. She brought her sleeve-covered hands to her mouth and giggled like a schoolgirl. "You look like that King guy," she said.

I increased the sneer for her benefit and gave her my best Elvis Presley imitation. "Thank you. Thank you very much!"

"No," she giggled. "The guy with the funny hair at all the boxing matches."

"I do not look like Don King."

We sparred like that until we came upon Buchanan Boulevard, where we swung right into Boulder City. We drove through modern suburbia: neat rows of Spanish-influenced townhouses and clean strip malls. All seemed to have drugstores, and the handicap parking spots were full. We kept heading south, with Angelica reading out directions, until the town-houses gave way to single dwelling homes. We followed the Boulder City Golf Club until she said to turn left up ahead.

"I haven't seen *nonna* for four or five years," she said excitedly, "when she came to the east house. The last time I was out here I was, like, nine years old or something."

"So you've been to Vegas before?" I asked, making the turn down a smartly landscaped street called Georgia.

"Well, not really. We landed at night and drove straight out from the airport to Boulder City. I don't even remember seeing a hotel or casino actually. It was dark, and I slept for most of the way. It was the same when we returned."

We drove past courts, crescents, and well-manicured boulevards named after famous golf courses around the world, hosting what looked to be extremely large, single-family homes or small mansions of at least 4,000 or 5,000 square feet.

"And your grandmother lives out here all by herself?"

"When she came out to see us back east a few years ago, she said that she was getting too old to do some things and that there was a woman from her original hometown in Italy staying with her. I remember she had a man that stayed in the garage loft that took care of the grounds and things like that."

We made one more turn, onto Pebble Beach Boulevard, and then Angelica shouted, "There it is! Over there. The big orangey one with the letter B on the gates."

The black iron gates were open, and I turned in and drove up a slight rise and through a small grove of Joshua trees, where a white swing for two hung in an octagonal gazebo made of cedar logs. The drive was circular, with a branch to the three-car garage attached to the house, both covered in salmon-colored stucco with clay-tiled roofs. I pulled up to the two-step natural stone porch, switched off the ignition, and sat there admiring the view.

"Those are the Black Hills," I pointed out to Angelica. "And if you look farther, you can see the McCullough Range." I shook my head in awe. "This is very impressive."

"It's all right if you like the outdoors, I guess," she replied, "but I think your place is way cool, too."

"True," I said, getting out of the car and stretching my legs. "I can see the golden arches from my place. If I look real hard, and jump up and down on my little balcony, I can make out the oil change shop."

I went around to the back of the car and popped the trunk while Angelica ran up the stairs and rang the bell. The door was opened immediately, and a middle-aged woman with a small towel in her hand smiled brightly and wished us good afternoon. She told me to leave the luggage where it was, that somebody named Vincent would be around shortly to take it upstairs.

I wasn't sure whether to hang around or leave, but after Angelica had introduced herself to the woman, whose name was Orsina, she called me up to the entryway and introduced me as Jake Morgan, and we all filed inside.

As I turned to close the door, I took one last look down the hill and the quiet street. It may have been my imagination, or maybe the aftereffects of being whacked on the head, but I could have sworn I saw a big black Cadillac go by us as we turned into the driveway.

# Chapter

We were led down a wide walkway and through a great room aptly furnished in Southwest and Mexican pieces made mostly of aspen and pine. We exited the house onto a flagstone deck with more of the same sturdy furniture but built for outdoor use. The view of the yard backing onto the immaculate golf course was broken by the eight- or nine-foot waterfall that cascaded softly down into a kidney-shaped swimming pool adjoined by a 10-person hot tub. Next to the change rooms stood a small cedar shack with a sauna sign out front. A number of smaller fountains were positioned around the patio, lending a sound much like a babbling brook.

"Do you think your grandmother would adopt me?" I asked.

"Maybe," Angelica said. "Ask her yourself. Here she comes."

We could see her through the windows of the great room sitting in a wheelchair being pushed along carefully by Orsina. They made their way through the doorway and to an elaborate set of western patio furniture.

Angelica raced over and gave her grandmother a long hug, looked her in the eye, said something softly, and gave her a light kiss on her forehead. The elderly woman beamed brightly, and her eyes moistened. She was in her 70s, relatively fit looking, with bright eyes and skin that had been successfully conditioned to ward off the wrinkled perils of desert living. Despite the obvious need for the wheelchair, she held herself with an air of grace, an almost regal appearance that demanded one's attention.

I remained standing until the two of them had finished their hellos;

then Angelica said, "Oh, *nonna*, I want you to meet Jake Morgan. He works for Uncle Julius. Jake, this is my grandmother."

I took the woman's hand. "Pleased to meet you. . . ." I then realized I didn't know her name, first or last. I remembered the letter B on the gates but thought it would be out of place to call her Mrs. B.

She picked up on it immediately and gave out a small laugh. "You can call me Olivia, Mr. Morgan."

"Okay, but only if you call me Jake."

We all smiled at that. Then I took a seat, and Olivia announced that Orsina would be back shortly with sandwiches and drinks.

"You play sports, Jake?" Olivia asked, looking me over.

"A little hockey, once in a while. I'm originally from Boston."

Angelica couldn't contain herself. "He didn't get that from hockey, *nonna*," she cried out. "On our way back from the airport, we were jumped by these two guys. Jake was awesome. He took both of them on. You should see the other guys."

Her grandmother wasn't satisfied with a synopsis. She was deeply interested in knowing exactly what had happened and what had been said. I noticed Angelica said she'd gone to the car for her wallet instead of a cigarette.

"This city," Olivia said, shaking her head. "The changes I've seen over the past 20, 30 years are incredible. It keeps getting bigger and bigger, and the crime gets worse and worse."

The lunch came, and we all had a meal of Calabrese salami, prosciutto, and Serrano ham, combined with a wonderful mix of provolone, Gorgonzola, and Toma cheeses, piled on freshly baked bread that was still warm. The conversation was light and consisted mostly of the grandmother catching up on all the granddaughter's news regarding the house back east, which I was now assuming was some kind of family estate, her various jobs in the fashion industry, none of which ever lasted a month, and the boys she was seeing and not seeing any longer. And, no, she told her grandmother, glancing first at me, she had not picked up the filthy smoking habit.

I learned over hot cappuccino that Olivia had lived most of the past 40 years out here in Boulder and that her husband had been a hotel partner/ manager back in the '50s. I complimented her on her beautiful backyard, and she explained that her regular groundskeeper and handyman, Stephano, had designed and built the swimming pool and waterfall.

It was all very interesting, but if the old lady wasn't going to adopt me I really wanted to get back home and take advantage of the downtime I'd have since Angelica was out here. I excused myself from the table, thanked everyone for lunch, and told Olivia I would find my way out.

Angelica remembered something all of a sudden and fetched her summer bag from beneath the table. "Here, I almost forgot. Uncle Julius had these waiting for me at the hotel. They're beepers. One for you, and one for me. Cool, huh? With text messaging, too. This way we can get hold of each other anytime, you know, like if I need a ride or anything." She handed me a piece of paper. "And here's a list of all the numbers the two of us can be reached at 24/7."

"Great," I said, lacking any real enthusiasm.

"Uncle Julius said to remind you to keep it on. Always. And to say *'Or you'll be workin' the big wheel.'*"

The big wheel was the stand-up wheel of fortune game found at the entrances of many of the casinos. It was the biggest sucker bet in the city, and whoever was working it was sure to be on some pit boss's shit list.

"Yeah, he says that often. If I keep working hard, I'll be a big wheel someday, just like him."

I shook Olivia's hand and thanked her again. I patted Angelica's shoulder and told her to keep in touch.

"Oh, don't worry, I will."

I left the patio, walked through the house, and found the front door. Outside, at the back of my car, stood a strange young behemoth in blue sweatpants and a sleeveless T-shirt with his back to me. The strange part was he had all six heavy pieces of luggage in his hands, and he was lifting them up and down, over and over, flapping his arms as he stared out ahead at the Black Hills. He had longish black hair, matted down with sweat, and his muscles popped out everywhere.

"You'll never take off with all those bags on board," I called out to him. "Wilbur and Orville started out light."

"Who?"

The young giant turned around, put the suitcases down, pulled his T-shirt front up, and wiped his face. The six-pack he sported on his stomach glistened with sweat just the way my six-pack did after a few minutes out of the fridge.

I realized now who he was. "You must be Vincent."

"Yo." He came striding up to me, wiping his hands on his sweatpants. "You must be the guy driving around the granddaughter."

He reached out a paw, and I took it, ready to kick him in the nuts if he tried to impress me with his grip. But it wasn't to be. He was obviously working other parts or just going easy on me.

"That's me," I said. "Jake Morgan."

We made small talk for a few minutes. I found out he had been here a month or so and, like Orsina, was from the same valley in Italy as most everyone else I'd met. He told me he took care of the grounds, some of the errands, and just about anything that needed fixing around the house. He lived above the garage in a comfortable apartment. He made sure I also knew he was responsible for the security of the premises as well by flexing his pecs like exclamation points.

"Well, it looks like the lady of the house certainly has the right man for the job," I told him. "Now if you'll be kind enough to lift my car and turn it around, I'll be leaving."

"It's a circular driveway, you just go around."

"Ah, thank you," I said. *"Ciao!"*

I wasn't sure if Vincent was a Vinnie or not, but I had a feeling I'd find out eventually. And unless I was mistaken, while he was lifting those bags, I could have sworn I glimpsed what looked like the leather of a holster in the small of his back.

I took off down the drive, got back on the street, and kept my eyes peeled for black Cadillacs and flying suitcases.

# Chapter

The drive home was uneventful except for the couple of times I drifted off into the warning ruts at the side of the highway. Hell, I was so damn tired that if I had gone off the road I may have just kept going over the flat desert, running over cacti, sagebrush, and the occasional rattle snake until I ran out of gas.

I made it home around 4 p.m., stripped down to my Calvins, and passed out facedown on my bed. My sleep was deep and rewarding — until I heard the smoke detector's loud, piercing warning. Some kind of internal gizmo was trying to ignite the synapses in my weary brain, while one group of angry neurons tried to convince the waking ones to go back to sleep. Eventually, the energetic faction won out when my olfactory nerves jumped up and set off their own alarm after detecting smoke.

*Holy shit, the condo was on fire!*

I jumped out of bed. The red digits on the clock radio displayed 9:02 in the just darkening room. I grabbed for the clothes that lay by the bed and slipped into my discarded pants. As I was doing up my belt, I noticed the smoke alarm sound was strangely emanating from my pants and not the hallway ceiling. I dug into my pocket and came out with the beeper Angelica had given to me at her grandmother's house.

"Son of a bitch . . ." I muttered, playing around with the buttons, trying to shut the damn thing off. Eventually, it silenced, and I held the LED display up to my face when one of the other buttons lit it up. It read "Hope you've had enough shut-eye, sleepy head, because the clubs await! Meet me at *nonna*'s at midnight. Ciao!"

I fell back on the bed for a few minutes, thinking vicious thoughts, trying to figure out how much sleep I'd actually managed. I grunted a couple of times at the calculation, swore, and closed my eyes. Just as that familiar cloud of unconsciousness was about to take over, a disturbing realization exploded in my brain, like the kid in class who shoots his arm up at a formidable question he just realized he knows the answer to and points his arm again and again at the ceiling, grunting and praying that you will pick him.

*Yes, Jake, what is it? Uh-huh . . . yes, good boy. You've just come up with the answer to the $64,000 question. If there's no fire, how come you still smell smoke?*

And that's when the earthquake hit.

The bed I was so comfortably resting in flew up in the air, and I flew ungracefully from it across the floor and into the wall. It was an 8.5 on the Richter scale.

I got to my hands and knees and tried shaking some of the cobwebs from my head. When I glanced across the room where my bed used to be, there was this giant black outline puffing on a stogie and trying to climb over the bed to get at me. As he got closer, so did the smell of cigar smoke. I could see the faint outline of white bandages across both sides of his nose and had the feeling we'd met before. Within the past 24 hours, as a matter of fact.

"I tode you I'd fuggin' kill you," he bellowed.

"Not yet, Lip," another voice called out calmly from the dark doorway. "We got some questions need answerin' first. Bring him out to the living room."

The one called Lip reached down to me, grabbed me by the belt and picked me up like I was a piece of baggage. He wheeled around and carried me out of the bedroom into the dark living room like it was something he did every day. Maybe it was.

"Put him in one of those kitchen chairs," said the voice in charge. "And tie him up with somethin'."

With his free hand, Lip grabbed my hair, lifted me up, and threw me into one of the wooden chairs. He kept hold of my head while rummaging around in the pantry drawers. Eventually, he came out with a roll of duct tape and did a Bob Vila on my wrists and the slats of the seat behind my back.

The brains of the outfit took one of the other chairs, placed it in front of me, spun it around, and straddled it.

"Go and check the bedroom," he ordered his goon.

He crossed his arms on the back of the chair and rested his chin on the sleeve of his suit. I couldn't figure out what these two hoods wanted with me. As far as I knew, I didn't owe anybody major cash, and I hadn't gotten laid in two months, so I couldn't have slept with anybody's wife. While his buddy tossed my bedroom, we played a little game of who could outstare whom in the dim light for a minute or so, but in the end he was no match for my baby blues.

"So you think you're a tough guy, huh?"

I knew he didn't really expect an answer. Even so, I couldn't keep my mouth shut. "I outstared you, didn't I?"

The back of his hand shot out, and one of his oversized rings caught me across the right cheek. The chair tilted slightly with the impact, then settled back again. Something warm trickled down my face.

"That was what they call a 'rhetorical question,'" he lectured.

"Well," I replied, running a damage control check with my tongue over the edges of my teeth, "you two jokers have the wrong bitch, and the sooner you figure that out the better it'll be for me. And even more so for you and your girlfriend over there later."

Now his other hand came across and hit me on my left cheek. This one was even harder than the last and was going to leave a mark for sure. There's nothing worse than an ambidextrous interrogator who doesn't know his own strength.

"Okay, bright eyes," he said, "let's take it from the beginning. What are you doin' hangin' around with the Bonello kid?"

"The Bonello kid?" I asked.

His hand twitched in anticipation.

"Ah, you mean Angelica."

He relaxed and rested his chin back on his forearm.

"She's a relative of my boss, out here to visit her grandmother in Boulder City for a week or so." In case it might have helped having a big connection, I added, "My boss owns the Oasis."

"Oooohh," he said. "I'm so impressed."

My eyes had gradually gotten used to the lack of light, and I could make out more of his features. I was certain he was the one who had introduced me to the swimming pool the night before.

His significant other returned from the bedroom. "Nope. Nothin' there, Tone."

My interrogator rolled his eyes. "You moron! I told you no first names."

The moron had a puzzled look on his face. "I diddin'. I said *Tone*."

"Tony, *Tone*," he yelled at him. "It's the same fucking thing, you idiot."

The idiot hung his head. "Sorry. . . ." A moment later he lifted it and said, "*T*," with a hopeful smile on his face.

"Jesus Christ!" Tony got up from the chair and went over to the glass coffee table, turning on a lamp after he sat on the edge of the sofa. He was as imposing sitting down as he was standing up.

But I was pretty sure he was too far away to hit me, even with a telescoping baton, so I asked him, "What the hell are you guys looking for?"

He lifted one eye up and looked at me; then he stretched both arms out and wiggled his fingers at me. "Clues."

"Clues? To what?"

"That's for us to know and for you to find out." Tony laughed. "'Member that? Didja used to say that when you were a kid?"

"Yeah, sure," I said, just to humor him.

"Fuck, I used to hate that. I always found out."

He pulled out an expensive-looking fountain pen, opened it, and started to empty the ink — except this ink wasn't black and wet; it was white and dry. He pulled a small blade from the end of the pen and began lightly chopping and rearranging the substance in a neat, narrow row.

"You religious?" he asked.

"When I have to be."

He laughed and nodded.

"I think it was Lennon who said, 'God is a concept by which we measure our pain.'"

"Yep, those fuckin' commies learned a lot about pain, that's for sure. Now the KGB thinks it can come over here and take over from the Mob. Yeah, right."

When he had the coke arranged to his satisfaction, he held the tube of the instrument to his nose, leaned over, and snorted until the table was clean again. He sat there with his eyes closed and a Cheshire cat's look on his face. When he landed back on Earth, he reassembled the pen, got up, and restraddled the chair once more.

"Sorry you weren't invited to the party," he said with a stupid smile.

"That's okay, I don't do the stuff," I told him. "I just like the smell of it."

He nodded in apparent understanding.

"Okay, numb nuts," he said to his partner. "Check the rest of the place while I confer with our host here."

I'd seen Tony's type before. The kind who tried to learn a new word every day but usually missed a bunch of days every week.

Numb nuts went into the living room and first looked behind my picture of *Dogs Playing Poker*; then he started tossing cushions and throwing books.

"And try to leave things neat, if you don't mind," I told him. "The cleaning lady won't be in for two weeks."

That earned me a smack that rattled my teeth again.

"Okay," Tony said, sniffling and wiping under his nose with the back of his index finger. "Where were we?"

Three times was enough for me. I wasn't answering any more rhetorical questions.

"So you say this Angelica is here visiting her grandmother. Any reason why?"

"She told me her grandmother was ill."

"We've seen her. She don't look so sick."

"I was told she had dementia. The early stages. It comes and goes, but it's not incapacitating."

He looked like he didn't know the meaning of the word but wished he did. "What else do you know about the old lady?"

"She has a very nice home in Boulder City. A couple of dedicated servants. No husband around. Don't know if he passed on or took off."

"What about the granddaughter?"

"She's a little weird. She works in the fashion industry. In New York. Maybe that explains it. I know she lives with some family members in New Jersey."

Tony afforded himself a little smile. "Oh, yeah, they're family all right." The look faded into one of puzzlement. "I'm perplexed, though. Why you?"

I almost said "Why me what?" but thought better of it as I'd already detected a loose tooth.

"Why would Contini ask you to shadow the granddaughter?"

"He didn't want to put some security cop on it. It wouldn't have looked natural, and I don't think he wanted to ring any bells or blow any whistles. I've got a pretty good feel for the city, know the ins and outs and what to look out for to show her a good time — without anything serious coming of it. I also owed him a favor or two."

Tony peered at me for a few seconds, and then he snapped his fingers. "That's right. Now I got it." He turned his head to the living room. "Hey, Lip, this is the guy who was working for Valentine when he got whacked last year."

Lip stepped around the corner of the wall with a bunch of my DVDs and a package of Oreo cookies. There were a few crumbs on his shirtfront. "Ya 'hink so, T?"

"Sure, it's him! I 'member the interview he did on TV. With the clowns and the elephants. Christ, that was funny shit."

Lip looked at me closely as he entered the kitchen and said, "It ith him! The guy thaved that showgirl. Thun of a bith!" He began opening cupboards and inspecting my boxes of Captain Crunch and Fruit Loops that I kept on hand for those mornings when I needed a sugar rush.

"So you don't probably know nothin' about the money. The family money?"

With the double negatives flying freely, I could have gotten away with saying "No" or "Yes" even if I did know. But I didn't.

Tony snorted lightly as if his nose was running. "Never heard of the Desert Ranch? Or the millions missing?"

I told him I had heard of the ranch but only stories of it hosting one of Elizabeth Taylor's weddings and eventually being torn down for one of the megahotels on the Strip and nothing about any missing money.

"Well, let me put it to you this way, friend. You are walkin' a fine line. Not only with my Neanderthal colleague and I but with those we serve — a rather large ethnic corporation specializing in activities that some might say 'skirted' the law."

Out of the corner of my eye, I saw the Neanderthal take a dish towel from the oven door handle.

"A select group of businessmen who once held the deeds to many of the Vegas hotels and casinos that flourished back in the '50s and '60s without much government interference, if you get what I mean."

From behind, the now rolled-up, rope-like towel was draped around my throat. Next it was crisscrossed behind my neck and slowly pulled taut.

"Now I just wanna make sure things are real clear between us. You can play date the princess for the rest of the week, but if you come across anything. . . ." He nodded, and the pressure tightened considerably.

I was starting to fight for air, but none came. Little white flashbulbs were going off behind my retinas.

"Anything at all to do with the past of the Bonello family, I wanna know about it. Anything about the old man, no matter how small it may be, especially if it has to do with the Desert Ranch or any other casino from back then."

Tony waved a signal, and the pressure eased. I took in as many big breaths as I could.

"And if you even hear a peep about some lost money, you let us know, pronto."

"How do I do that?" I croaked.

He got up from the chair and motioned for his strangling gorilla to follow. "Hang your doormat over your balcony railing if you have anything. We'll be keeping an eye on your place."

He reached inside his jacket, pulled out what looked like a Beretta Vertec, and held it under my jawbone. "And you keep our little visit to yourself. If we see the cops sniffing around, that little girl might not make it home, and the old lady won't have to worry about her . . . whatever that sickness is she's got." He shoved the barrel up and in until I winced. "And then we'll come for you."

Tony left me to consider that and walked through the living room. The two of them stood at the doorway surveying the damage.

"Pity," Tony said. "And he was such a tidy housekeeper."

"You shoulda lemme kill da prick, T," said Lip.

Tony waved Lip through the door. "Go on, go on. You might get your chance sooner than you think."

"Guaranteed!" I shouted as the door began to close. "Fucking guaranteed."

"Mamma's boy," I heard Tony say, and then something about "old lady and her house."

When the door shut, the apartment fell into an eerie silence. The lamp by the sofa had been turned off when they had left, and, except for the faint light coming from the street between the blinds, the place was as black as the ace of clubs.

I tried to stretch the tape by pulling and twisting my wrists, but to no avail. I slowly tried to stand and lift my arms from behind the chair and eventually managed to do so. The problem was going to be getting the tape off. I might be able to work the door open, even though my hands and fingers were practically numb, but notifying the neighbors meant notifying the police, and right now I didn't want to do that.

It wasn't going to do any good with my hands behind my back, so I tried to work my arms down, under my butt, and out along my legs. The plan was feasible. The feat was plausible. The ass was just too big.

My next thought was to cut through the duct tape from behind. There were a few pieces of broken glass and shards of plastic lying around but none that I would be able to hold and saw through the tape like in the movies. I could probably manage to switch on the front burner of the stove, but I guessed the taped distance between my wrists at about three or four inches. There was no way of accomplishing that without searing my skin. It would remain as a final choice.

I looked around the kitchen for some idea. The electric can opener was a possibility, but when I tried to negotiate the moves I couldn't get the tape close enough to the turning wheel. I tried to jam a steak knife into the space between the counter and the stove, but every time I ran the tape over the blade the knife would fall over.

Then I spotted the toaster. I pulled the little two-slicer out to the edge of the counter, cranked her up to high, and pushed down on the plastic lever. I stood on my toes and lifted my arms up as far as I could, until the tape rested over the top of the two-slice opening. I was pretty sure the heat wasn't going to be enough to burn through, and I was right. Eventually, though, the oily gum in the tape began to give and allowed the fabric to stretch farther than expected. After a couple of rounds with the toaster, I had the space between my wrists stretched out to nearly eight or nine inches. I got down off the counter and put all my effort into pulling the still warm tape farther. When I finally tired, I felt as if I had managed another inch or two.

I bent at the knees and tried to move my arms down my torso. Close, but no cigar. They held once more at the gluteus maximus, and I swore off chicken wings for a month. I went over to the sink and used my mouth to pick up a bottle of dish detergent. I placed the bottle on the kitchen table, turned around, and grasped it upside down. I squirted the soapy liquid down the small of my back and shot some down my butt and the back of my thighs. When I finished what was left in the bottle, I tossed it aside and went through the entire process of getting my arms out in front of me.

*Hallelujah!* My arms slid around my big old ass, and I eventually got my hands around my feet. I took a minute to recuperate; then I got the steak knife, put the hasp against my chest, and pushed the point into the drywall. It took only a few hearty strokes against the knife to break through.

I ripped the tape from my arms and shook them until the feeling came back. The whole experience had left my apartment in shambles and me in a sweaty mess. I trudged off to the bathroom for another much-needed shower. And why not? I was already lathered up.

# Chapter

It was just after 10 p.m. when I left my apartment, now dressed in my second-best set of dancing clothes. Although my living quarters were a total mess, I wasn't the worse for wear. One of Tony's smacks had left a bit of a bruise on my left cheek but nothing that a five o'clock shadow wouldn't hide. His ring had caught me on the right cheek and left a small cut. A couple of dabs with a septic pencil, and I was as good as new. Well, almost.

After making sure the door was locked, and looking up and down the street before walking to my parked car, I realized I had a little time to kill. I decided to drop in to the Oasis and see how the Anaheim Mighty Ducks had done that evening.

I parked the Chrysler 300 in the midst of the chaotic collection of vehicles and showed the valet my employee pass, my official-looking comp card, and a picture of Andrew Jackson on a $20 bill as I told him to leave the car out front.

The Sports Book was winding down for the night. Most of the bettors had left after a full day of horses and the busy schedule of NHL and NBA games. I always liked the Sports Book. You could plunk your lazy ass down into one of the most comfortable seats ever made and wager all day while being served free cocktails and sandwiches by scantily clad wenches. If there was a better life, I hadn't come across it.

The big electronic scoreboard told me the Atlanta Thrashers had been thrashed 6-1 by my Mighty Ducks of Anaheim. I found my betting slip and happily made my way to the cashier, who gave me back my original $185 along with another crisp $100 bill of profit. Although it was closing in on 10:30 p.m., it was a great start to the day.

I dropped in to the Ali Baba Deli, flashed my comp card, and sat down to a breakfast of bacon and eggs, scrambled, a side order of sausage, a bagel with cream cheese, an order of whole wheat toast, a glass of freshly squeezed orange juice, and a pot of strong Columbian. Getting the crap beaten out of you a couple of times a day, you work up an appetite.

I left a few bucks on the table and made my way through the busy casino. It was no accident that most, if not all, restaurants and shops in hotels were located at the ends of their casinos. As a rule, the food was fairly cheap; it was running through the gauntlet of gaming tables where they really wanted to get a shot at you and your bankroll. Luckily, as an employee of the Oasis, I was not allowed to play at the regular tables. The casino and gaming commission did not want to take a chance on "friendly" working dealers cheating the house by wrongly paying off other dealers who might sit and play during their off-hours and then split the profits later. Like most of the casino security, the regulation was in place to protect the casino from its own more than from the public. As intuitive as he was, Bugsy Siegel might have died of old age instead of a gunshot if he had placed even some basic internal security systems to watch over his own people. Siegel opened the Flamingo back in the '40s, and because his employees were stealing from the chip trays, the kitchen, and the bars he never had a money-making month.

I peered through the tinted glass of the lobby until I spotted the valet I had shown the Andrew Jackson. As soon as he ran off to fetch another vehicle, I ambled over to my car, slipped another valet an Abe Lincoln, and drove away.

A little while later I turned off Flamingo and onto Boulder Highway.

The dash displayed the time as 11:17. I had about 43 minutes before I had to pick up Angelica and about a 27-minute drive left. That left me with around 16 minutes to put out the fire that $500 was burning in my pants pocket, less the two C notes Contini had given me, of course. I whipped the wheel hard left and entered the parking lot of Sam's Town. I beat out a couple of cars that were trying to park in a space by the side entrance, clicked the doors locked with the remote, and ran inside.

Sam's is a throwback to the old days. The floors weren't sawdust, but the decor was extreme rural, the music real country, and the costumes denim, leather, and snakeskin. There was a lot of noise coming from the crap tables, and I homed in, contemplating buying a Stetson so I wouldn't feel out of place. I just as quickly rejected the idea, figuring that, with all the bumps and bruises I was sporting, I could easily blend in as a rodeo cowboy. Or clown.

I bellied up between a couple of good old boys who were just watching. An old-timer in a dusty, weather-beaten fedora was rubbing the dice back and forth on the green baize while a large group stood watching, mesmerized, and a bunch of others were whetting their chapped lips in nervous anticipation.

"Ya come atta good time, sonny," he cackled gleefully. "Imma hot! Just threw three passes and made mah point eight times inna row."

"Mighty impressive," I acknowledged, throwing the stickman three crisp hundreds. "Make 'em black."

And it was impressive. A pass was when the one throwing the dice, the shooter, rolled a seven or 11 on his first roll. If he rolled a four, five, six, or eight, nine, 10, that became his "point," and he had to roll it again before he rolled a seven and "crapped out."

The stickman exchanged my bills for three black chips.

The shooter was still playing with the dice, and the players at the table were starting to yell and shout, working themselves into a frenzy. There was about $20,000 or $30,000 in chips spread out on the pass line.

Another cowboy waved his Stetson in the air wildly and whooped. "Baby needs a new pair of boots!"

I squeezed in farther to the back corner of the table and plunked my chips down as the shooter picked up the dice and shook them close to his ear, listening for just the right moment.

Just as he dropped his arm and went to flick his wrist to launch the two clear cubes, somebody screamed out, "Who the hell bet the don't?"

I neglected to mention there is another bet that can be made prior to the first roll called the don't pass. It's a tiny square hidden at the back of each end of the table, and it wins if the shooter does the opposite of the pass. A two or three on the first roll, or a seven when trying to make the point, and the don't pass bettors win. A 12 would be a push or tie. Almost all players bet "with" the shooter, giving them some kind of camaraderie they could all cheer about even though they weren't the favorite. Even more unfortunate was that I was the one and only player who had bet against them all. I had taken the slight advantage in odds and bet negatively on don't pass, much to the chagrin of my fellow gamblers.

As the shooter opened his hand to fire the dice down to the other end of the crap table, his eyes caught my bet, his face contorted, and his mouth parted as if attempting to speak. As he tried to stop his forward motion, the dice fell feebly to the table and rolled halfheartedly across the center.

"Three, craps," droned the stickman.

"Ah, shit!"

"What the hell?"

"Sonnavabitch!"

"What stupid prick bet the don't pass?"

The stickman answered by sliding three more black chips up to my original pile and began collecting everyone else's bets.

"Ya dumb shit!"

"What an a-hole!"

"I'm goin' out to the car and switchin' to hollow points. . . ."

I didn't look to see who was saying what. I was getting out of Dodge. I grabbed my chips and headed for the cashier's cage. As I stood in line, I looked back and saw six or seven of my fellow crap players marching down the aisle in my direction. Well, screw 'em if they couldn't take a joke. I'd come back later and cash out. I then realized things sometimes did come in threes, but I couldn't take another beating and walked quickly toward the side exit.

At the door, I looked over my shoulder and spotted the posse closing in. I beeped myself into the Chrysler, fired up the horses, and reversed out of my stall. As I shifted into drive, a black boot bounced off the hood. I hated being treated like the big bad wolf.

I put the pedal to the metal and shot through the parking lot and fishtailed out onto Boulder Highway. I'd had enough excitement for one day. I punched the scan button on my nifty stereo and waited until it locked in to a light jazz station, then I slipped the cruise control on, adjusted the power seat to a leisurely position, flipped back the moon roof, and aimed the big shiny nose of the Chrysler toward Grandma's house.

# Chapter

It was just before midnight when I arrived at the Bonello estate. The street was quiet, and everything seemed to be in order, except for the black Cadillac parked just past the driveway entrance. I pulled over on the opposite side, turned off the ignition, and watched from about 50 feet away.

The gates were open as if expecting someone, probably me, and the driveway and entrance area of the house were well lit. I sat there for about five minutes looking for movement on the premises and wondering what to do. I slipped out of the Chrysler and made a circle, coming out behind the other vehicle. Still nothing stirred. I took out a pen and jotted the plate number on the back of my left wrist; then I thumped the back fender. No one home. I walked up to the driver's side and tried the door. Locked.

I went to the driveway and peered through the open iron gate. When nothing jumped out at me, I slid around the gate and to the right of the property with my back against the iron fence and cedar hedge. I made my way through the grounds until I came to the garage, where I tried to stay in the natural shadows cast from the estate's eaves.

Somewhere in the distance, two cats hissed. I jogged softly across the open driveway and buried my back into some six-foot bushes. The property was well landscaped, allowing me to stay behind foliage while I followed the wall of the house toward the backyard.

As I approached the corner, I heard a creaking sound from the rear of the yard, behind the waterfall and close to the border between the Bonello property and the adjoining golf course. As if on cue, a spotlight situated on the flagpole by the cabana snapped on and illuminated the area where the noise had come from. There was a rustle and the movement of a figure dropping down behind a bush, then a moment later two dark shapes running for the far corner.

A minute later the light went out as if it had lost interest. I studied the grounds for a while, seeing nothing out of the ordinary and hearing only the sounds of crickets singing in the warm night air.

I took a moment to let my nerves and the muscles in my neck relax. I started to turn toward the front of the house when the metallic click of a round being chambered in a pistol sounded directly behind my right ear, and a low voice growled, "Sweet dreams, motherfucker." As I was about to water the garden unintentionally, the same voice rose an octave and asked, "That you, Morgan?"

"Damn straight," I replied, turning my head slowly around to find Vincent pointing a very large, shiny pistol at my head.

"What the hell are you doing out here?" he asked, lowering the barrel to a safer position. "You scared the crap outta me."

"I almost beat you to it," I said, relaxing against the brick of the house and lighting a cigarette in my imagination.

Vincent, who was now looking more like a Vinnie and one of the *boys*, placed the pistol into an old-fashioned leather shoulder holster he was wearing over a white sleeveless T-shirt. "I saw the motion light come on by the flagpole. What were you doing at the back of the property?"

I blew out a lungful of imaginary smoke. I was starting to feel better. "I wasn't." I told him I was supposed to pick up Angelica, which he was already aware of, and I had noticed a suspicious car out front of the house. "I heard some commotion around back and saw some bodies heading over the fence to the golf course."

His head cocked at that. "You mean there was more of 'em?" He tugged his buddy out of the holster again and strode heavily across the flagstone in his bare feet, muttering, "What the fuck?"

After a few minutes of pointing his pistol and posturing his pecs, Vinnie came back across the patio and motioned me to follow him along the driveway. When we arrived at the walkway that connected the house to the three-car garage, he told me to wait.

He returned shortly and said Angelica would be waiting for me out front in about 15 minutes, so why didn't the two of us get to know each other a little better up in his apartment? He said I looked as if I could use a stiff one. It sounded a little kinky, but although he was carrying the gun and outweighed me by about 60 pounds I was pretty sure he meant "a drink."

We entered a side door and walked through the garage to an open staircase between the second and third stalls. The first held a big black Explorer loaded with all kinds of gadgets and antennas, which I figured was his. The second was a silver van equipped with a loading ramp for wheelchairs. It was the third that really caught my eye. Parked with its long nose pointing out toward the door was a majestic, classic sedan, its black skin polished to a sheen and its chrome so bright the numerous garage lights sparkled like diamonds on an ebony backdrop.

"Very, very cool," I remarked, admiring the vehicle. "You don't see too many of those around today. It's a Bugatti, right?"

Vinnie stopped and turned on the stairs. "Yup. A 1939 Bugatti Type 57. That was the old man's. Still runs like a charm. Mrs. Bonello kept it cleaned and tuned all these years."

"Like maybe he'll come home to it?"

"Yeah," he said, dropping his voice. "Some say he took off. Some say he took off with one of the casino girls. Some say he's on some beach where nobody'll find him." He turned and resumed his walk to the second level. "That's what some say," he said over his shoulder. "The old lady . . . she don't wanna believe none of it."

At the top of the stairs, we came to a small hallway that led to an open door.

"It's really a great apartment," Vinnie said. "I think it was built by Stephano, the guy I'm filling in for. He's back home taking care of some business problem or somethin.'"

It was a spacious, open-concept room with a double bed at one end, a kitchen and bath at the back, and a well-furnished living room looking out over the drive. A number of Native American rugs were tastefully laid out over a polished cedar plank floor. The walls were tongue-and-groove pine paneling, and a huge pine beam traversed the entire room. And instead of *Dogs Playing Poker*, intricate Navajo tapestries hung discreetly on the walls.

What I hadn't seen behind the open door when we'd entered was a long, business-like desk and leather captain's chair. The entire tabletop was covered with electronic gizmos and machines. Above was a wall of monitors showing a number of different locations around the Bonello estate.

Vinnie saw me eyeing the different shots. "Besides the cameras, there's infrared at various key entry and cross points around the property. I picked you up as soon as you crossed the beam through the front gates. Didn't know it was you, but I wasn't taking any chances, you know? I knew you were coming here tonight, but I figured you'd just drive in like you did last time, not park out on the street. When I went out to see who you were, I saw the light come on in the rear section of the yard." He leaned across the desk and flicked a switch, and a flashing red light in the bottom section of the screen in one of the monitors went out. "That was the sensor that went off when whoever hopped the back fence and crossed the beam."

"Once again, very, very cool." I wasn't sure what an elderly lady had to do with all this high-tech security, but I was still impressed.

Vinnie went to the kitchen and came back with two glasses and a bottle of lemon liqueur. He half-filled our glasses and motioned me to a seat on a sofa. "Okay, enough of the tour. We only got 10 minutes, so I need you to explain everything that went on when you got here and, if you can, why."

I sat as instructed. "You're going to debrief me?" I asked, sipping the sweet drink.

He sat on an ottoman opposite me and looked me in the eye. "You can call it whatever you want. I just wanna know why you parked out on the street and why you came in here all hush-hush and all." He could stare much better than Tony. "You just better hope it all makes sense to me. You got nine minutes left. Don't let me down."

I told Vinnie about the encounter Angelica and I had had with the two goombahs last night by the swimming pool and about the big black Cadillac. I also told him that, on our drive out earlier that day, I'd thought I'd seen the car following us on Boulder Highway. I explained that, when I'd pulled up tonight and saw what looked like the same car parked near the Bonello house, I'd thought I'd use a little caution and sneak in to make sure everybody was okay. I went on to describe my venture around the house and out back, where I'd thought I'd seen the same two guys. Vinnie sat quietly and nodded in all the right places.

"Why they'd be out here I don't have a clue," I told him.

For the time being, I left out the little cataclysm at my condo. As far as I could see, that was between my visitors and me. But I was piqued as to why all these little occurrences and violent flare-ups were happening to me and the Bonello family since we had linked at the airport.

"Vinnie, how come all the homeland security?"

"It's Vincent," he corrected. "And the 10 minutes are up. I saw the granddaughter earlier, and she was pretty excited about going for a night on the town. We don't want to keep her waiting."

I followed Vincent back down the stairs, through the garage, and around to the front of the house. Standing on the front entryway were Angelica and her grandmother, who balanced herself with a chrome four-legged walker. Orsina stood discreetly inside the open doorway with both hands on a blanketed wheelchair. Vincent asked for my keys so he could bring my car up the drive.

Surprisingly, Angelica was modestly dressed down for what I thought she might have had in mind for clubbing the Strip. Then again, it made sense, because the only time I'd seen her dress as "herself" and in today's style was when we'd met at the airport. Not only did she have to hide the fact that she smoked, but she had to dress down for her family as well. Her wardrobe tonight consisted of a plain, small-patterned cotton shift with a fairly high collar and a hemline just below the knees. There wasn't much that could hide the package contained beneath, but this outfit did a pretty good job of attaining the desired nonsexy effect.

"Mr. Morgan," the old woman demanded when Angelica had run back into the house for a jacket. "You are to have my granddaughter home at a reasonable time — before sunup, I would think. And care should be taken that she not wander off with one of the animal-like types that might frequent these establishments. Her family back east has worked very hard to keep their little angel as chaste and virtuous as can be in a world growing so immoral and dishonest. They, not to mention Julius Contini, would be terribly offended should her innocence become sullied."

*Was she talking about drugs? Booze? Her virginity?* Terrific. Chalk up a couple more items to the job description. Not only was I her tour guide/body guard, but now granny was holding me responsible for her morality as well. That was out of my control. And, to be honest, there were times when her flirtatious ways reminded me I was just a man, even if I was almost old enough to be her father.

Angelica came bouncing out of the doorway and gave her grandmother a hug and a peck on the cheek. "'Night, *nonna*. Love you."

Vincent drove up in the Chrysler, left my door ajar, and walked around to open the passenger door. The two of us climbed in and waved as we pulled away. I gave the horn a little toot.

As we headed down Buchanan toward Boulder Highway, Angelica pulled out a pack of cigarettes and fired up. I used my master controls to electronically crack open her window. She pulled out a compact from her purse, flipped down the visor with the lit makeup mirror, and started applying this and that. After a minute or so, she took a couple more puffs from the cigarette resting in the ashtray; then she reached into her jacket and pulled out a flask.

I gave her an admonishing look. "My, my — what would *nonna* say?"

Angelica gave me her sexiest smile while she unscrewed the cap and placed the opening between her recently glossed lips. When she'd taken a healthy sip, she pulled the flask away and made a face. "Wow . . . ," she breathed hotly, handing me the container. "Have some Jack, Jake?"

"Uh, no thanks," I said, too late.

The flask was in my hand, and Angelica was taking another drag while she scanned the stereo and settled on some loud Latin music that pounded out a sexual frenzy. She leaned over and lifted the flask to my lips. "Drink, silly. Get in the mood. I am." The tensions of the past 24 hours seemed to hammer away at me. While I tried to decide, she pried my lips open and poured an ounce or two down my throat.

She laughed, undid her ponytail, pulled out a hairbrush and a can of hairspray, and began brushing and spraying. When she finished a few minutes later, I'd taken another sip, or two, and left the flask on the console. She took another healthy swig and sprayed a small atomizer of perfume around her. It was a blend of jasmine and cinnamon, both intoxicating and stimulating on their own but an invigorating powerhouse of aroma when combined.

"Hey," I said. "While you've got your purse open, let me see your ID."

"Why?"

"Well, unless you've got some, you're not going to get into any of the clubs."

"Believe me," Angelica said with a laugh. "I never get turned away from the door. Actually, they usually let me in ahead of the line."

"Okay, I can understand that. But I know this town. There'll be lots of great-looking ladies in sexier clothes than what you're wearing. It's Vegas. No ID, no entry."

She huffed, rummaged through her purse, and handed me two cards. "Here's my birth certificate and photo ID."

I scanned the cards and learned she'd been born Angelica Marie Bonello and was in fact 21 years of age. I passed both back to her.

"Feel better knowing I'm old enough?" she asked with a smile.

"Very much so."

By the time we hit the highway, Angelica had her cosmetics applied and put away. She was getting into a groove, bouncing and moving to the Latin beat. We passed the flask a couple of times, and for the first time in days I felt the tensions slowly eroding and a warm relief taking their place.

Without warning, Angelica leaned over and gave me a peck on the cheek. "Thanks for taking me out to see some of the clubs tonight, Jake," she giggled good naturedly. "You're not as old and stuffy as you try to be."

"Well, you're in Las Vegas for a good time. And Big Julie is taking good care of me. It's my honor to show you around. As long as you don't expect me to get up there on the dance floor and make a fool of myself."

She laughed, took another shot of Jack, and sat back in her seat smoking a cigarette. After a moment she moaned, "God, I'm getting soooo hot!" She turned her back to me. "Unzip me, Jake. Then pull over so I can get out of this dress."

I did as I was told.

# Chapter

When the dust finally settled, we found ourselves on the grounds of a deserted trailer park. A couple of outbuildings shared the property with a family of sagebrush that bounced and roamed about the enclosure like a herd of horses in a corral. The only dim light showing was coming in from a standard on the highway.

Sure, I'd had a rough day, or two, and, if the truth be known, the smooth Tennessee Old No. 7 whiskey had rounded off some of the jagged edges and clouded some of my senses, but enough was enough. At least now I was sure Angelica was of legal age, for drinking or fooling around, but I was even more sure that, if this went any further and Big Julie or the folks back east found out, some future contractor would excavate some now remote desert lot for a new house foundation and stumble across my corpse.

"Look, Angelica," I pleaded.

"Shush," she chided gently. "Now close your eyes."

"Angelica . . . please."

"I said close them."

I shut my eyes reluctantly. "This isn't right. . . ."

"Don't be silly."

The sounds of her clothes rustling as she removed them seemed to warm the inside of the vehicle even more.

"Have you thought about what would happen if your family finds out?"

"Look, we'll just say it was my idea. It was, so I'll take the blame. And besides," she laughed, "who's going to tell them anyway? You?"

"Well, it's just that —"

The interior light snapped on, and there was a faint opaqueness through my eyelids.

"Ta-da," she sang out. "Okay, what do you think?"

"Angelica. . . ."

"Open your eyes and tell me if you like what you see."

"Ah, jeez."

"Open!"

I cracked open one eye and squinted in her direction.

"Wider!"

I opened both eyes and gaped.

"Sweet, huh?"

"You look . . . great," I answered. And she did.

She was wearing a pair of hip-hugging white shorts with loose thread fringes and embroidered every once in a while with little silver stars. A thin black rope with two bullets for a buckle acted as a belt but was obviously only an accessory. Her top was white leather, a partial jacket that hung dangerously apart, fastened with a thin gold chain and leaving very little to the imagination. The bottom rested three or four inches above her navel, where a tiny pair of dice chained to an ace and jack of diamonds pierced her perfect little belly button. Her lush blond hair floated freely around her face and to her shoulders in an untamed style that coincidentally matched her manner.

"Well, what do you think?" Angelica asked. "Front of the line or not?"

I fell back on the headrest and let out a hearty breath, then took a moment to settle my heart rate. "If I had a daughter your age, and I don't, I'd never let her wear that in public. However, compared with what I

thought you might be changing into, ahem, I approve of your selection."
I took a quick sip of Jack. "One hundred percent."

"Cool, then let's get going."

First up, around 1:30 a.m., was the Ghost Bar at the Palms. Angelica had a great time dancing with a number of available young men and women on the glass dance floor, 55 stories above the Vegas desert, while I looked down every once in a while and tried not to lose my equilibrium or my drink.

We hit the Green Valley Ranch around 2:45 a.m., and I sipped another beer while Angelica checked out the music and the people in the busy Whiskey Sky nightclub. We left shortly after 3:30 when I caught her sneaking outside to fire up some funny stuff with two young studs and another girl who already had a sizable buzz on.

The evening was rounded off with a stopover at Baby's in the Hard Rock, where even I got into the mood when a couple of early Stones tunes took over my legs and tried to make a fool out of me. Later, during a slow dance with a delicious bank teller I'd met at the bar, Angelica came over, tapped my dance partner on the shoulder, and asked, "May I?"

My dance partner looked at her, then at me.

I raised my eyebrows. "Again, later?"

"Maybe." She reached into a pocket, slipped me a business card, and sashayed away.

Angelica draped her arms over my shoulders and around my neck. "This was one sick night," she told me.

"You're not feeling well?" I asked.

She laughed and pressed herself a little closer. "No, silly. Sick means excellent. You know, like most awesome."

"Ah. Well, I'm glad you had a good time." I glanced at my watch. "But we better be going. The sun will be up in less than an hour, and I don't want to find your *nonna* at the gates with a sawed-off."

She snuggled her head into my shoulder. "Mmm. But only if we can do it again. We still missed a bunch of clubs I want to see before I leave."

"Okay," I said, disengaging the two of us. "One night at a time."

As we left, I waved a good-bye to the bank teller, but she took one look at who I was leaving with and shot me a glower that a Kevlar vest wouldn't absorb. At the coat check, Angelica retrieved her large cloth bag she'd snuck out of the house in her coat and asked me to wait while she went to the washroom to clean up and change.

I hung around watching the partygoers filter out slowly in pairs, even the ones who had earlier arrived single. I fumbled around in my pockets and came out with the bank teller's business card. I studied it and wondered what might have come about had we extended our encounter. Her name was Eileen Hanover, and her title was financial advisor. That was enough for me. I crumpled the card and tossed it into a nearby waste receptacle realizing it never would have worked. Sure, I'd heard opposites attract, but with her being a money-saving wizard and me being a money-spending fool we wouldn't have stood a chance.

"Hey, handsome, you lookin' for a little company?"

The voice had been debilitated by one too many unfiltered smokes and a few too many whiskey sours. She was late '40s, early '50s, with a lot of miles on her, an aged lioness looking for her youth in a cougar preserve. The bleached tresses were piled high, the façade hardened by the sun, and she looked like she didn't bother removing her cigarette to apply her lipstick.

"Uh, no, not right now, thanks," I stammered.

"I couldn't help but notice all those bumps and bruises. They turn me on. I like it rough, too." She gave me an exaggerated wink with a heavily covered, purple mascara eyelid.

"I, uh, play for the Anaheim Mighty Ducks hockey team. Right wing."

Just at that moment, Angelica came prancing out of the washroom. "Let's go, Jake!" She hooked an arm through mine and announced "Buh-bye" to the shocked woman.

We began walking away to the sound of "cradle-robbin' son of a bitch" echoing from behind as we parted company and left the building.

# Chapter  JACK

Thankfully, the drive back was uneventful. With no one following us, I spent the time playing with the Map Search and GPS onboard computer system while little Miss Partygoer snored lightly in the passenger seat. I thought about stopping at Sam's Town and cashing in my chips, but the morning sun was peeking its head over the Sunrise Mountains, and *nonna* had me on a tight leash.

The iron gates were closed as I pulled up, but as I contemplated whether to toot the horn or ring the intercom they swung silently open, and I followed the drive up to the house. I pulled up to the entryway, put the car in park, and turned off the ignition. The opening of my door caused the overhead interior light to come on, and the sudden brightness brought Angelica awake with a start. "What's up?"

"We're here," I told her. "Camp Bonello."

It took her a moment to collect herself and her belongings; then she opened the car door and bounded up the steps. The front door opened, and there stood the grandmother, apparently unarmed. I stayed on my side of the Chrysler for an extra second or two just to make sure.

"Good morning, *nonna*!" Angelica wrapped her arms around the old woman and gave her a light squeeze.

Olivia smelled her granddaughter's hair and nodded approvingly. "Not too much smoke and no hint of alcohol." She kissed Angelica's forehead and looked my way. "You've done well, Jake. You can come out from behind the car. I've no reason to shoot you," she said with a smile. "Yet."

"Oh, *nonna*," said Angelica. "Jake was a perfect gentleman."

To prove it, she bounced my way and planted a kiss on my cheek. I thought I heard her say "Maybe too perfect," but I couldn't be sure. She put her arm through mine and escorted me up the two stairs to the entryway.

"Thank you for taking good care of my granddaughter, Jake."

"It was no problem, Olivia. She was a perfect little lady, which I am sure runs in the family. And most likely your side."

"Oh, come on now, Jake," she chided, with a wave of her hand. "Cousin Julius warned me about your bullshit." Her smile told me she was more amused than upset.

"But you didn't have to wait up, Olivia," I assured her. "There was no need to worry."

"Oh, but I didn't," she chortled. "At my age, this is just when you get up."

"Excuse me, you two, but I'm going to bed," said Angelica. "It's been one phat night. Thank you both so much." She gave us each another peck and bounded off to her room.

"You took her out to a lot of eating establishments rather than musical ones?"

"No," I chuckled lightly. "She means p-h-a-t, phat. I think it means awesome."

The old woman laughed good naturedly. "I'll never understand these young people and their misuse of the English language." She had obviously worked very hard at learning English when she'd arrived in the country and was proud of having done so.

"Well, I better be going," I said.

The old woman looked at me with lucid eyes that defied her age. "How about a cup of coffee, Jake?"

I could tell right away that there was more to her invitation and hesitated.

"Orsina just made a pot of her special blend," she added.

My nose twitched at a new smell coming from inside the house, but it wasn't coffee.

"Ah," Olivia said. "That would be her freshly baked Tuscan bread and croissants."

That was enough invitation for me. I started up the steps.

"Join me in the library," said Olivia as she turned, retrieved her walker, and entered the house.

Before I followed, I took a look around the property in the early morning light. Nothing seemed amiss. And if Vincent was out there hiding behind a bush watching, I couldn't see him. I gave a little hidden wave to either side just in case he was out there and thought I hadn't spotted him.

"Here, take a seat."

We were in what had to be the library; being the bright detective I was, I noted the thousands of books that lined the walls from floor to ceiling. The octagonal room was windowless, with one of its sides wholly devoted to thick double doors and the opposite containing a fieldstone fireplace and mantel. The other six walls featured a dozen levels of mahogany shelving each, all entirely filled with thick leather and hardcovered tomes. Two narrow, matching mahogany ladders on wheels and attached to the wall allowed access to the books near the 16-foot ceiling.

Olivia directed me to one of the two burgundy leather wingback chairs that sat facing the unlit fireplace, discarded her walker, and took the seat kitty corner to mine. When Orsina arrived a moment later, she brought in a cart filled with steaming coffee, freshly baked bread, and a crystal bowl filled with freshly diced fruit. She poured our coffees into delicate bone china cups and left the room.

Olivia broke off a piece of Tuscan bread, and I helped myself to a warm croissant. The two of us sipped our coffee black. We made small talk for a few minutes, and I learned that the room had once been her husband's office, which explained the massive mahogany desk off to one side. When she filled our cups again with coffee and cleared her throat, I could tell the conversation was about to slip into second gear.

"What do you know about our family, Jake?"

That sort of caught me off guard. "Um, you seem like a real nice bunch of people, uh, you, Angelica, Orsina . . . even Big Julie and Vincent, I guess."

Her lips tightened, and then she said, "Jake, if we're going to trust each other, and I do believe we are going to have to, we will need to leave the bullshit aside." She took a sip of her coffee. "Do I make myself clear?"

"Yes, Olivia." I sat back in the chair. "What I know is that you and your husband moved out here in the '50s, and he worked for one of the casinos back then. I'm not sure where he is now. I assume you have at least one child since you have at least one granddaughter in Angelica. I also know that you are related in some way to my employer, Julius Contini, who got me involved in the first place. And you also have a need for a fair amount of security around here."

"And that's it?"

"For the most part."

"What about those two men who assaulted you and Angelica?" She sipped her coffee and asked, "Have you seen these men again?"

I breathed in deeply a couple of times to give me room to think. "Yes."

Olivia nodded her head in understanding. "I am old, Jake, and a lot of things about me, mentally and physically, are not what they once were, but my eyesight is still pretty good. I knew some of those cuts and bruises were newer. Tell me about it."

I gave her a rundown of what had happened at my apartment and told her everything I knew.

"Yes, the Desert Ranch was one of the casinos my husband, Carmine, ran. Along with a few others. His employers were rather well diversified in the hotel/casino management area at that time."

I finished my coffee and placed it on the cart. "Olivia, I thought we agreed not to bullshit each other?"

"Right you are, Jake," she chuckled. "Right you are." She collected herself for the real story I knew was coming.

"Carmine worked for the Accardo mob out of Chicago. He was Tony Accardo's right-hand man. When Vegas began booming in the '50s, Tony told Carmine to move us out here and take over his operation. Almost every hotel was run by Chicago, although none of their names were on the paperwork. There were a couple owned by the families in Detroit and New York, but Chicago ran everything else.

"We were just a young married couple then, and Vegas was such an exciting place to be. Carmine was based out of the Desert Ranch, but he had lieutenants in another five or six casinos he was responsible for as well. *Everyone* seemed to report to Carmine. We had the run of the town. Rubbed shoulders with all the big names back then. It was party time 24 hours a day. Every once in a while you had to remind yourself that this was all an illusion put on for the customers who traveled in for a few days a week. It was very easy to let the lifestyle take over one's state of mind if you weren't careful. One night we'd go out to listen to Nat King Cole and then end up having drinks with Danny Thomas. The next night we'd go see Paul Anka and have drinks with Sinatra. It was one heck of a time to be alive and quite the town to be living in."

Olivia took a moment to collect her thoughts.

"You probably know the casinos were not totally legitimate. They never reported to the government what they really made."

"How'd they get away with it?"

"I never knew all the ins and outs. Carmine never went into detail with me. The men who held high positions in the mob never really opened up about their work. I think it was something they counted on. No one could expect to get information out of somebody's wife if they didn't know anything."

"That's amazing, though. The casinos were already profitable back then. They must have been making a killing on everything else."

Olivia afforded herself a little laugh. "Bad choice of words."

I was afraid she might be referring to her husband's disappearance, but then she continued.

"There was a lot of killing going on, too. At the point Carmine went missing, the news of somebody buying a bullet in Vegas was almost a daily item or at least a rumor. I think that's why Carmine was having second thoughts."

"About staying in his position?"

"Our daughter, Sofia, Angelica's mother, was born a couple of years after we arrived out here. I think it had a bigger impact on Carmine than I would have ever imagined. For a man who dealt with the things he had to deal with on a daily basis, you would never have believed the tenderness and love he could express the moment he saw her face. As the weeks and years went on, and then Sam Giancana taking over for Accardo, I think Carmine realized that at some point his number would come up.

Eddie was still in the background day to day, but Sam was calling the shots. And no matter how well Carmine may have been doing for the boys in Chicago, he wasn't hand-picked by Sam and would probably have been replaced."

"That's still not the real story, though, is it?"

Olivia looked down at her lap and brushed away a crumb of bread. "I suppose I'm trying to bring about some kind of explanation, or answer, to why you and Angelica were accosted earlier."

"What does anything to do with the mob 50 years ago have to do with me being used as a punching bag?"

Olivia went to pour each of us another cup. "I believe it has everything to do with it, Jake, but you'll have to hear me out."

I took the coffee and took a long drink, embarrassed at how I held out my pinkie. Then I grabbed two more croissants. I listen better on a full stomach.

"I have to believe Angelica's abduction, your home invasion, and the breach of our property's security have something to do with my husband."

That caught me off guard. "Your husband? But he's. . . . I thought he was. . . ."

"I know, I know. I probably sound like my medication is wearing off." Olivia settled back in her chair. "Carmine has been missing for 45 years. He went to work back in October of '59 and never came home." She looked at me for a reaction. "He just fell off the face of the Earth."

"No good-byes? No notes? No explanation?"

"Not a thing. And I will be very frank with you, Jake. Most people believe Carmine took off from everybody, everything, and that he's probably out of the country, basking on some beach and surrounded by native girls serving rum punch."

"And the others?"

"A small group thinks he was killed." Olivia held her body stiffly. "I'm not a convinced member of either camp."

I tried imagining what running a mob casino must have been like back in the early days of Vegas, and my initial opinion of his whereabouts leaned the same way. But I did remember the old Bugatti in the garage and the care it was given to keep it maintained.

"And you believe he may still come back?"

"I don't know what to believe. But I know what I *want* to believe." Her eyes moistened slightly. "There was talk when he disappeared that he may have left with a fortune in cash and another woman. That he was stealing from the people he worked for. But I can't resign myself to believing he would leave me to spend the rest of his life with someone else. Especially without any warning. Especially without Sofia.

"He was the father of my only child, Jake. And as I said, despite his reputation as head of the mob's Vegas operation, he was a wonderful parent and a loving husband. As to whether he was seeing someone on the side, I could not say for sure. When you are the wife of a made man, someone so high in their chain that they would entrust a new cash-yielding frontier like Vegas to him, you sometimes had to force yourself to look the other way. Back then it seemed that everyone who was anyone had a girlfriend stashed somewhere. It was almost a part of the job description. But they always knew where their home was. And the people they worked for expected them to always remember that. They were big believers in having a little something on the side, but they were even bigger believers in the love and respect one should hold for one's family. It was a credo they would not allow to be broken.

"And Carmine truly was a family man. He loved his little Sofia as much as a father could, and if anything had changed Carmine in any way it was becoming a father. I would watch him playing with Sofia on Sunday afternoons, whispering and cooing into her ear, telling her that someday he was going to take her and momma away, to a place far away from Las Vegas, a place where he could spend seven days a week with the two of us, not seven hours. That sounded so wonderful to me. Occasionally, I would ask him what he meant. He would smile, give me a kiss, and tell me it was already planned and in motion, to just be patient and trust him. And I did trust him, Jake. I still do. We were madly in love and brutally honest with each other. I will never accept that he left me and his child for another woman. Not without a single word to me. Never."

Olivia had become very emotional, and I thought about getting up to comfort her. She dabbed at the corner of her eye with a fine lace handkerchief. "No, never." We sat like that for an uncomfortable moment.

"Olivia, I know there is something wrong with this picture, and I'll probably regret asking, but where is your daughter? Why didn't she raise Angelica?"

She collected herself and then said, "Sofia was a product of Las Vegas. She was everything my husband didn't want his family to be tainted with by remaining in this city."

"She *was?*"

"I lost my husband suddenly one day in October 1959, Jake, but I lost my daughter right before my eyes over the course of five or six years."

"I'm so sorry, Olivia, I didn't mean. . . ."

"It's all right, Jake. It's something I've dealt with. Something I've gone over and analyzed a million times, but the ending was already written years earlier. Sofia was one of those who got caught up in the Vegas lifestyle. You probably know what I'm talking about, Jake. This place was built so the average person could come and let their hair down for a long weekend or two every year. That's fine. You always had time to recover when you got back home. But if Vegas *is* your home, well, you have to learn to watch out for the pitfalls lined up everywhere to snare you."

My expression probably showed I knew exactly what she was talking about.

"Well, Sofia never learned. Or didn't want to bother to. No matter what she was told or advised, she went the other way. First it was the booze that almost did her in. There were times I wouldn't see her for days and worry myself sick. Stephano, my husband's old friend and family protector, would see my distress, leave, and come home a day or so later carrying a passed-out Sofia from the car to her room without a word. I tried rehab, private counselors, everything I could think of, but she wouldn't listen or adjust. She was a fire cat, and Las Vegas was made for her. When she had money, she blew it. When she couldn't get any more, she'd sit down with any drunk who could afford her.

"I was pretty sure she was doing mild drugs then, too. I'd found rolling papers and pipes in her room on numerous occasions. But then in the '80s — she was in her mid-20s then — she started taking harder drugs. She ended up in the hospital after an overdose. The paramedic said they were able to revive her heart in the ambulance or she wouldn't have made it. She tried to clean up her act after that scare and seemed to be making some inroads. Then she met another guy from out of town who professed his love for her after two days in Sin City. They celebrated by knocking back a couple of bottles of bourbon and conceiving a baby to commemorate the occasion.

"Well, you guessed it, the father took off after a few months, never to be seen again. The two girls stayed with me. Fortunately, I think Sofia had kept herself fairly clean for the pregnancy. But after that, I swear, I didn't recognize the being I'd brought into this world."

Olivia stopped and sipped her coffee.

"I don't even know when I really lost her — that period of my life drifts in and fades away. It was hell on little Angelica growing up. The one birthday her mother actually did remember and plan a party for, I think it was Angelica's fifth, we had to go downtown and bail her out. Her baby daughter watched as Orsina and I threw out her mother's clothes and washed the vomit and booze from her. Sofia wasn't even around for Angelica's sixth birthday. The week before Angelica turned seven, I had to go down to the morgue to identify Sofia's body."

"Drugs?"

"Yes, in some kind of combination that should never be taken."

"I'm really sorry, Olivia." And I was.

"Angelica stayed with me for a few months, until we got all the paper-work done, and then she went back east. She stayed with a couple of aunts and uncles who had a bunch of kids her age on a huge estate outside New York. Carmine's 'family' was quite insistent that they would take her in. And honestly, I just didn't think it was right to try to raise her myself, especially out here. The city had taken everything I had ever loved, but I couldn't leave. I still can't. Not until Carmine is put to rest."

"And Angelica had no problems with that?"

"She accepted them in every way and they her. She had as normal a childhood as she could have had under the circumstances. And she seems to have turned out nicely. I would have hated to see what this town might have done to her. She's been out to visit a couple of times, and I went back east as often as I could. But with my present health, it is impossible for me to travel well. I thought having Angelica come out to visit one last time would be nice."

"One last time? Don't think that way, Olivia. I've heard people with dementia have lived with it for years. And look at you. Listen to you! You barely have any signs that it is debilitating you."

Olivia smiled. "That's very kind of you, Jake, very kind. But stories of my illness have not been altogether accurate."

The confusion must have shown on my face.

"I chose dementia for just those reasons, Jake, that my symptoms could come and go and be hard for anyone outside to monitor. The truth is I have cancer. The doctors have given me six months. Outside of the hospital, you and Orsina are the only two who know. I would like to keep it that way."

The shock must have shown.

"Jake, I have been dying a slow death for almost 45 years, ever since Carmine disappeared. I have had plenty of time to tidy up my affairs . . . to get ready. Believe me, it is not a totally bad thing. As I said before, I just wish Carmine and I could have escaped and raised our daughter elsewhere. I dream about where we might have gone and the things we might have done. And what Sofia might have made of herself."

Thankfully, we were back on a topic I still had questions about. "What do you think your husband meant by that, Olivia, that someday he would take you and your daughter away? Did he ever discuss it? Go into any details?"

"No, not really. We often joked about how wonderful it would be to live near water, where there were trees and the sand was a beach and not a desert. How it would be far better for our daughter to be raised in a somewhat normal environment as opposed to life for a child in Las Vegas."

"Would it have been that easy for him to just leave any time he wanted to?"

"No, actually, it probably wouldn't have been that simple. But something told me Carmine had a plan already in place for us. Whenever the subject came up, he would smile at me and assure me that things were being taken care of in order to fulfill our dreams."

"I expect he was making good money. Would it have been enough to keep the three of you going elsewhere on such an early retirement?"

"Sure he was making a good income. But so much went into his lifestyle. I think that was part of how the organization kept its people. They paid them well, gave them costly expectations, but at the same time gave them things like homes, cars, and accounts so it made it that much harder if you wanted to get away. If somehow you managed to leave, you'd lose all the large perks they'd bestowed upon you."

"Would he have tried to pick up a new profession?"

"Carmine was only 35 years old, but he had lived a lifetime. He made it sound like he wanted to spend all his time with us, to make up for time lost in the last few years. I remember early one morning, it had to be around 4 a.m., I awoke from a dreadful dream about the three of us running away from some unknown terror. I came downstairs, and there he was sitting at his desk, carefully painting a clay model of his Bugatti. It was his pride and joy. A creation he'd had commissioned from one of the best sculptors in Rome. Meticulous down to the finest detail.

"I told him about my worries and asked him what we would do for money if we left Las Vegas. He stood, kissed me, and placed a finger on my lips, telling me not to worry, that I'd never have to worry about anything again. Especially about money. He kissed me again warmly, told me to return to bed, and went back to his painting."

She laughed lightly at the memory.

"I still have that car. It's upstairs in our daughter's old bedroom. A beautiful piece, really." Her face went solemn for a moment, and then she added, "He never liked to get his picture taken, but there's a photograph leaning against the model car of Carmine and I, with him holding our infant daughter in a blanket while we stood proudly next to his car. He loved that picture. He called it his 'prides and joys,' the three things he loved most in his life.

"But you know, Jake, even though I've lived much of my adult life wishing and praying for him to walk through those doors and take his place at his desk, I would almost prefer that Carmine was dead than to believe he left for someone else. I realize I don't have a lot of time left in this world, but it hurts me so much not knowing. It almost paralyzes me with fear that I'll die and never know why the only man I ever loved left me. Did he really take off with some Vegas showgirl without a thought of Sofia or me? Or did he die on some empty parcel of desert sand, unable to say good-bye?" She wiped at her eye. "I am so afraid that not knowing may prove to be crueler to me in the end than my death could ever be."

I let her collect herself while I thought about what she had told me; then I said, "Olivia, there has to be more to it. What's the association with what happened 50 years ago and the recent incidents?"

"If there is, Jake, I don't know what it could be."

I had an idea — but I'd keep it to myself for now.

"Olivia, I know this is hard for you, but think back to when this all happened. What did the people he worked for say? They must have had some thoughts."

"*Il mio dio!* Those bastards. They hounded me day and night for weeks. It was bad enough that my husband had disappeared, but then I had to have them around me day and night. At first, they tried to console me, those ugly apes, but none of them knew how. They didn't think I saw their snickering at the thought that Carmine had left and taken off with some young dancer."

"Why did everyone seem to think that?" I asked her.

"As I said earlier, most men in my husband's position tended to have something going on on the side. Some companion to look good with when the boys visited from back east and wanted to be entertained until the wee hours. Most of these men didn't want their wives involved in the business side of their lives. They knew the sleaziness. The booze. The drugs. Most of the floozies they hung around with were a step up from whores, and no made man would be respected for having a wife who fell into their category. It may not have been right, Jake, but that was the way it was.

"And the icing on the cake as far as they were concerned was that his car was found at the airport a few days later."

"The Bugatti?"

"Yes. The airport wasn't like it is today, with high-rise parking lots and tickets printed with the time you arrived. There was just a big outdoor parking lot with hundreds of cars, and you parked where you wanted for as long as you wanted. No charge. With Vegas having a 24-hour airport, and the hundreds of flights that arrived and departed, there was no way of tracking where he may have flown to."

"If he in fact flew."

"What do you mean?"

"Maybe it's just me, but, if I was going to make myself scarce and wanted to throw the hounds off my scent, I might park at the airport too, then take a bus, rent a car, or thumb my way off into the distance."

Olivia looked off into the dark fireplace, now aware that the airport may have been a ruse; then she said, "Or someone else parked the car, and Carmine didn't go anywhere."

That was just as likely.

"Olivia, didn't any of the senior people in his organization ever speak with you? To get your side of things? You know, like were the two of you getting along, were there any problems at home, did he have debts to people that they may not have known about?"

"I was visited many times. Some, the earlier ones, were friendlier than others. At the beginning, they were apologetic and almost sensitive. But as the days and weeks passed, they became more confrontational. Men I'd never seen were being sent to my house. They started asking me questions about money that Carmine may have been putting away for a rainy day. Of course, I told them he hadn't, and as far as I knew that was the truth. As time went on, more senior men arrived, saying that Carmine may have been withholding on the money he was responsible for sending back to Chicago.

"Now they insisted on looking around the house and the grounds. The goons they had searching were not light-handed, careful, or even respectful. Bookshelves were emptied and holes drilled to look for hidden compartments. The sofas and furniture were poked and prodded, mattresses and cushions slit, and drawers overturned into a giant mess. Every nook and cranny was poked and prodded. They even dug holes out back.

"I pleaded with them to stop and tell me what it was they were looking for. When they had finished and not found anything, they sat me down and asked if I knew anything about hidden cash, bank accounts, a map, or paperwork that might help clear up this matter. There was no need for me to lie to them. I had no information to give them, and I told them so.

"Eventually, the visits dwindled, but for years I knew I was followed. The grocery store, the gymnasium, and especially when holidaying, here or outside the country. It was as if they were expecting Carmine to appear out of thin air, taking me in his arms and showering me with kisses and $100 bills. Even now, almost 50 years later, I can't help but feel like my phones have been tapped and my life monitored on some remote chance that I find something, or learn of something, about the day my husband disappeared."

"What was your relationship with your husband's people in the end?

Were they still there if you needed them? I realize there's no official pension fund in the mob, but would they look out for you if needed?"

"Carmine had an adequate insurance policy. It just took longer than usual before it was all straightened out. In the meantime, things *were* taken care of. The house was paid off, there were no debts, and every once in a while a check would come in the mail. Orsina and my regular man-around-the-house, Stephano, who has been with me since my husband vanished, have been taken care of by someone in the Jersey family. They even arranged for Vincent to be here for Stephano, who had to go back to Sicily to clear up some family matters."

"Sounds like a very creepy setup. A love-hate relationship. They want you around, but only because you might unearth something immensely valuable to them."

"It's the way it's always been, unfortunately."

I managed to glance at my watch. It was just past 7:30 in the a.m. My body ached, my head still hurt, and the episode back at my apartment hadn't done much for my machismo. My entire system felt like it was about to go on standby.

"I better be going, Olivia, it's getting early."

"Or is it getting late?" she replied with a smile.

I got up from the chair and stretched. "One or the other, I guess."

Olivia rose as well and took hold of her walker. "Well, I do appreciate our little chat, Jake. And I want you to know that I do know a bit about your past, that you were once a police officer, and I feel very comfortable with you looking after my Angelica while she is here. I'm not sure what is going on with the mysterious assaults, but if there is anything you could find out, or discover, I would be forever in your debt."

"I'll do what I can, Olivia, but for the most part I'm just Angelica's tour guide and escort. I think these guys that jumped us are pretty much convinced we have no idea what they are talking about. I'm sure this is going to blow over soon, if it hasn't already."

"I hope so," said Olivia as we exited the library and made our way to the foyer.

We had reached the entryway, and when I opened the door the bright sunlight flooded in and attacked my pupils until they went pinpoint sharp. The heat hitting my body made me even more tired, and like a zombie I said my good-byes and shuffled to the Chrysler.

I sat down, enveloped by the warm leather, and turned on the ignition. I cranked up the AC to keep me awake and rolled down the passenger window to wave good-bye.

"Jake! Wait up!"

*No, please no.*

Angelica was giving her grandmother a big kiss; then she shouted, "I slept like a total log while you two yakked away. Now I'm starving. Let's get some breakfast!"

She waved back to *nonna* as she bounded down the steps, opened the door, and jumped in; then she punched me playfully on the shoulder and gave me a big smile. "So, didja miss me?"

I thought about punching her back, but granny was still waving and watching. "Like a nerve misses a sloppy root canal."

# Chapter

Angelica was no dummy. She knew I was pissed and didn't push her luck. We did the drive back to Vegas with a minimum of conversation, and what small amount we spoke was brief and polite. She even did her little costume change at a service station restroom when I stopped for gas. This time she changed from jeans and a baggy, long-sleeved sweater into a hot pink silk halter top with spaghetti straps, matching cotton short-shorts, and white tennis shoes and ankle socks with little pink pom-poms on the backs. Not that I noticed. The package was rounded off with her hair in a ponytail, which made her look even younger. Lucky me.

The sugar daddy thing was wearing a little thin, especially since I would never do anything about it. On top of that, Angelica was crowding my style with some of the available ladies out there. It was bad enough that the last woman I'd fallen for was the sex goddess showgirl Rachel. And, well, as good as I am sure I was, I didn't want to lose practice.

Angelica decided on the Palms for breakfast because somebody at the Hard Rock had told her last night that Britney, or Christina, or Beyonce was supposed to be staying there. With Angelica, it was hard to tell if she wanted to actually meet them or be seen near them, where she might stand out as being even better looking and be discovered by some talent scout snooping around.

It was just as well that we were off the beaten path, because there was no way in hell I was going to chance taking her, dressed the way she was, to the Oasis or anywhere Big Julie might see us. He would undoubtedly find me responsible for her attire.

I directed the friendly coffee shop hostess to a table near the back, where we could be inconspicuous. She gave me a knowing wink for being the sleazebag she took me for and told me she understood. I explained to her that the young lady with me was the infamous Angel, that I was her manager, and that we were just trying to hide from the public for a quiet breakfast. She promised us anonymity after requesting that Angelica sign a paper napkin for her daughter.

"Why do you do that?" She pulled out a pack of cigarettes, stuck one in her mouth, and rummaged around in her purse for a light.

"What?" I asked. I found a package of matches, lit one, and held it out toward her.

"You know what I mean." She pointed the cigarette at the flame and puffed until she got it going. "Thank you."

"You're welcome."

"But you always do that."

"What?"

"You act like you're disappointed with the way I look. Like you're embarrassed to be seen with me."

"Oh, come on. Of course I'm not. You are a beautiful and stylish young woman, with *young* being the operative word."

A waitress came over and gave us menus and a carafe of coffee. She gave a little curtsy to Angelica as if the hostess had told her they had royalty sitting in the back. She said that she'd return in a minute to take our order.

"Look," I told Angelica. "If I was 21 again, I'd probably be fumbling and bumbling around after you, too, like that kid at the airport parking."

"That *was* kinda cute. . . ."

"But let's get serious. I'm older. Not to mention wiser."

She blew out a puff of smoke. "I'm not clueless about my family's background, you know. You're really talking about the fact that I'm a Bonello."

"Ah, bingo has been called."

"And Uncle Julius would be offended?"

"Uh-huh," I said, opening my menu. "Unless there's a stronger word that means 'He'd cause me misery and pain.'"

Angelica opened hers, and I heard her say, "Hmm. Well, I could have sworn I saw you fumble a couple of times since we met. . . ."

I closed my menu and stared at her over it. "Girl, do you have any idea what your uncle might do to me if I stepped out of line? Construction companies are coming up with buried bodies out in the desert two or three times a month while they dig sites for new homes. Hell, I'm even afraid to think what *nonna* might do to me if she found out you were smoking, drinking, and changing into outfits like you're wearing now. And Vincent looks like he would like the target practice, too."

The waitress returned and happily took our orders. Angelica had two Pop Tarts coated with peanut butter, a bowl of strawberries, coffee, and a Bud Light. I went out on a limb and had bacon and eggs with a side order of toast. I capped off my breakfast with a glass of freshly squeezed orange juice, and Angelica had another Marlboro. We eventually left without seeing any stars and none of them seeing us.

Angelica explained that she just *had* to pick up some new clothes while she was in Vegas, so I killed a little time by giving her a half hour tour of the Strip until the Fashion Show mall opened at 10. I found a parking spot close to the high wall of Saks Fifth Avenue that would provide me with shade for a while and told her to go knock herself out for at least two hours because that was how long I planned to sleep. I also told her to pick up a book or magazine because, when we left here, I had something to do downtown that would take a half hour or so. She started to argue, but I gave her a look that stopped her in midsentence, and she wisely backed off.

"Okay, fuddy-dud, I can tell you need a nap or you're going to be cranky all day. Two hours should do me just fine."

I made sure Angelica knew exactly where I was parked in relation to Saks and what exit to take on her return. If anything looked in the least suspicious inside, I told her, she was to go to the cashier of the nearest store, ask for help, and call me on the cell phone or pager. She told me she'd be fine and made sure she wiggled her way to the entrance of the store. Of course, I couldn't help but notice.

I called information on my cell and got the number I needed for my appointment. One more call and everything was arranged for 12:30 p.m. I opened all the windows, reclined the seat, and closed my eyes. I think I drifted off at the count of the eighth Angelica jumping over a short fence, but it may have been just a dream.

The loud thud of something hitting the trunk of the car brought me out of a deep sleep; so much for relishing the merits of being the only male on a college cheerleading squad. Unfortunately, when I woke, I thought I had drifted off somewhere out on the highway. My body stiffened, I grabbed the steering wheel for all it was worth, and started pumping the brake like a madman.

"Jake, will you pop the trunk, puh-lease. . . ? It's hot as hell out here."

When I finally realized that the wall of Saks wasn't getting any closer, I relaxed, looked in the rearview mirror, and pushed the trunk release button.

Angelica was back there with two or three security types from the mall and a colorful collection of boxes and bags. When the guys had finally got everything put away and were on their final round of flexing, posing, and flashing their pearly whites for her attention, Angelica played her part to perfection, giving them two-fisted handshakes of gratitude, with lots of touching and the hope of future prospects. When she finally got into the car, the three of them walked around with shit-eating grins, bumping into benches and each other.

I started the car and closed the windows. She fired up a cigarette, and we made our way out of the parking lot.

"You know how to work a crowd."

"Don't be silly," she said, cracking the window to let the smoke out. "They were just coming to the aid of a poor helpless tourist."

"That was a lot of bags. I hope it didn't leave you poor."

I came to Las Vegas Boulevard and made a left, heading north and downtown.

"No, *nonna* gave me a credit card earlier and told me to have a good time shopping and not to worry what it cost. But there are some things that I can't show her."

"Granny wouldn't approve?"

"No way. Not in a million years. But I bet you and Vincent would," she cooed. "You should see me in the Body Glove swimsuit I got. It's totally hot. Do you like thongs?"

"Uh, yeah, sure," I answered, trying to concentrate on my driving.

"And did you know the mall has a Victoria's Secret *and* a Frederick's of Hollywood? I couldn't decide who had the sexier lines, so I got a big bag from each. You wouldn't believe some of the things they're coming out with. I'm in the fashion industry, and I couldn't believe it. But I bought some anyway." She gave out a little giggle and muffled what sounded like "And one toy."

Enough was enough. I was being forced to bring out the heavy artillery. "Did you know I can name every team in the NFL and their starting quarterbacks?"

Angelica had put out her cigarette a moment earlier and was firing up another. "That is really whacked, man. I'm talking about all this sexy stuff I bought, and you wanna talk about basketball?"

"Football."

"Whatever. But it sure sounds — Jake! Stop the car!"

Luckily, I had just practiced this; I stomped on the brakes and corrected our spin. The rear end came up, and I heard the bags and boxes toss around in the trunk. We had barely cleared an intersection on a yellow, and fortunately there were no other vehicles behind us. As I looked around in panic, I realized there were no cars to the left, or to the right, or even in front of us. There was no baby stroller that had rolled out onto the road, no elderly person who had inadvertently walked out into the traffic, not even a child's ball that had bounced in our path. I pulled over to the curb to catch my breath.

"What the hell was that all about?" I demanded.

"Jake, look me in the eye and tell me the truth." She was turned right around in her seat facing me. "You're not gay, are you?"

I bit down on my lower lip, counted to 10 by twos, and looked her in the eye with my eyes as wide as casino chips. "Do you mean am I *happy?*"

She gave me a quizzical look. "No, like in, do you like —"

"I know what the hell you mean!" I yelled. "Is that why you almost got us killed? For Christ's sake, what the hell ever made you think that I was gay? Not that there's anything wrong with it. . . ."

"Well, I don't know," Angelica said, sitting back in her seat and trying not to pout. "There I was talking about all these sexy clothes and things, and then you start talking about sports, and guys, and stuff. And then I thought about how uncomfortable you were when I was changing in the car the other night, and I don't know. It would have explained it, I s'pose. I guess I just put two and two together. . . ."

I checked my left and pulled the Chrysler back out onto Las Vegas Boulevard. "You put two and two together and got 'gay'? You better work on your math, little lady."

"Well, I was just having a little fun with you, and you were talking about men's sports and tight ends —"

"Quarterbacks!" I shouted. "I was talking about starting quarterbacks. It was a joke. Get it? I was using the sports metaphor as an example of when a man and a woman are having, uh, relations and the man, well, he doesn't want the relations to be over too soon, so to take his mind off what's going on, well, he thinks about sports, baseball scores, you know."

She was looking at me as if I was nuts. "I don't have a clue what you're talking about, Jake. I've had boyfriends, you know, and I'm not going to say how far — hey, hold on. Is that where you guys get that baseball stuff from?"

"I don't know what you mean."

"You know." She put on a husky male voice. "So, Bob, how'd it go last night? How far did you get? First base, second base? Oh, too bad, it was rained out?"

I couldn't help but chuckle. "No, but that's a good one."

"Well, all I can say is that no guy has ever talked about sports when we've been alone and fooling around."

"Okay, okay, enough is enough. Let's forget the whole thing, all right? Rest assured, I'm a 100 percent, all-American, grade A heterosexual. Case closed."

"Uh-huh."

"I mean it!"

"All right, already."

We had just arrived downtown, and I finally found a parking spot just off Stewart Avenue in front of some stores. It wasn't the best of areas, a bunch of pawnshops, some bail bond offices, and some seedy storefronts that didn't advertise what they offered inside, but the Las Vegas Metropolitan Police Department was just down the street, and that had to mean something. I told Angelica I wouldn't be long, a half hour at the most, and she said it was no biggie. She said that she had some magazines and a bottle of water in her bag and that she would be fine.

"And you don't open the car for anyone," I told her. "Do you hear me?"

"Yes, I hear you."

I left her the car keys in the ignition. "You've got the radio for company, and that's it. Leave the windows and the roof open a bit, but if it gets too warm start the car up and run the air-conditioning."

"Don't worry. If I have a problem, I'll beep you. I think I'm going to call Uncle Julius and see if we can stop by the Oasis later and use the pool."

"And try out your new swimwear, I bet." The kid might be in for a shock. There were always gorgeous showgirls and hookers who used the pool area to touch up their tan lines. Their outfits looked like they were made out of dental floss and cotton swabs and might give Angelica a run for her money.

"Sure, why not?" she said. "I won't be able to wear it at *nonna*'s, that's a guarantee."

I might want to talk with Big Julie myself after I was finished down here. I got out of the car, leaned my head in, and pointed a finger at her. "Don't forget what I said."

"Go, go, go already."

I shut the door and heard her use the power lock. The music went on and then up, and I shook my head as I walked quickly down the street.

⟨❖⟩

I entered the LVMPD building and walked up to the front desk. "Jake Morgan to see Lieutenant Oakley."

The desk sergeant gave me the once over, wondering if the bumps and bruises posed any threat, then told me to take a seat. He kept one eye on me while he spoke into a phone. I thumbed through an issue of *Police Marksman* without a lot of interest. Next was an issue of *Women Police*, which I took a little more time with because of my love for women in uniform. If there had been a centerfold, somebody had got to it before me.

A door opened down the corridor. "Morgan, down here." A big, thick hand prompted me to come its way, so I did.

When I got to the doorway, the same voice said, "The coffee is still where it was last time you were here. Grab a cup while I make a quick call."

I went back to the front desk and into the little nook that housed the coffeemaker. I took a Styrofoam cup and poured two-thirds full; then I added a little whitener. As I was stirring, I noticed a tray of washed cups and one I remembered in particular. It was big, white and read "World's Greatest Dad." I took it and filled it up, leaving enough room for three sugars. I carried the two cups past the sergeant, who was looking to make sure I hadn't walked off with any spoons or tea bags.

Oakley was wrapping up his telephone call when I reentered his office and closed the door. He nodded his thanks at the sight of his cup, took a sip, and gave me a thumbs-up.

The lieutenant hadn't changed a bit. He was still his thick, well-built self, six-two or -three, topped off with a full head of thin blond hair. Young, at 35, I had always thought, for a homicide detective. He had been the lead investigator in the Valentine case last summer, and we had first met while he was trying to arrest me for the murder.

"Yes, captain. I'll look into it. You've got my word. Thank you, sir."

He placed the receiver into the console.

"So what brings you here, Shamus? You got a speeding ticket needs fixing?"

I did have a couple of parking tickets in the Vega glove compartment. "You can do that?" I asked.

"No. Of course not. I was just shittin' you." Oakley sipped his coffee again. "But you did get my java right. Very observant of you." He pulled out his notepad. "So you wanna file charges?"

That caught me off guard. "For what?"

"On the girl guide that beat the crap outta you." He shook his head slowly. "What the hell happened?"

"Ah, the bruises, right. . . . Would it help if I told you 'You should see the other guy?'"

"I doubt it, but let me hear it."

I went into detail telling him about my assignment regarding Angelica, the run-in with the boys outside my apartment as well as the one inside, and a general overview of the Bonello family history or at least what little I knew and understood of it.

"I don't have anything to do with the Organized Crime Unit, but it sounds like some kind of mob retribution has reared its head. Did you get a plate number on that black Caddy?"

I told him I had and dug around in my pockets until I finally found the scrap of paper.

"Lemme run it." Oakley turned to his computer, cracked his knuckles, then started typing with a practiced flair. He finished by punching the Enter button with a flourish of his index finger. "There, let's see what happens."

We filled the moment by catching up on old times. He asked if I was still seeing Rachel and was good enough not to pry further when I just pursed my lips and shook my head once. Before he could ask anything else, a little bell sounded from the computer.

"The plate matches a black '88 Cadillac Sedan de Ville."

"You got an owner and address?"

Oakley glanced over to me. "Now listen to me, cowboy. This is for informational purposes only. I don't want you taking this matter into your hands, paying them a visit, and having them bust you up worse than they already have. After all, you weren't that pretty to start with."

"I promise I won't do anything stupid without letting you know first. Who's the owner?"

Oakley turned back to his computer screen. "Hmm, it's not a 'who'; it's a 'what.' The car is registered to a Perrotta Meats and Poultry. Right here in Vegas." He typed in a few things and then said, "Okay, I've sent an inquiry e-mail up to the guys in OCU. The mob might not be openly involved in the ownership of the hotels and casinos anymore, but nothing is grown or manufactured here in Vegas, so everything like food, furniture, clothing, booze, I mean *everything*, has to be shipped in. And that's where you'll find *da boys*. Behind the scenes."

I asked the lieutenant what he knew of the "old days" in Las Vegas and, more specifically, about how the mob ran the casinos and how they profited from them in illegal ways. Especially about their skimming operations.

"Not my area of expertise, Morgan. But it's an interesting bit of local history, that's for sure."

"I guess I could try the library, research it there."

"It'll take you forever to find the right books. I know who the department uses when it needs back info on stuff like that — the Gambler's Book Store over on 11th Street at Charleston. Guy named Howard Schwartz, been there for years. What he doesn't know about Vegas, or gambling, he'll know where to find it."

"I might give it a shot later. I doubt it'll help me understand what's going on with these two jerks following me, but from what Mrs. Bonello was saying it was an interesting venture that the mob had going on back then. Sorta like a win-win situation."

"Good luck. I'll let you know if I learn anything from upstairs. You still at the same phone number? In the meantime, Morgan, don't do anything dumb. Boston PD didn't prepare you for guys like this. They still think of it as their town, and they're really good at proving it. Let *us* show them who really controls Vegas now. You get anything, or they go any further without killing you, give me a call, and I'll take it to the right people. You've got no one to watch your back, and to them blackjack dealers are a dime a dozen."

"Poker. I'm a poker dealer now."

"Okay, sorry. . . . Poker dealers are a quarter a dozen."

Oakley and I finished up, and on my way out I thought about Angelica all alone in the car and probably bored out of her mind, and I started to feel a little guilty. Maybe I'd take her to Baskin-Robbins and give her a treat.

I came around the corner and could see the Chrysler four or five spots down. But I couldn't see Angelica. I figured she must have gotten tired and decided to lay back and crash for a while. I walked toward the car and noticed that the butterflies in my stomach seemed to multiply with each step.

When I got to the Chrysler, I saw that the windows were up and the engine quiet. I gave the passenger side a double beep with my remote and opened the door, poking my head into the back when I found the front seats empty. "Damn!" I shouted, loud enough for anyone a block away to hear. I looked up and down the street two or three times, then across the street. I started to check out the signs and window fronts of each establishment in case she'd gone in to use the facilities or something. But no luck. Like I said, the stores here were all bail bonds places, pawnshops, and . . . oh, crap, *sex shops*.

If Angelica had gotten out of the car for any reason, most males in this end of town would have tripped over their feet trying to meet her. Unless it had been the boys in the Cadillac. *Damn!* Very bad thoughts started to enter my mind, and the disgusted faces of Big Julie and Olivia Bonello started to flash around in my subconscious.

My head was spinning, and I was about to call Oakley, when through the dusty, dirty window of the Hell's Bells tattoo parlor three doors down I thought I saw Angelica. I started walking that way with hope pounding in my heart when all of a sudden reality kicked me in the ass. *Tattoo parlor?*

A bell sounded as the door opened, and Angelica stepped out onto the sidewalk.

*Oh, shit. . . .*

"Hi, Jake!" she shouted, pointing to her upper left arm. "Wait'll you see what I got."

# Chapter

Two blood-red hearts were inked to her upper left arm; a purple banner draped over them read "Bad Girl."

I grabbed her arm with both my hands. "What did you do? I told you to stay in the car."

"But Jake —"

The bell sounded from inside the parlor again, and out from the doorway stepped this big, hairy throwback to the '60s in a white T-shirt and bib overalls. "What's going on out here? You okay there, Angel? 'Cause if this guy is bothering you —"

"No, it's okay, Ernie. He's supposed to be my body guard," she explained.

"That's right!" I yelled. "And I want to know why the hell did you go and get that done to your body?"

"Relax, dude," said Ernie. "It's a temp tat."

"A what?"

Angelica started to giggle. "A temporary tattoo. You know, like a removable kind."

"Stuff'll wash off with baby oil or rubbin' alcohol," advised Ernie. "Maskin' tape will work, too."

I let go of her arm, still not totally convinced. The stale traces of marijuana on Ernie's clothing made me wonder if he was a full-time artist or just preyed on people who didn't know better.

"Look, dude, I've been doing this for almost 30 years, and I know better than to ink some chick who isn't totally ready. Of course, if the two of you wanna talk it over and come back —"

"Yeah, right, Ernie," I said. "Maybe tomorrow."

I took Angelica by the elbow and turned to walk toward the car.

"Sure thing, dude," he said, pulling a handkerchief from his overall pocket and wiping the back of his neck. "Gotta real nice 'ex-cop' tat I can do for you. . . ."

I stopped and glared at him over my shoulder.

"Yep, knew I was right," he laughed. "Seen that look plenty of times before." He turned and went back to his door.

"I didn't know you were a cop!" Angelica shouted. "That's so cool."

"Come on, *Angel*," I told her. "Let's get in the car."

I held open her door, and she got in. I walked around, opened the driver side, and sat down, rearranging the rearview mirror so I could see the tattoo parlor. Old habits.

"Why didn't you tell me you used to be a cop?" Angelica asked again, lighting up a Marlboro to help hold her excitement.

"I don't have to tell you everything," I said, more relaxed now at the situation than I was five minutes ago. "I'm allowed a few secrets."

"Sure, I s'pose," she replied, blowing a trail of smoke upward. "But then I get to have some from you, too."

"Sounds fair to me," I said, starting up the car and pulling out into the light traffic.

"Well, then, good. Because the bad girl tattoo wasn't the only one I got."

"What do you mean?"

Angelica giggled like a bad, bad girl. "I got a real cool tat of the Tasmanian Devil, too."

"What are you talking about? You're not exactly overdressed, you know, and I didn't see another tattoo."

"Exactly," she explained. "Now use your imagination while I keep *my* little secret."

I started to laugh. "That's fine, really it is. What do I care what you do? It's your body." I looked over nonchalantly to see if I had missed it or if she'd hidden it in the nether regions.

Angelica casually crossed her left leg over her right, exposing even more skin than the original short-shorts were made to do.

I drummed my thumbs on the steering wheel as we made our way back up the Strip.

"Front or back?" I finally asked.

◆

We got to the Oasis without further trouble. I called Julius Contini on his private line and let him know Angelica was going to use the pool and I was going off on an assignment. He said he'd have someone from Security keep an inconspicuous eye on her and told me to come by his office when I was finished. He informed me that the Contini and Bonello families were gathering later that evening with a bunch of other relatives and that I was invited. I explained that I appreciated the offer but that I had other plans. He said the invitation would be left open in case I changed my mind. He was close. I would have to *lose* my mind.

Angelica dug around the trunk of the Chrysler 300 until she found her new bathing suit. She also came up with a silky floral cover-up, which I suggested might not be a bad idea to wear through the hotel on her way to the pool and up to Uncle Julius if she should drop in to see him. She closed the trunk and told me she would be fine, that she'd bought a couple of more conservative outfits for occasions just like this and the family get-together.

I told her to be careful at the pool and that, even though it was October, the sun could still do a number on the uninitiated.

"Are you sure you don't want to come with me?" she asked.

"Uh, no, thanks."

"If you're so worried about me getting burned, you could help me put on my sunblock. . . ."

"Now it's 'No' for sure," I told her, opening up my door. "Have fun. I'll be back in a couple of hours, but I've got some things to do around here, too. Don't forget, you've got the pager if you need me." I checked my watch. It was just after 1 p.m. "Try to be out of the pool by 3 or 3:30."

"Yes, sir," she said with a crisp salute.

"Later."

As I was entering the car, Angelica shouted out, "Oh, Jake!"

I jumped back out. "What is it?"

"On the back."

"What's on the back?"

"You know," she said with a laugh. "The other tattoo. . . ."

# Chapter

I found the Gambler's Book Shop where Oakley said I would. I parked in behind, walked around, and entered through the front door. The main part of the store was L-shaped and divided into two rows, with section after section of books just about gambling. I decided to take a walk around to familiarize myself with the place.

And what a place it was: a treasure trove of information on my favorite pastime, current love, and addiction. I felt like a drunk touring a distillery.

There were not only books on how to play every game known to man, but also, in most cases, historical perspectives on each. Books on horse racing, dog racing, and how to handicap properly; books on keno, bingo, craps, slots, and every card game and casino game invented. Blackjack and poker had their own large sections, with poker being subdivided into Hold 'Em, Omaha, Stud, and Others, divided again for low, medium, and no limit, and then divided once more for the fast-growing tournament crowd. NFL and sports betting held a large area all its own. There were books on snooker, billiards, magic, and how to look out for cheaters. And if you wanted to be a showgirl, dealer, pit boss, or anything else to do with employment in the gaming industry, they had that, too, right down to sample application forms. I worked my way to the wall next to the display counter where the bookcase was marked History of Nevada.

The shelves were filled with hundreds of books with gaudy, neon-depicted covers, solemn, filthy-clad claim diggers, and stern-faced mafiosi that looked like they'd cut your heart out if you were late on the juice. Seeing that I'd centered in on a subject, an attentive clerk behind the counter came around and asked if I needed any help.

"Actually, I'm here to see Howard Schwartz."

"I think he's out back finishing his lunch; he shouldn't be too long."

"Great. I'll wait. Lieutenant Oakley from downtown said Howard was the man to talk to."

I could sense the clerk weighing whether I was a cop or not. In case it might help, or get me a discount, I didn't bother to enlighten him.

"I'll let Howard know you're here, anyway." The clerk hurried off.

There was an interesting mix of subjects and topics in front of me, so I began picking up and flipping through books that had a "mob" or a 1950s, early '60s, look to them. In a short while, the clerk returned.

"Howard says to come on back, and he can give you a few minutes. Follow me."

I did as I was told, and I found myself being led through a maze of narrow hallways with various rooms full of furniture, books, and papers piled high. A full offset press area was also visible and hundreds of cartons of paper and the store's current catalog. A few women were busy packaging shipments of gambling books, magazines, DVDs, and computer software. Back in the warehouse's shipping area, seated at a large table surrounded by outgoing boxes waiting for a courier, was a man reading a huge, worn, black hardcover tome balanced with one hand as the other fed him a piece of sandwich from a cellophane wrap. He looked to be in his early 60s, fit as a fiddle, and challenged only by his spectacles and thinning hair.

"Here's the guy asking for you," announced the clerk.

The man at the table put the heavy book down and wiped his hands with a paper napkin as he stood to extend a hand.

"Hello, I'm Howard, have a seat."

I returned his firm grip and exchanged names.

"That's quite the book there," I said.

"Oh, this thing," he said with a laugh. "Yes, but don't be fooled. You and I should look so good at 150 plus years old."

"Really? But what's it about? They couldn't have had books on gambling way back then. And look at the size of that sucker. It has to be two feet tall."

"I get books like this quite often. Collections, too. Families donate them to me because they don't want to see them discarded and tossed away in some trash bin. They aren't excessively valuable, but the family members know they meant something to the owner, and they know my reputation with such things, that it will have found a good home. This one came from an estate in France and is reportedly the first book ever written on horse racing, the sport of the kings. That's worth a lot, to me."

I glanced around and saw that he had shelves upon shelves of older books as well as some newer ones that were stacked this way and that, many of them having large yellow Post-It notes poking out from their pages.

Howard saw me looking and laughed out loud. "Those shelves over there are my reading list for next month. These two bookcases are this month's. Then they have to be reviewed and categorized."

"Are you kidding me? There's gotta be 100 books there. And we're already well into October."

"Nope," he said, taking a sip from his water bottle. "And there's around 140 there. I read about 1,500 words per minute, so that only makes it around five or six a day. If I get caught in a bad traffic jam on the Strip, I can knock one off on the way home. I guess I might have to cut down on my pleasure reading, but they'll get done." He laughed again. "They have to get done. It's my business. Who else is going to do it?"

I shook my head in amazement. "I usually read one edition every day, too, but I don't think studying the *Daily Racing Form* is the same thing."

"So what brings you to GBS?" asked Howard.

"Well, I was speaking with a friend of mine over in Homicide, a Lieutenant Oakley, and he said you were the man to talk to regarding Vegas of yesterday."

"I'm one of them. There are probably others at the newspapers or hanging around the Sports Book, but I'm more approachable, that's for sure. I get customers in here who are screenwriters looking for background material, world-class poker players who want to ply a book or see what the competition is writing and maybe pick up "a tell" on them. I once had a guy call me from one of the poker rooms. He was in a $20-40 Hold 'Em game and phoned to ask me if he should draw for an inside straight on the river. After I stopped laughing, I told him he was about an 11-1 dog to make it, so if the pot was laying him more than $500 he was getting his "pot odds" — his return on investment. He said it was over $1,200, and I heard him call. I hung up, but apparently he must have hit his straight because he came by the store the next day and spent $400 on books and videos."

"Incredible."

"So what can I do for you?"

I told him I was doing some background research on mob history and that one of the areas I was most interested in specifically was the casino skimming operations.

"Well, I'm no expert," admitted Howard. "Most of what I know is a little bit about everything."

"Then tell me what you know. How'd they go about it? Where did it go?"

"You're probably already aware that running the casinos was not on the up-and-up. There weren't the regulations and laws on gaming like there are today. Up until '55, the Tax Commission oversaw the day-to-day responsibilities of the reporting and monitoring of casino revenue. But the city was growing so fast and the gambling was so furious that there was no way for the commission to control issues or attain accurate numbers.

"Although most of the casinos were making money on their reported earnings, they were making even more on what wasn't reported. For example, if a casino filled out all the paperwork for a certain day that stated they made $100,000, then they probably really made around $140,000-150,000. This pilfering of the unreported profits was called 'the skimming' or just the 'skim.' These were the real dollars as far as the owners cared. Not only could they 'wash' or launder money into and through the casino, but it gave them an undisclosed, tax-free income that totaled hundreds of millions."

"How'd they get around the procedures the government had in place?" I asked.

"It's not much different today. Look at the computer. One day somebody puts up some kind of firewall protection, and the next day the hackers are all over it, like a dog on a bone. Somewhere somebody is putting up a wall, and somewhere else somebody is taking one down."

"Some of it must have been obvious. There had to be a paper trail."

"Oh, they had paperwork coming out the wazoo. And with every new government regulation issued, the *boys* would outfox them in some other way. It was like a game."

"But how'd they do it, Howard?"

"Well, one of the easiest ways was to just falsify the forms. In a lot of cases, the coinage was weighed, so it didn't take long before the weights were adjusted or marked lighter than they actually were. That way even the personnel doing the counting didn't know it was being done. Another was to not report the money going down the slot in the table games.

"Manipulating wealthy gamblers was an art form. They'd give credit to a high roller and, when he went bust, not report it on the official books. When the good fellas specializing in 'accounts receivable and broken kneecaps' would eventually collect the outstanding debt, it was never recorded. It went right into the boss's pocket. And there were some big debts. Some of them from the same voices who were singing in their showrooms."

"And this went on at the majority of casinos back then?"

"No, Jake," he corrected. "It went on in *all* the casinos back then."

"That's amazing. They must have been making a fortune."

"No question about it."

A door opened, and the clerk stuck his head in. "Howard, when you've got a minute, there's a guy here who says he's got a sure-fire, guaranteed system to beat the lottery. Says he's got a two o'clock appointment to talk to you about publishing it."

Howard hung his head and waved at the clerk. "Tell him I'll be out in a minute."

We both started laughing.

Howard said, "If I had a dollar. . . ."

I added, "Yeah, and if I had a guaranteed system, I sure wouldn't be sharing it!"

"You just hit the nail on the head, Jake. But it's the business of the business I'm in. For every guy with a system, there's a thousand who want to buy it."

We chatted for a couple more minutes, and then Howard took me out to the store and pointed out a few books that had articles or stories related to my area of interest. We shook hands again and wished each other good luck, like two gamblers passing in the night.

A portly, middle-aged man with a bad complexion and sweaty brow was waiting for Howard by the register, with both arms wrapped tightly around a beaten-up leather satchel and a tic so palpable it was starting to make me nervous.

Howard held open the door for the man to go through; then he turned to us, wiggled his eyebrows up and down as if he was entering *The Twilight Zone*, and was gone.

# Chapter

I meandered back to the Oasis, turning onto Fremont and heading out to Sam's Town, where I cashed in the chips I'd won the other night at craps. It was mid-afternoon and fairly quiet, and apparently, with my Raiders cap and sunglasses on, no one recognized me or cared.

Back at the Oasis, I left the Chrysler with Valet and entered the crowded casino floor. It always seemed busy. The atmosphere was very relaxed, and although it was definitely not geared toward children the luxury hotel featured a small theme park, a giant arcade, shark and whale tanks, as well as numerous shows, like the ever-popular *Ali Baba and the 40 Thieves*: real horseback battles where Ali and his men fight to liberate their country. But I was in the "adult" section, which I so loved, with all the green felt tables, the clicking of chips, the constant sound of bells and whistles, and the clinking of coins being paid off in the mammoth slot area.

I waved and nodded and said hello to a number of dealers and pit personnel I knew so well from my blackjack days. BJ was my way into the Oasis a couple of years ago, but dealing out of a shoe wasn't something I wanted to do for the rest of my life. I thought I'd done a good job. And I didn't mind the people, really. But it was such a robotic routine that, with six decks, automated card shufflers, and a large cutoff of cards not to be used at the end of the shoe, most of these poor schmucks didn't stand a chance.

The only really exciting times were when some new "card-counting" team snuck into the casino and wanted to pit their MIT degrees against our dealers. They would bring in their counters, who would sit at a table playing for five dollars, keeping track of which cards had been exposed and which had not. This is not an easy feat, believe me. I've been there, done that. When the count of a shoe became positive for the player and not the house on a certain table, the counter at that table would signal the "money man," who would come in and start betting $5,000 or more each hand until the count reverted back. These altercations rarely got off the ground as the casino heads determined that the counting and keeping track of all cards coming out of the shoe, even at high speed, comprised some kind of cheating. It wasn't, of course, but these teams could do a lot of damage to the bottom line in the matter of three to four minutes, and the house would refuse to deal to them and charge them with trespassing if they didn't leave immediately.

To keep the gaming industry informed, their photos would be sent to the people who kept the Griffin book, an insider's photo catalog on the who's who of cheating. The folks at Griffin would then update their files and make the faces of these personas non grata available to every casino in the world.

I made my way to the poker room, averting my eyes as I passed the panels of glass that lined one wall of the expansive swimming pool and sunbathing area. Thong or no thong, I wasn't buying. Hell, I wasn't even window shopping. The ultimate price could be extremely high, and I was still hoping I had another 40 years to go.

At the poker kiosk, I put my name down for $20-40 and $30-60 Hold 'Em. Hank, the poker supervisor, put my name on both lists and told me I had about a 40-minute wait. I gave him my pager number and asked him to beep when I was "on deck"; then I hurried back the way I'd come, once again avoiding the crowded sunbathing area. I went down a hallway marked Employees Only, past the dealers' break room, and slipped out a side door at the end of the corridor. I jogged across the parking lot and crossed the street, which brought me to the side entrance of the Rendezvous Hotel and Casino.

Although I wasn't allowed to play table games at the Oasis, regular poker was different since the house had nothing to lose. Poker was a game pitting player against player, and the casino simply supplied the dealer, the equipment, and the ambience, including security. It was extremely hard for a dealer to cheat at a casino poker room and not very viable. For my table game fix, I usually went to the Rendezvous.

I took out $200 and sat down at an empty seat at Caribbean Poker. This is a player against the house game where the best poker hand wins. The game doesn't have a lot going for it as it has a healthy five percent house advantage, but it was a slow game without a lot of thinking or decision making, and for a minimum five dollars a hand you got a lot of bang for your buck. I also liked that, for an additional dollar, the player had a shot at the progressive jackpot for a royal flush and 10 percent of the jackpot for a straight flush. Because of the odds, break-even points, and overlays, I only played when the jackpot exceeded $250,000, and right now it was paying $273,511 and calling my name. In addition, a quarter of a million was also the sum that I figured would clear me of debts, new and old, and set me up nicely with a big down payment on a neat little two-bedroom bungalow and still leave me with 40 or 50 big ones for a lively bankroll.

I hung around for half an hour or so playing cards, chatting up the cute dealer Katie from Kansas, frequently appreciating the ladies my own age who ambled by, and nursing a couple of free beers that ended up costing me about $85. At the sound of the beeper, I cashed out and made my way back to the Oasis poker room.

"A set of aces!" I announced proudly. "American Airlines, cleared for take-off!" I flipped over my two black aces in front of the board, which showed A-6-K-4-5, reached my arms toward one of my all-time favorite dealers, Ben, and wiggled all my fingers and thumbs for him to push the pot in my direction.

I'd been playing $20-40 Hold 'Em for almost an hour and was up about $1,800, counting the $1,000 in the current pot. A good day's work. After this pot, I decided, I'd play a couple more hands until my blind antes, take the healthy win, and decide how to celebrate tonight seeing as how Angelica was busy with her family. Perhaps I'd stop back at the Rendezvous and see what Katie from Kansas was up to.

"Sir, can I have your cards, please?" Ben asked the old guy down at the end of the table who looked like he was still trying to figure out his hand.

You could almost see him thinking on his fingers until finally he said, "Well, I guess you win . . . ," and tossed his cards in front of him, where the 2 of hearts and 3 of clubs cart wheeled and turned faceup.

I widened my arms to accept the pot.

"Straight," the dealer called out.

I didn't know what the hell Ben was talking about, but I had three of a kind, not a straight. What did I care, he could call it whatever he wanted, just give me the pot.

The dealer gathered the chips and pushed them with both hands to the old guy at the end.

"Ben!" I shouted. "What the hell are ya doin'?"

"You know the 'cards talk' here, Jake."

The entire table seemed to be wondering, until some wiseacre remarked, "Michael Jordan shoots down American Airlines once again."

And then we all saw what only Ben had seen.

"He went for the perfect, perfect, inside straight!" somebody shouted. "Holy shit!"

The old fart collected my $1,000 in chips and began stacking them. A goofy grin filled his face as he took congratulations from around the table. Except from me, of course.

"Well, I just started playin' this game," he admitted, "and I figured I was gettin' my whadjamacallit!"

"Pot odds?"

"Yeah, that's it. I seen it on the television."

Ben looked over at me as he washed the cards and said softly, "Remember, that's why we play here, Jake. The competition is loose."

"Yeah," I said, as if awakening from a coma. "Thank God for TV. . . ."

For anyone who has played on a pinball machine, the term "tilt" is familiar as your unruly, disruptive, amateurish behavior and performance that will result in the game shutting down. And you feel angry with yourself for losing your quarter. Well, let me tell you, when you go on "tilt" playing poker, the consequences can be far more devastating, and you will likely lose thousands and thousands of quarters. But you make a lot of friends.

And that's what I did. I threw a party for the next 20 minutes, raising on every hand, and reraising when anybody challenged me. I was the perfect host, and when the smoke cleared and the party finally ended I'd made a lot of new friends and lost the $800 I'd been up as well as the $500 I'd bought in for. Thankfully, it was getting late, and I had to be going, or I would have had to hit the ATM and make even more friends at the credit card companies.

I called up on the house phone located near Contini's private elevator and took the quick ride up. Big Julie met me as the door opened, wrapped an arm around my shoulder, and escorted me to a leather couch. He explained that Angelica had just left but would be back shortly. She'd complained how her hair had looked after coming out of the pool, so Uncle Julie had sent her down to the Curl Up & Dye Salon to have them do a quickie on her tresses.

Just like Olivia, Contini was sharp enough to notice my new bruises. He got me a cold beer from the refrigerator and asked me to recap the whole situation. I began where we had left off at the hospital and took him right up to my meeting with Oakley. I left out Angelica's smoking, her unhealthy diet, the costume changes, the endless sexual innuendos, and her removable tattoos.

"Well, I'm glad things are going so well with you and Angelica, sport. I'm sorry I didn't give you too much info when you were here last, but I knew we didn't have a lot of time, and plans had changed quickly."

Big Julie had been pacing during my little debriefing, and now he took a seat in a worn leather armchair that he sank deeply into.

"You see, Jake, there's a whole other story out there about what's happening right now. All this crap, going back to Carmine's working at the Desert Ranch and his managing the rest of the outfit's casinos. . . . Some stories we'll never know. A lot of the others are filled with lies and bullshit. And a whole lotta allegations.

"I know I wasn't totally upfront with you when I asked you to help me out with this, but you're going to have to trust me on some things. Some I can talk about. Some I can't. There are things about our families, my wife's and mine, that are better kept quiet or at least kept from the public. A lot of history's facts are never documented and get lost over the years. Much of it can be opinions, or views, tales told over a fire or a table in a café, retold so many times through the generations that the original truth is so distorted it would hardly be recognizable from the real story if it was ever discovered."

I think Contini could see he was starting to lose me by talking in riddles.

"Okay. Let me tell you what I can; and about the rest you can speculate. But first you must understand what I tell you here stays here. Between you and me. *Capice?* This office is swept once a day and always after I have guests I don't know or don't trust.

"First off, I appreciate everything you're doing for me. My wife and I have always had a soft spot for Olivia and her situation, and our two families, the Continis and the D'Amatos, along with the Bonellos, go back many generations. That is why we are getting together tonight, to celebrate our bond and our friendship. Although the majority of our relatives are back in New York and New Jersey, there are still a number of the older ones who have moved out here to keep the eastern chill from their bones."

Contini took a sip from his crystal glass, got up out of his chair, and took a seat at his desk. He removed a cigar from a wooden box and made a big deal of snipping off the end and firing it up.

"And to be honest, it will probably be the last time many of them will get to see Olivia alive. We have a private villa near Red Rock where we will all be celebrating her life. There's a few private jets coming in this afternoon for the event, from Chicago and back east, which I am sure is going to have the FBI running around in circles trying to find out what the hell's going on."

"They still keep an eye on everybody?" I asked.

"Nah, not really. . . . But this much traffic might raise a few eyebrows."

"How could they possibly be watching everyone?"

"You kidding? With the computers today, they just load in every name that's ever come up, and when that name is used at an airport check-in, gas station credit card, or overheard at a rub 'n' tug that's under surveillance it gets red-flagged. The red flag gets sent to whoever requested it, and bingo! You can keep track of anybody."

I could see how Big Julie might be right. Angelica had been caught

coming into Vegas by the goons who had jumped us. Things started connecting in my brain, but Contini made it too hard to concentrate, so I
filed what I was thinking for later.

"So, getting back to these two *babbos* that have been bothering you.
Where did you say their car was traced to?"

"Perrotta," I said. "Perrotta Meats & Poultry."

"Jesus Christ. . . ."

"You know them?"

"Yeah, you could say that." Contini blew a stream of gray smoke toward
the air filter built into the ceiling, and it quickly dissipated. "You have to
understand, Jake, that in my position with the Oasis there are a lot of things
I have to know about. But as far as many of the investors in this property
are concerned, there's a lot of things out there that they never want me to
speak of, associate with, or even hint that I know anything about."

"Perrotta, for one?" I asked.

Contini gave me a frustrated look; then he pointed a stubby index finger with the thumb up at me like it was a gun. "If I ever hear any of this
got out of this room . . . God help you."

I nodded my head to let him know I understood.

"Perrotta is one of the probably hundreds of companies owned by the
Chicago outfit. When things went tits up with hotel ownership in the '60s,
they bought into all kinds of suppliers and outside distributors."

"Then Perrotta is owned by the same people who put Bonello out here
in the first place."

Contini nodded. "Generally, the major families worked together.
Maybe they didn't trust each other 100 percent, but they were in the same
business, and there was enough to go around for everybody — if no one
got too greedy. Chicago controlled most of the Vegas action back then.
New York and Detroit had only a small piece."

"But the family thing, the connections between the Bonellos and the D'Amatos and the East/Midwest breakdown . . . it's not really clear to me."

"Okay," said Big Julie with a sigh. "Here's how things were. As I said, Chi town was the major player out here in the '50s. Carmine Bonello was a trusted member, and his boss, Tony Accardo, promoted him to *capodecina* with the intention of giving him Vegas to run. Although Carmine's loyalty was to Chicago, he had connections to New York because of his recent marriage to Olivia D'Amato. There was no problem with that as everyone knew everyone else, and, if the truth be known, little connections like that could help iron out more serious problems between the families should they ever arise.

"Now, I don't know what went on with Carmine while he was operating out here, but I've heard all the rumors. And as far as I'm concerned, it's all speculation. Did he run off with some piece of ass? . . . I don't know. Was he skimming from the skim? . . . Don't know, don't care. Is the poor bastard buried somewhere out in the Mojave? . . . Your guess is as good as mine."

"But if he was skimming from his bosses, that could have added up to a pretty penny."

"Sure it coulda," agreed Contini. "But only if you got a chance to spend it."

"And once the word was out that Carmine could have been holding out on the take, they tried to get the information out of Olivia, to no avail."

"Nope, never found a cent. Then the D'Amatos took her under their wing."

"What about Orsina and that Vincent kid with all the security? That can't come cheap."

"No, the boys back east pick that up. They weren't happy with the way

Chicago treated Olivia and her daughter, Sofia, trying to find out about Carmine, so they sorta stepped in and drew their line in the desert sand. Nobody from the Midwest wanted to start anything with the East, what with all the changes happening in Vegas, so they let it rest. And as far as Vincent goes, he's just a hired Young Turk, on loan and trying to make his mark. He's filling in for another guy, Stephano, who's been with Olivia since Carmine went missing. He's in his 70s now but right from the hills of Sicily. Don't let his age fool you. He's as hardcore Sicilian as they come, and you don't want to fuck with him. He's practically dedicated his life to looking after Olivia's welfare. Had to go back home about a month ago to look after something, or someone, but as far as I know that was taken care of, and he might be flying in tonight. If you're lucky, you'll never meet him."

The telephone rang, and Contini took the call. "Sure, Princess. Come on up. Yeah, Jake's here, too."

"Well, that's about it, sport. For some reason, these two guys following you and Angelica have a bug up their ass for you. But you've done good so far. I don't think they're going to bother you much anymore, but keep your eyes open. Angelica will be gone in another few days, and things should go back to status quo."

Contini opened up a side drawer of the desk and took out a white business envelope. He double-checked its contents, got up, walked over, and handed it to me. I peeked in, and five or six crisp hundreds smiled back. "Keep up the good work."

"Thanks, Mr. Contini," I said, placing the bills in my pocket and giving them a loving pat. "I'll pick up more iodine and bandages at Walgreen's on my way home."

Big Julie gave me a smile and a look full of pride. "I mean what I said. You've done a good job. So far. And these two guys who tossed you? I think they know by now that you don't know — hell, even *I* don't know

— what they're looking for. Things'll die down."

The elevator bell sounded softly, and the door began to open.

As Angelica exited the car, Contini said, "Don't forget, Jake. This is between you and me."

"Good evening, gentlemen." Angelica strode toward us as if she was here for a business appointment. Not only was her walk straight and purposeful, but her outfit screamed Madison Avenue. She was wearing a peach-colored pantsuit that accentuated her long legs. The matching jacket was a cross between business and military, cut clean and crisp with button-down pocket flaps and thin epaulets covering a lightly patterned white blouse with a small neat bow. The salon had put her hair in an up do, and the transformation from hip hopper to ad exec was mesmerizing.

Angelica came to a stop before Contini and me and twirled around once for our benefit. "You like?" she asked.

I just looked and nodded, meaning it.

"You look great, sweetheart," said Contini. "Just great."

Angelica seemed pleased with the response. "Thanks for letting me shop downstairs, Uncle Julius. I thought I'd wear it tonight, but I wanted to see a reaction first. I think it'll work."

"It'll work," Contini and I said in unison.

# Chapter

The two of us left Big Julie's office and loaded the car with more boxes and bags. We took a quick swing through my neighborhood — just to check for vehicles that didn't belong. The streets were busy with cars and people, but other than old man LeBlanc, who was walking around on his balcony in his unbelted robe, nobody seemed suspicious. I toured the area once and was about to exit the complex when I noticed the black Caddy sitting in a private parking lot down the street and across from my unit. I didn't bother to alarm Angelica.

A few minutes later we were on Flamingo, heading west, when we both looked at each other, remembering we hadn't had anything to eat since morning. It was now approaching 5 p.m.

"I'm getting hungry," I said. "How about you?"

"Yeah, I could use a bite and something to drink. We aren't getting together tonight until eight, so dinner will probably be late."

We were driving through a long section of town filled with commercial properties and numerous bars and restaurants.

"What do you feel like?" I asked.

Angelica shrugged her shoulders. "Doesn't matter much to me. I'll eat just about anything."

I couldn't help but laugh. "Yeah, I've seen what you have for breakfast."

"Hey, that looks cool. Let's try it."

Angelica was pointing out a place called Naughty Mike's Love Shack &

Oyster Bar, brightly colored and featuring long, fin-tailed cars filled with teenagers from the late '50s, early '60s, on its neon billboard.

"I can dig it, daddy-o," I said.

"What's that supposed to be, hippie or something?"

I pulled into the gravel driveway of Mike's. "It's beatnik, actually."

Angelica scrunched up her nose. "Beatnik? What the hell's that?"

"You know, bongos, hep cat, gimme some skin."

"You're weird. And you can't be that old."

"Age has nothing to do with it," I explained. "It's part of our history. Do you think your parents listened to that rap crap when they were your age? No way. Haven't you ever watched reruns of *Dobie Gillis?*" I asked.

"Never heard of it. My aunts used to watch reruns of *Golden Girls* and *Lucy.* I've seen them."

We parked in the relatively crowded lot and headed for the door. Speakers in the empty outdoor patio were blaring out the Clovers singing "Love Potion No. 9."

"You hear that?" I asked. "That's 50 years old. In another 50, when you're in your 70s and your grandchildren come over to visit on a Sunday afternoon, are you going to have Lil' Flip singing 'I Came to Bring the Pain' or 50 Cent doing 'P.I.M.P.' on the stereo for them while you serve milk and cookies?"

Her brows furrowed, and she bit her bottom lip as if she was trying to picture herself at 70.

"Of course not!" I pointed out emphatically. "Even if you only have the radio on, it'll probably still be playing Sam Cooke's 'Only Sixteen' or something by the Beatles."

"Will the Rolling Stones still be touring then?"

We came to the door, and I held it open for her.

"Forget about it. Let's get some chow."

The interior was a mixture of what could only be described as "surf and turf." The engaging bar area, fairly busy for this time of day, I thought, was 50 or 60 feet long, made of worn oak, and adorned with fishing nets, lobster traps, buoys, lighthouses, and mounted fish. The designated dining area was about half full, mostly couples except for a large party of 20 or so who were celebrating something. The mahogany tables and chairs were dark and solid looking, a good match for the plank floors and barn board walls. A small stage was at the end of the room, and the dance floor, complete with disco ball, had actually attracted four or five couples.

"Let's sit and eat at the bar, Jake. It looks so dope."

"Okay, but don't ring the bells or anything," I told her. "I think they're just for decoration."

We hopped up onto a couple of stools, the kind that spun around and had wooden backs to them and brass rails near the bottom for your feet. No sooner had we sat down when a skinny bartender wearing a goatee, gray T-shirt, and jeans came up to us.

"Hey, daddy-o," he called out. "My name's Woody. What'll it be?"

"Oh, God," cried Angelica.

I just laughed, and then I said, "I'll have a Corona. Extra lime."

He looked Angelica over and said, "The young lady looks every bit a lady in that outfit, but unfortunately I'll need to see some ID."

"All I wanted was a '57 T-bird," she said in a sultry voice.

Woody looked over at her with a newfound respect. "Just a '57 bird?"

"Of course not, silly," she admonished him. "With Hawaiian license plates."

"I think I'm in love. I'll be right back with your drinks."

When he left, I said, "A '57 T-bird . . . well done. That certainly turned his crank."

"I thought it might. It helps to be prepared."

"Have you had it before?"

"Sure. An ounce each of Vodka, Amaretto, and Grand Marnier. The rest pineapple juice. It's not bad."

The drinks came along with the menus, and we decided on an assorted platter of seafood. We knocked that off and another drink each during the next half hour, and then Woody and Angelica thought it would be fun for me to have something called 1-900-FUK-MEUP.

"Friends of mine at TGIF in Tallahassee came up with this little number. It'll take me a few minutes," explained Woody, "but it's worth it."

"Wow," said Angelica. "This guy knows his shit. I've heard of that drink, but I never would have known who came up with it. Nobody would lay claim to it in case somebody got hurt."

"Oh, please. I've been enjoying the fruit of the vine and by-products of the barley and oats for longer than you've been alive. There's no drink out there, except for maybe moonshine or Newfie Screech, that could knock me on my ass." I laughed out loud at the idea. "And especially from a bunch of drinkers at a TGIF, for God's sake. And Florida to boot!"

The drink came, and it wasn't bad. Woody, wise beyond his years, had cut the volume of the ingredients down by half because he knew I was driving, even though he admitted that my size and experience probably would have handled one of them. To be honest, though, I was getting a buzz on by the time I finished the concoction. It was close to six o'clock, and the bar area had filled, and the music had been turned up. We were nibbling on nachos and chicken wings and having such a good time we were trying to decide whether to have one more drink, a coffee maybe, or head for Boulder City.

My decision was practically made for me when a sugary voice said, "Excuse me, 'scuse me, please." She was trying to get the bartender's attention to order, but with her soft breast bouncing back and forth against my back and arm, and the sweet scent of French Vanilla intoxicating the remainder of my brain, it was my attention starting to rise. Woody saw her too and came running over.

She was one of the most beautiful women I'd ever seen, a mix of Asian, African American, and white, a combination at odds with each other but evolving into an incredible result. She was almost six feet tall, the way I like them, full-bodied but not fat, and dressed in a tight-fitting black dress that hugged every inch of her curves, all touched off with a pair of stiletto heels. Her black hair was thick and long, and her lips were moist and naturally full and filled with anticipation. At least I thought so.

"I'd like an Attitude Adjustment, please," the soft voice said.

"I could use one, too," I said to her after Woody left. I realized she wasn't wearing a bra because I could feel her nipple hardening against my bicep.

She laughed as if I was the funniest guy she'd ever met; then she held out her hand and said, "I'm Darling."

"Of course you are," I told her, taking and kissing the back of her hand.

She put her left hand on my shoulder. "And you are?"

"Drunk and stupid," Angelica answered for me. "And in deep shit if he doesn't get me out of here and on my way home in the next five minutes."

I gave her a reproachful look. "Angelica, why don't you go check out the songs on the jukebox?" I gave her a handful of quarters and other loose change. "Put a dollar in for every group named after an animal, bug, or bird."

She got up and stomped away, telling me I should order a Blue Balls, because that's what I had coming to me.

"The name is Jake," I said, standing and inviting her to take Angelica's vacant seat.

"Your daughter?"

"No, no, no," I said, shaking my head. "Babysitting for a friend."

Her drink came, and she clinked it against mine. "Some friend," she said, holding up her drink. "To new friends."

"To new friends," I cheered out loud, almost spilling the remainder of my drink. "Yes, siree. The world always needs new friends." Okay, maybe I was really buzzed. But I could hardly believe that this vision of beauty had walked into my life. If I played my cards right, who knew where it would lead?

We made small talk for about five minutes, and we'd already got to where she was playing with my fingers and forearms with her freshly done French manicure. Each nail was done with a different face of a playing card, and I was beginning to think the two of us were made for each other as each hand made a royal flush. Her left was in hearts, and her right was in diamonds. It was the most romantic thing I'd ever seen.

Woody came by, dropped off our tab, and said he'd be by in a couple of minutes to see if we'd like anything else. *Damn!* I knew we had to go soon, and I started to think of ways in which I could get out of it and stay here with Darling. I was still miffed about losing my shot with the financial advisor from the club the other night, and here I was getting the shaft again.

I looked across the room at the jukebox, and there was Angelica staring at me with her arms folded in front and a scowl on her face. I'm no body language expert, but that stance was easy to translate. She held her hand up and pronounced "five minutes"; then she stalked off toward the restroom.

I thought about sending Angelica home in a taxi and knew how that would look. And besides, she had so many boxes and bags in the Chrysler I didn't know how we would transfer them all. I could always tell Darling I'd be back in an hour, but what were the chances some other stiff wouldn't pick her up by then? All of a sudden I came upon the brilliant idea of taking her with us. I'd drop off Angelica and then have the whole night to play with my new friend.

"Are you having another drink?" I asked.

She gave me a sexy look that I was afraid was going to make me hyperventilate, and then she moistened her lips. "What I'd really like is a Slippery Dick," she breathed hotly. "Or maybe A Sloe Comfortable Screw Against the Wall." She began to get out of her chair, and her dress rose to the point where I couldn't tell if she was wearing anything else underneath. "But right now I have to go water the flowers." She put a hand on my leg and ran her nails along the inside of my thigh; then she whispered so close that I could feel her lips against the tiny hairs on my ears, "And then I'd like to grind out a slow song with you on the dance floor."

With that, she rose to her full height, straightened out her dress, and walked the length of the bar, with every male watching her ass swing by and even a couple of females, too. I took out some cash to pay the bill, closed my eyes to the sounds of the Honeydrippers singing "Sea of Love," and pictured Darling and I in a heart-shaped Jacuzzi surrounded by rose petals and bubbles.

I made up my mind. I'd invite her with us and give her a night on the town she'd never forget. I was trying to decide whether to pick up a bottle or two in case we ended up back at my place when Angelica came racing down the aisle of the bar with a shocked look on her face.

"Jake, let's go," she shouted. "Now."

"Hold on, we're not going —"

"Jake! I said right NOW!"

She saw the money in my hand and the tab on the bar. She read the bill and grabbed a hundred from my hand and slapped it on the bar; then she gave out a shrill whistle using two fingers to get Woody's attention and showed him the money.

"Angelica," I protested, "I don't —"

She took my face in both her hands. "Do you trust me?"

"Well, yeah, I guess . . . but —"

"I promise you, you have to listen to me, Jake. I swear on my *nonna*'s life. You have to leave right now."

I knew then she wasn't kidding. "You didn't kill anyone in the restroom, did you, Angelica?"

"I don't think so. Now let's go!" She grabbed me by the elbow, and we hightailed it out the front door.

I started up the Chrysler. "What the hell was that all about, Angelica?"

She kept looking back to the restaurant. "Let's get out of here first."

"No." I turned off the ignition. "We aren't going anywhere until I get a satisfactory explanation."

Angelica took a big gulp of air. "Jake, you are not going to believe this."

"I'm so pissed off that you better hope I believe it, young lady."

"Remember when I held up my hand to signal you for five minutes?"

How could I forget the body language? "Yeah, so? Then you went to the can."

"That's right. And when I was finished in there, I passed what's her face going in."

"Her name's Darling."

"Yeah, right. Well, anyway, she gives me this glare and calls me a 'biatch.' Then she knocks me aside and goes into the restroom. I take a few steps and then realize I left my watch by the sink. I was the only one in there, so I knew it wouldn't be gone, but I didn't want to run into your new 'girlfriend.'" She started to laugh.

"What the hell's so funny?"

Angelica looked back at the restaurant door. "I sneak back in without a sound and go retrieve my watch." She put both hands to her face, and it took me a second to realize she was laughing again. "So I look over at the cubicle, and I can see her black heels in the space at the floor."

"Yeah, so? She said she had to pee."

"But, Jake, that's the part that wasn't right."

"What do you mean?"

"Well . . . the heels were there all right, but they were facing toward the toilet, not out."

I tried to picture what the hell she was talking about.

"*Jake!* It was like a friggin' waterfall. I'm trying to tell you she stands when she pees."

"She *what?*"

Tears of laughter were starting down her cheeks. "That's right, Jake. *She's a he!*"

"Oh, come —"

"I swear on my grandmother's life! She, I mean *he*, was standing there pissing and started singing 'Feelings,' for God's sake."

"Well, lots of —"

"He sounded like Barry White! And when he was just about finished, he ripped one so loud the mirrors rattled!"

"Oh, for Christ's sake!"

"I know."

"No, I mean 'for Christ's sake, there she, or he, or whatever is!'"

The door to the restaurant was wide open, and two men were holding a disheveled Darling on each side. We both slid down in our seats and watched them from just above the dashboard as they surveyed the parking lot.

"Angelica, you said you didn't hit anybody," I whispered loudly.

"Actually, I said I didn't *kill* anybody."

"Jesus! What the hell did you do back there?"

"Nothing they can trace back to us. Unless they have cameras in the restrooms, which legally —"

"What did you do?"

"Well, I was pissed off at her/him for leading you on like that, and if it was true, you know, that she was a he, well, I didn't think that was right. And I didn't like being shoved and called a biatch, either. So I had to be sure. I stood in front of the cubicle, and when the toilet flushed and the latch clicked open I ran at the door full tilt and rammed it with my shoulder and with all my weight behind it. I must have caught him right on the forehead because he was down and out right away. I pushed the dress up with the toe of my shoe, and, sure as hell, he had his salami taped to his leg. . . ."

The trio at the door got bored with the parking lot and turned to walk back inside. I noticed one of the guys had his hand low on Darling's ass, so maybe her night wasn't wasted after all.

I looked over at Angelica, who was still trying to suppress her laughter at what was and could have been. We uncoiled ourselves, sat up, and started out of the parking lot.

"We better find a restroom, fast," I stated curtly.

"Why, you okay?"

As we pulled out of the lot and onto Flamingo, I started laughing like I hadn't for years, and Angelica joined in. "If I don't get to a washroom right away," I said, tears now rolling down my cheeks, "I'm going to piss myself!"

# Chapter

The ride to Boulder City was lighthearted, with the majority of the laughing and giggling revolving around my taste in men.

"Can you imagine," asked Angelica, "if she'd come with us and the two of you went out and then later, you know, you guys got like, you know. . . ?"

We turned to each other and made faces. "Gross!" we said in unison, like two schoolgirls.

That's about how it went for the 40 minutes until I pulled into the driveway of the Bonello estate.

"Angelica," I said firmly. "Don't forget what we promised. I don't mention anything about your smoking, drinking, or taste in body art, and in return you don't mention anything about you-know-who."

She fanned herself with a small kerchief from her purse and, in a credible southern belle accent, said, "Oh, you mean Dah-Ling? Why, Mr. Morgan, whatever are you concerned about? I'll have you know that our little secret is locked and sealed away forever. . . ." Then she stopped fanning, looked me in the eye, and said in a deep, dark voice, "Unless you don't do what I say. Then, I hang you out to dry." She leaned over and gave me a peck on the cheek. "Just kiddin'!" she said as she opened her door and added what sounded like "Maybe."

I shook my head and popped the trunk; then I got ready to unload it.

The door to the house opened, and Orsina stood waiting in the archway. "My dear Angelica," she said. "You look so . . . so much older!"

"Thank you. Wait until you see some of the other outfits I bought."

Vincent came around the house.

"Oh, Vincent," said Angelica. "Be a *darling* and help me with all this stuff."

The emphasis wasn't lost on me.

Vincent started looping string and plastic handles around his thick, muscled fingers and began carrying the bags inside.

"*Nonna* is getting ready for this evening," Orsina explained. "She is very excited about seeing so many of her friends and family."

"She's such a *darling*," said Angelica. "She'll have so much fun."

"Will you be joining us, Mr. Morgan?"

"No, I'm sorry, I can't." I looked at Angelica and said, "I have a date with a special someone tonight." Just to rub it in, I added, "She's a show-girl."

"Oh, Orsina, she's absolutely *darling*," announced Angelica. "I've met her; she's a dancer at La Cage."

For those who don't know, La Cage is the hugely successful show featuring female impersonators. Unfortunately, Orsina's brow furrowed, and I started to worry that she was putting two and two together. Luckily, Vincent stepped between them, picked one up in each arm, and lifted them up as if they were pillows. "Okay, ladies, time to get ready for tonight." He turned and put them down in the foyer.

"So, Jake," he said, coming down the steps once we were alone. "I hear you're not staying."

"Nah. I'm still feeling the effects of these bumps and bruises. I think I'll use the time off for some beauty sleep."

"Well, I wanted to tell ya, I seen that car around here again. A few times."

"The Cadillac?"

"Yeah, the big black one. Couldn't get close enough to see who was in it, but I'm sure it's the same car."

"I saw it, too. Just an hour or so ago. In a parking lot across from my place."

Vincent shook his big, thick head. "I'd like to get my hands on those guys."

"I'd pay to see that," I told him. I also told him about the expandable steel baton and the effects it could have on you.

"Yeah, well," said Vincent, "I'd like to ram it down his throat and expand it out his ass."

"They'll get theirs. I haven't forgotten what they did to Angelica and me or to my home. There's some payback in order; I'm missing a couple of my favorite Foreigner and Barenaked Ladies CDs, and my *Gladiator* DVD is gone, too. Not to mention the package of Oreos the guy called Lip finished off while I was getting my molars rearranged."

"Double-stuff?"

"Yep."

"Sons of bitches. . . ."

We both seemed to fall into a reverie for a moment, and then Vincent said, "Hey, why don't we hang together for a while, you and me. See if we can run into these punks."

I sort of wanted to keep this between me and the two sons of bitches and try to take them down myself, but Vincent was certainly in a motivated mood and could definitely come in handy.

"You're not going to the big function tonight?" I asked.

"Nah, it's almost all family. Me? I'm just fillin' in for the other guy, Stephano. He's supposed to be coming back from Sicily tonight. If he does, then I'll probably hang around for a few days and see the city, pick me up a nice piece of *culo*, maybe two."

I told him about the license plate run I had done and the connection of the car to Perrotta Meats.

"You got that from the cops?" he asked incredulously. "You ain't got nothin' to do with 'em, though, right?"

"No," I said with a laugh. "I used to be a cop back in Boston, but that was a long time ago. I know this guy downtown because of this murder case I was involved with last summer."

"No shit?" Vincent looked at me with newfound respect. "Well, why don't we go take a drive down to Perrotta and see what we can find out?" He saw me trying to decide and continued, "We can drive around here and your place, too. And swing by Perrotta if we don't come up with anything. What do you say, Jake? Could be fun."

I wasn't sure how much fun it was going to be, but I was looking forward to some payback with a little frontier justice. "All right," I said. "Let's do it."

Vincent slapped me lightly on the left bicep, but I was braced and prepared for the collision, so I got knocked only a foot or two. "Cool. Let me get my stuff."

He turned and started around the house when all of a sudden he spun around. "Hey, Jake, you need a piece or somethin'?"

I shook my head. "Nah, I don't think so."

"Ever have to use one?"

"Yup, once."

"Oh, yeah? What happened?"

"The guy died. . . ."

"Whoa." Vincent was taken aback. "And this was when you were a cop?"

"Uh-huh."

"How did it happen?"

"Maybe some other time," I told him.

"Yeah, sure." He seemed to understand and started off. "I'll be back in a minute."

Vincent left me with old memories trying to poke holes through walls I'd worked very hard to build. The only one I'd ever told the entire shooting story to was Oakley.

No, I wasn't planning on discussing the past anytime soon. The nightmares had practically stopped, and I wasn't about to invite them back.

# Chapter

We drove around the Bonello neighborhood a couple of times and checked the few strip malls and restaurants in the area for signs of the Caddy. Next I pointed the Chrysler north, and we took in the nonscenic sights of Boulder Highway in the early dusk that was just beginning to fall.

Vincent and I made small talk during the drive. I learned that he was a 26-year-old dedicated foot soldier of the eastern family, and he had been living with and working for them for the past seven years after coming to the United States from Italy. His one goal was to become a "made man." Outside of learning I was a poker dealer at the Oasis, he got very little about me. He flipped through some of the books I'd bought earlier but seemed more interested in the pictures than in the words.

Eventually, we turned down Spenser, and I told Vincent to keep his eyes peeled for our friends. As we circled the block for the second time, the Cadillac passed us going the other way. I slowed down to watch, but the other car kept going and appeared to turn into the heavy traffic going west.

Vincent looked at his watch. "It's 7:30, maybe they're going to go eat."

"Maybe. But I'm pretty sure they saw us. I'm going to go around back and park. We can look for them from inside my place. Then, if they show up, maybe we'll sneak out and give them a surprise."

Vincent seemed to like the surprise part. "Yeah," he chuckled. "Cool."

"Those guys really did a number on your place," Vincent said, surveying the wreckage of my apartment.

"Yeah, excuse the mess. Our little Angelica has been keeping me pretty busy, and I haven't had time to tidy up."

"No problem."

"I'm going to clean myself up." I peeked through the blinds, but there was no sign of our friends. "There's beer and stuff in the fridge, so help yourself. The big screen is hooked up to satellite, so if those two a-holes didn't steal my remote watch what you want, and I'll be back and ready to rumble in about twenty minutes."

I started to empty my pockets of money, keys, pagers, and phones, when I heard the television click on.

"You got any milk?" asked Vincent.

"Yeah, but you better check the expiry. I don't want you getting sick on me later."

"Okay. Don't worry."

I peeled off all the clothes I'd been wearing since yesterday and threw them onto the closet floor. Then I heard Vincent.

"Aw, shit!" he yelled. "Goddamn it."

"What is it?" I asked.

"I was checking for the Caddy through the window. When I turned around, I tripped on a cushion and spilled the milk all over the rug."

"Don't worry about it. I'll take care of it later."

"Nah, I'll clean it up. But the rug's going to be a bit wet."

"No problem, it'll dry. I won't be long."

"I'll take care of it. . . ."

I laid out an outfit conducive to a good street brawl: loose black jeans, a snug, dark gray, short-sleeve sweatshirt, and a pair of steel-toed Dr. Martens. And then, for good measure, I rummaged through my old hockey bag until I found my jock and strap and, after deciding that they weren't too foul smelling, tossed them onto the rest of the pile.

I grabbed a pair of shorts, and as I was walking bare assed down the hall to the shower I heard Vincent open the front door. He was probably getting a better view of the street. I was beginning to like Vincent more and more.

◆

The hot water felt exquisite. I'd read somewhere that average Americans liked their water at 105 degrees when showering. If that were true, then I must have had mine around 115 to help fight the abuse my body had taken over the past 48 hours. I rested my forehead on the tiled wall and let the water beat on my back as I drifted.

Somewhere all hell was breaking loose.

And then I realized I had already turned off the water and wasn't dreaming. Yelling and screaming and swearing filled the air, secondary only to the sound of medium-caliber gunfire that was probably responsible for the sounds of breaking glass throughout the unit and the ricocheting of bullets embedding themselves into wood and drywall at this end of the hallway.

*What the hell!*

I went to the bathroom doorway to look at what was happening, but the whizzing sound and breaking of the hallway light suggested I shouldn't. I looked through one of the vanity drawers and found a mirror with a long handle; then I went back to the doorway, held out the mirror, and looked up the hallway.

Vincent was crouched behind a thick old armchair, firing his gun from around the side as well as occasionally from over the top of his cover.

From the far end of the hallway and across the living room was the front door, where I could see an arm come around and fire off a few and then pull back. Judging from Vincent's two lines of fire, he was holding off someone in the living room as well as at the door. The smell of cordite filled the air.

"Vincent!" I shouted, still looking via the mirror. "You okay?"

He fired one shot at the door and another somewhere off to the right.

"Yeah, wonderful." He was facing me as he slapped a new clip into his automatic. I could have sworn he was smiling. "You got any way out from back there?" he yelled.

"No. There's a storage room right across from me, and that's my bedroom you've got your back to."

There were no windows in the bathroom large enough to attract attention through and, except for a razor and a pair of eyebrow and nose hair scissors, not much in the way of weaponry or protection. But there was a baseball bat in my bedroom closet.

"Vincent, there's a door at the end of the kitchen right across from you that leads down the back way of the complex. Go for it and get help. I'll lock up back here and try to hold them off."

Shots rang out from both the door and the living room. I watched Vincent hunker down and then watched as the mirror took a direct hit and disintegrated in my hand.

"Forget it!" he shouted as he calmly fired two shots to each of his assailants. "You'll never last."

"Okay, if you can cover me, I might be able to make it to my room. I only need three or four seconds. From there, with one more set of covering fire, I can make it to the kitchen, and you follow with me."

"Sounds like a plan."

I took a couple of breaths. "Okay, Vincent, on the count of *three!*"

"Got it."

Since the only way of calling the play was to shout out loud, the opposition was fully aware of our plan as well, and I would probably be spitting blood halfway up the hall. This called for a quarterback audible.

A couple more gulps of air. "Okay, one . . . NOW!"

Vincent caught on a split second before they did and fired off two sets of double shots at each of the bad guys. That gave me a full four seconds to go flying along the hall and headfirst into my room, reminding me I hadn't put on my shorts. I grabbed another pair and jumped into them; then I felt around the back of the closet until my hand wrapped around my Louisville Slugger.

The sound of opposition gunfire increased considerably, and I could hear the bullets as they punched the thin drywall of my room and the occasional round as it made it through. And then it became strangely quiet.

"Vincent!" I shouted.

No response. No sound at all.

And then testing fire by the enemy to see if Vincent would answer.

Still nothing.

Then I remembered the heating and air-conditioning vents that led to my room as well as to the area where Vincent was located. It was the same ductwork with vents on both sides. It came to me because it was the hiding place I'd used the few times I'd won enough money that I didn't feel comfortable leaving it lying around in my pocket. Most gamblers have a hidey-hole, and most are empty.

I got down on my knees and popped the cover off with one pull. I stuck my face to the hole, and through the wire mesh on the other side I could see Vincent's empty eyes looking at me. His mouth was still shaped into a smile, but now blood was leaking from the corner closest to the carpet. It looked as if he'd fallen on his gun.

I heard voices in Italian, and it sounded like each was trying to convince the other to enter the room of Vincent's last stand. And then I heard, "If he's dead, no witnesses."

*Jesus Christ!*

I jumped up and quietly closed my door. It had a lock, but it wasn't worth shit. I took a five-foot-high dresser and pushed it across the room and up against the door. Then I took a shorter dresser and mirror and pushed that up to the first. That still left me with about four or five feet of space between the second dresser and the wall, so I flung my mattress off my bed, took the box spring and frame, and wedged it on an angle from the dresser to the baseboard.

Just as I was surveying my work, a shot fired out, and the handle of the door flew apart. Pressure was being applied to the door, but it wouldn't budge.

"Open up, Morgan! We just wanna talk to ya!"

"Yeah, right."

I went to the window that opened to the courtyard, opened it, and looked out. There was a group of teenagers laughing and smoking and drinking up a storm, sitting around a big old ghetto blaster that was belting out whatever it was at a high volume. But it was the back of the complex, where a lot of people entertained at the pool and sauna, and nobody had bothered to complain. Now I wondered if the sound of the gunfire had been heard over the so-called music.

"Morgan, you asshole," yelled Tony from the other side. "What did you want to talk about?"

"You're all fucked up, *Tone*. I didn't want to talk to you!"

I went back to the window and started to yell to get the party's attention, but nothing doing. I went to get the Louisville to smash the window as the thumping against the door began. Obviously, it was Lip and all his weight, because the barricade of furniture I had built was actually starting to shake. Fortunately, the hallway was only about 40 inches wide, and he wasn't able to get up a head of steam.

"So why didja leave the goddamn rug out if you didn't wanna talk, Morgan?"

Lip tried punching the door, and there was an ugly sound of a crack. These doors weren't meant for high security, but you would think they would hold up to a punch. A few more were thrown at the door and then at the walls, where the drywall caved in to his big fist. It still had to get through the drywall on my side, but he gave it a try. Fortunately, on his third attempt he hit a two-by-four stud, which splintered along with his knuckles.

When his screaming settled down, Tony told him to go to the door and check on the neighborhood. If the coast was clear, he was to go to the car and get a sledge hammer.

I shouted, "What are you talking about a rug for, you dumb shit?"

"The rug! I told ya to hang the rug over your balcony when you had something about the Bonellos you wanted to share."

*Oh, shit, no. The wet rug! . . . Vincent, what have you done?*

If there was ever a reason to cry over spilt milk, this was surely it. And I was almost on the verge.

"Morgan, come here, listen to me."

Tony must have hoped I wanted to hear what he had to say, because a couple of seconds later three rounds came shattering through the door in a parallel pattern.

"You're a dead man, Morgan." Two more shots came through on an angle, and I flung myself against the wall. "Dead as dead."

*Screw this!*

I spun around and found the baseball bat; then I turned and crawled on my hands and knees toward the vent. Vincent was still wide-eyed and smiling, but the blood around his lips was starting to congeal. I was truly hoping they could keep that boyish smile for the funeral home viewing.

I took the Louisville and put it into the vent hole, clenching it with one hand halfway and the other on the end, as if I was paddling a canoe; then I started ramming it into the screen on the other side of the wall as if my life depended on it. Because it did.

The screen bulged considerably after the first two strikes, and then the screws popped from the wall, and the mesh hit the back of the chair. I nudged Vincent's head over and back a bit until I had a clear view of the gun; then I used the business end of the bat to slide it within my reach. I dropped the bat and stretched my arm through the hole as far as I could. I managed to grab the bottom of the handle, but it slipped a few times because of all the blood. Finally, I had two fingers around the butt and was bringing it in when three quick shots sounded and Vincent's mouth and right eye exploded. There would be no open casket after all. The third must have hit the Louisville because the bat jumped and rolled.

I yanked my hand back inside and slid on my ass into the corner. I popped the clip to Vincent's Glock, found there were still five rounds left, and slapped the clip back home. I could hear talking outside and then the moving of Vincent and furniture. Two shots came through the bedroom door, as if to get my attention, and then I heard some thumping and scraping coming from the vent. The nose of a pistol came through the hole on my side, seemed to sniff the air, and then burped off three or four shots around the room.

I calmly rested my hands on my knee as I sat in the corner and took careful aim. One shot clear through the back of the leather-gloved hand and the gun stopped its belching and fell to the floor. An incredible scream came from the other side of the wall. The noise from behind my door ceased, and I heard what sounded like Tony trying to comfort what sounded like Lip. I headed over to the door.

"I'll kill that sunna va bith, Tony, tho help me."

"Sure, Lip, sure."

I pushed the taller dresser sideways as quietly as I could.

"You thwear he's mine?"

"He's all yours. Come on, let's get the hell outta here."

The door swung open about a foot and a half, and I edged my head and right arm into the hall. I could see four legs sticking out. Two were toes up, which I assumed had to be Vincent's, and the other two were pointed toes down. I figured these belonged to Tony, who was trying to help Lip up. The sounds of approaching sirens could be heard in the distance. I rested the piece up against the doorframe, aimed, and fired. I saw the material of one of the pant legs twitch and tear open, and then I heard another long wail and swearing.

"Get the fuck outta my house!" I yelled and fired off another round just for the hell of it.

I saw them scrambling to get up and then fall into the kitchen. I slipped back into my room, slid the dresser back into place, and waited for the boys in blue to come roaring in.

# Chapter ♛♛

A nightstick, or the butt of a rifle, slammed twice into the bedroom door.

"This is the Las Vegas Metro Police," a gruff and angry voice shouted. "Open up!"

To make sure everybody remained calm and I didn't get shot by some trigger-happy cowboy, I called out, "This is Jake Morgan, tenant of this apartment. I'm ex-cop, Boston PD. Two perps, both in suits and injured, just fled down the back stairs through the kitchen. They came in the black Caddy out front."

I heard whispered orders, and a couple sets of young legs took off down the back exit.

"I know there's at least one DOA out there," I continued. "Since you're going to have to call in Homicide anyway, you might as well call in now and ask for Lieutenant Oakley. He'll vouch for me."

The nightstick or rifle banged again but not so loudly or urgently. "Okay, already. Open the fucking door!"

I'd been on enough assignments, just like the guys on the other side of the door, to know how badly these things could go. Once, on a call much like this one in a small, dark warehouse on the Boston waterfront, a hissing cat jumped out and had all nine lives snuffed out right there and then.

"All right, but everybody stay cool. I'm going to push away the barricade and put my hands up against the wall; then I'll call out 'Enter.' There are two guns on the floor by the door, clips pulled."

I laid both pieces and clips on the carpet, pushed away the dresser, walked over to the adjacent wall, and stretched my arms up high. "Okay, enter!"

The door slammed open and came off one of its hinges, and then, just as I expected, nothing happened. They weren't going to fall for that old trick of coming in on the count of some deranged shooter only to have him sitting there behind a hunk of metal with an Uzi pointed at the door. No way.

They did one of the two things I would have done on a gunfire call to an apartment that had been shot up like Swiss cheese. They waited and then, instead of a gas canister, sent in an angry-looking German shepherd that, since its training is to go for the target's clothing, had its eyes aimed at the flimsy material covering my quivering white ass. He came charging, barking sharply, not exactly sure what to latch onto. He did a quick and effective search of the rest of the room looking for another bad guy or someone else better dressed. Coming up empty, the dog came running back to me. He sat down in front of me, nudged and sniffed my family jewels, and barked out something that probably meant "Checkmate" in doggie talk.

A few moments later what seemed like 30 or 40 arms hauled me down to the floor, twisted my arms behind me, and slapped on a set of cuffs.

"Good boy, Barney," said one of the cops to the dog. "Good boy."

Two of them picked me up, and the dog's handler started laughing. "You better put those away, buddy. Barney loves Burger King."

Not having any idea what the hell he was talking about, I looked down and saw I had thrown on a pair of underwear an old girlfriend had given me years ago. The front read "Home of the Whopper."

They let me put on a pair of jogging shorts before taking me out into the living room. I had seen my abode in moments of disarray before but none quite like this. Furniture and paintings and books were lying everywhere, but that could be cleaned up. I hoped my insurance covered bullet holes, because practically every wall showed punctures that would have to be repaired, and the entire unit would need repainting.

Feeling as if I might be acting insensitively, I looked over into the other room and saw Vincent's lifeless form sprawled out. I reflected on our short association and realized he was the kind of guy you'd want watching your back if you were caught in a foxhole. Seeing him also reminded me that I'd have to get the carpets cleaned.

The boys in uniform took down all the usual information. When they had everything I could possibly remember, from the time Vincent and I had entered my apartment, they said: "Great, now go over it all again. Right from the beginning."

All of this took about half an hour. Uniforms and suits were moving about doing this and that: dusting and bagging, prying and collecting. A couple of young patrolmen showed up and told the sergeant they hadn't been able to track the bleeding runners — darkness made it impossible to follow the trail. The ME was doing what medical examiners do and recording everything into a mic on his lapel.

"Well, if it ain't the Sherlock Holmes of Glitter Gulch!" boomed out a voice from the front doorway.

We all looked up.

"Hey, Lieutenant," said the cop with the writing pad.

Most of the others nodded hello.

Me? I just sat there looking like an idiot, with my love handles hanging over my shorts and my arms behind my back.

Lieutenant Oakley shook his big blond head at me. "You can unhook him, Lloyd."

"If you vouch for him, Lieutenant, sure thing." Lloyd took off the cuffs, and I rubbed some circulation back into my wrists.

"Good to see you, Lieutenant," I said. "Glad you got the call on this one."

He smiled down at me. "I didn't. But when I heard the address and your name, well, how could I refuse? And since I couldn't pin you for the Valentine murder last summer, I thought, 'What the hell, maybe I'll have better luck this time.'"

The other cops looked me over again, and one of them said, "So this Jake Morgan is *that* Jake Morgan?"

"The one and only," said Oakley, looking around the apartment. "Jesus Christ! I haven't seen this many bullet holes since the last time I was at the shooting range."

He walked over to where the ME was examining poor Vincent. They shared a few words, and then Oakley wiggled his finger at me to follow him.

We ended up sitting at the small table in the kitchen, where it was relatively quiet and we could talk alone. The lieutenant took out his notebook, pen, and a package of Juicy Fruit, offering one to me before he put the gum away. The two of us sat there smacking our lips for a short time, and then Oakley said, "Okay, what happened?"

I took him through everything again, starting with who Vincent was and how the two of us were going to try to get a closer look at the guys who had been bothering us. I told him we had spotted the Caddy driving by us outside.

Oakley called out for one of the uniforms to go and look for their car out front or in the parking lot across the street and quarantine it if it was located.

He used his cell phone and made a call repeating the license plate from earlier that day. "No good on the Caddy," he told me. "Reported stolen about half an hour ago."

I nodded my head. "What a coincidence. . . ."

"Yeah, really. Go on with what happened."

I told Oakley how I'd heard the gunfire and made it to my room with the help of Vincent covering me. Then I told him about barricading myself in and how I ended up getting my hands on two guns. I also admitted I may have, in self-defense of course, put a teeny, tiny hole through the left hand of the one they called Lip and that a ricochet may have nicked the so-called Tony in the calf.

Oakley called out to the ME that he wanted separate samples of all blood locations out there and to look for multiple injuries.

I also told him how the whole thing had probably gone down while I was in the shower, explaining how Vincent had spilled a drink and unknowingly signaled the bad guys that I had something to talk to them about.

Oakley was shaking his head as he kept writing. "Wow. Can you imagine the look on all their faces when the door flew open and three arms lifted up firing off rounds?"

As if on cue, one of the suits stuck his head in the kitchen. "Looks like O'Reilly wins the pool again, Lieutenant. We counted up 123 slugs, and he was closest at 125. We also got 127 spent cartridges. So, with what looks like three to the victim, that leaves one slug traveling with the pair this guy says left here."

I thought back to my three shots. I was certain the first had gone right through the gloved hand, hit the gun butt, and ended up on the floor. The second had flicked the other guy's pant leg, and the third I had fired in the air.

"No," I said, remembering one other shot. "They got away clean. Check the barrel end of my baseball bat. All the slugs that don't match up to the two guns I gave you will match each other and belong to the piece that's missing."

"Go check the bat, Carl," said Oakley, scribbling in his notebook.

"And just the two of you were going to try to find these two guys and have a discussion with them?"

"Yeah, you know, try to find out at Perrotta Meats what the connection was to the goons following us."

Oakley looked around the place. "I can imagine how that discussion would have gone."

A couple of cops came by and whispered in Oakley's ear, and he had me clear up a few things, such as the jockstrap laid out on my bed. Carl came by with the bat and showed the slug to the lieutenant. The medical examiner called Oakley out to have a word with him while paramedics put Vincent into a body bag, placed him on a gurney, and wheeled him out.

At about 11 p.m., Julius Contini showed up puffing on a stogie, full of piss and vinegar and wanting to know how his boy was.

After making sure I was okay and learning about Vincent, he talked to Oakley alone for a few minutes. Then we all got together, and the lieutenant informed me they were going to shut my place down for the night as a crime scene. Contini told me to pack up some clothes and toiletries because I was going to be a guest of the Oasis for as long as it took. He also told me to write down the landlord's name and number and to give him my house insurance policy so he could have his secretary look after having my place cleaned and repaired when the investigation was completed. Then he walked out of the kitchen and surveyed the living room-dining room area.

"Look at all the fuckin' bullet holes!" he yelled out in amazement. "There's gotta be 100."

"One twenty-four," someone announced.

"The Oasis. Sweet deal," said Oakley, tapping the end of his pen against the table. "I guess I can let you go stay at the Oasis instead of with the city

. . . as long as you're sure there's nothing you aren't telling me." He studied my baby blues with his own. "Don't shit me, Morgan. There's one dead guy pulled outta here tonight and traces of blood from two others. This is serious business, and you better make sure you've treated it that way. If there is anything that you're holding back, and I mean *anything*, you better tell me now. I may know you, and you may think we're pals, but I've got a job to do, and I'll carve you a new one if you take advantage of our acquaintance."

I could tell he was serious, and I tried to think if I'd missed anything, but in all good conscience I didn't think I had, and I told him so.

"Okay, then go and get your stuff together and get out of here."

I got up and was almost out of the kitchen when Oakley called out, "Oh, and by the way. . . ."

I stopped and turned around. "Yeah, I know," I told him. "Don't be crossing any state lines."

**Chapter**

I'd driven back to the Oasis by midnight and found that Big Julie had arranged for a small suite for me on the executive floor. Thursday night had just become Friday morning, and the place was jumping. I took my luggage and went straight to my room, avoiding the call of the casino. I was exhausted, sure that the emotional stress of getting involved in a shootout had made things even worse.

The room was ornate yet functional. It had a small bedroom, behind sliding double doors just off the living room, and a full kitchenette with a separate dining area. It also came with four telephones and an equal number of televisions, all with DVD players for the extensive collection of Hollywood hits and, dare I say, more "adult" selections. There was a big screen in the living room, a 16-inch in the eating area, a 28-inch in the bedroom mounted from the ceiling, and a 12-inch built into the wall at the end of the two-person Jacuzzi tub.

I didn't even bother to unpack after chugging back a bottle of cold Corona. I took a bite of an apple from the fruit basket, and it only reminded me how hungry I was for some real food. Again, almost getting killed can work up a tremendous appetite.

I stripped off my clothes down to my undies and flopped onto the king-size bed without pulling back the covers. I decided that I'd lie there in the dark just long enough to catch my second wind and to think what to order from room service. Maybe I'd feel good enough after something to eat to go back downstairs and play a few hands with the loosey-goosey tourists who were probably checking in right now for the weekend.

♦

I must have been thinking about food so much that I had willed various favorite aromas to fill my nostrils. I knew the sweet smells were just in my imagination, but I was having a difficult time ignoring the grumbling sounds being made by my hungry stomach.

Then I realized a bunch of things all at once. First, I wasn't dozing at all. I could see through the crack in the heavy bedroom drapes that the sun was up and that the day was well on its way. The clock radio confirmed it by displaying 9:06. Second, there must have been food nearby, because my eyes were partially open and I could still smell the wonderful aromas. Third, my stomach wasn't making funny noises at all; the giggling was coming from Angelica, who was leaning against the bedroom door with her hand covering her mouth and staring.

"I like Burger King as much as the next girl, but I didn't know they super-sized."

I looked down, embarrassed to find that I was unfortunately experiencing a "seven o'clock silly," and here it was well after nine. My foggy brain began to log on and receive messages from my senses outlining what the current situation really was.

"Jesus H. Christ!" I screamed, trying to cover up on top of the bed I'd been lying on all night. I reached up and yanked one of the pillows out from under the cover, slapped it to my midsection, and sat up. "What are you doing here?"

Angelica collected herself finally and said, "I couldn't sleep last night when I heard what had happened. Uncle Julius called the house this morning to give *nonna* and me an update. I begged him to let me come to the Oasis so I could check on you and also try to work on my tan a bit more. I think he agreed that under the circumstances I would probably be safer here while you recovered today. Not that the old bodyguard Stephano can't look after us; on the contrary, he seems to be as tough as they come."

I rubbed some of the sleep from my eyes. "How the hell did you get in?" I asked, tousling my hair and stretching until I shivered to a stop.

"Uncle Julius gave me the room next door to use for whenever I'm here. You know, a place to change or have a nap. My room's a connector for when more people stay in yours."

I sat there considering that for a moment.

"I know what you're thinking," she said. "That the connecting doors are usually locked. Well, Uncle Julius walked me to my room this morning, where the maid had just finished cleaning. He told her who I was and to make sure I got whatever I wanted." She hunched her shoulders up high and then let them loose. "Now the door is unlocked, and here I am."

"Uh-huh."

"Wait'll you see what I got us for breakfast." Angelica turned and skipped into the dining area. She was wearing a white Minnie mouse T-shirt, black track pants, and pink runners. Her hair was up in a ponytail. "Just be glad I had your appetite in mind and wasn't some kind of crazed sex maniac."

"Yeah, you, too," I mumbled under my breath and looked for where I had put my clothes.

I went out to the dining area after finding a pair of jeans and UNLV T-shirt. I'd taken the time to brush my teeth and splash myself with water but decided I wanted a hot breakfast now, although a cold shower might have been in order.

Angelica had pulled two of the dining room chairs up to a lavish room service cart laden with food.

"I hope you don't mind what I ordered," she said. "I just picked a bunch of stuff I thought you might like."

She had done a good job in her selection. There was coffee and freshly squeezed OJ as well as a choice of cereals, bacon, sausages, scrambled eggs, and four or five bakery products. And three cute little roses in a crystal vase.

"You did great," I told her when I'd sat down and started to attack the food.

"So," she said, dunking a piece of English muffin into her coffee cup. "Tell me all about it."

I gave her a rundown of what had happened, keeping the shooting to a minimum and excluding the naked running altogether. She sat there quietly while I explained how I had outfoxed the foxes. Her eyes welled up at the mention of Vincent's demise, and she seemed genuinely concerned that my situation had seemed so helpless that I might not have made it out alive, although I was sitting right there telling the story.

"We were all so worried when Uncle Julius got the phone call and told us what had happened." She sniffled while she dabbed at her eyes with a napkin. "All we knew was that there had been a shooting at your apartment and that one person was dead. Uncle Julius said he was going to your place, and Stephano insisted he go along, but he was ordered to stay close to *nonna* and me."

I suddenly realized what they, and especially Angelica, had gone through. "Well, don't worry yourself sick about this. We lost a good man in Vincent, but I promise you I'll get to the bottom of what's going on. Their biggest mistake was not finishing me off."

"And you promise me you're okay?"

"Yup. Thanks to Barney, I'm still all in one piece."

Angelica had found her appetite again and was applying peanut butter to a helping of scrambled eggs. "Who's Barney?" she asked. "One of the cops?"

"Yeah, sorta. But it's another long story. Could you pass the ketchup?"

I changed the topic to her grandmother and, after learning she was concerned but okay, told Angelica I was going to drive out to the Bonello estate to talk with Olivia and meet with Stephano so I could give him a heads-up on the overall situation. "You wanna come for the drive?" I asked her.

She was finishing off her eggs with the remainder of a can of Clamato juice and seemed to really think about it for a minute. "Nah, but thanks for asking. I've only got another few days, and I'd like to get what little sun there is. If you're back later in the afternoon, do you think we could go for dinner or something?"

"Sure," I said, plunking the last sausage into my mouth. "A man's gotta eat, right?"

She wiped her lips but seemed to have a dispirited look about her.

"And what the heck," I said, trying to cheer her up. "Except for when you're beating up cross-dressers who are trying to pick up the old Jakester, you're not bad company."

We both started laughing.

"I'll be fine here, really," she finally said. "You go ahead."

"Is there anything you want me to bring back from the house for you?"

Angelica thought about it. "No, I brought a suitcase of different out-fits. I should be okay for a day or two." Her eyes went wide. "And there's always that *hellamall* downstairs. They have some very cool shops!"

"That mall is solely for the tourists," I said with a laugh. "Sometimes I wonder if they built it for the big winners, so their wives can spend a good chunk of it back on overpriced haute-couture. I remember looking at a tie there once that would have cost me a week's pay."

"Yeah, well, judging from what I saw earlier, you could use some new underwear."

"Okay, that's enough," I said, tossing my napkin over my empty plate. "I thank you for taking care of breakfast, but off you go. I've got work to do."

We pushed the cart out into the hallway for room service to pick up later. I walked Angelica to the connecting door and held it open for her.

"Leave it unlocked, please," Angelica said softly. "I still feel a little scared."

"Okay," I said with a generous smile, although I knew I'd prefer easy access to her room if anything went wrong, even here at the Oasis. "But I was going to ask you the same thing, you know, because I've seen you in action, and I could probably use the help myself."

She gave me a playful punch to the belly; then she stepped on her tiptoes and gave me a peck on the cheek. "Later, alligator."

"In a while, crocodile."

She turned, closed the door gently, and was gone.

# Chapter

I sat by the window that looked out over the Strip. I hadn't thought this hard since back in Boston. Then I'd just been kicked off the police force for borrowing confiscated drug dealer money to finance my gambling habit, and I was trying to figure out how to straighten out my spiraling life.

Not even Internal Affairs knew everything. Oh, sure, they got the gist of the poker game shooting and had determined, in their minds, why I was such a misfit, caught where I was: an underground card room where four people had been shot, one fatally by me.

And, yeah, IA knew I'd lost a Vice partner six months earlier. Karen Bulloch and I had been working together for 14 months and dating for nine of them. We had a meeting planned with a drug informant one night, and she ended up going it alone. The meeting was scheduled for 6 p.m. at a downtown bar. She called me around 5:30 to make sure I was on my way, and when I told her I was stuck large in a big poker game and to give me another hour she decided not to believe me. She had reason; I'd let her down before.

Karen was still alive when I arrived at the bar at the promised time of 6:30, but despite my encouragements and the sounds of the ambulance rushing down the street she died in my arms. IA wrote if off as a bad decision on Karen's part by going in alone, and the Boston PD acknowledged that they'd lost a good officer. They had no idea how close the two of us had been or that we were making plans to move in together.

There was a lot that nobody knew and would never understand. Hell, I was having a hard time understanding it myself. But I was making progress.

I sat there mulling, jotting down notes, and scribbling down names and bits of information. It's what I did when I worked undercover investigations — tried to fit pieces of the puzzle together. Little things I knew for sure would be underlined. Those that were uncertain received a question mark. For the most part, I sat there wondering what the hell a couple of gangsters really wanted from the Bonello family. I knew I wasn't the focal point of their questioning and accepted that I was just the wrong guy in the wrong place at the wrong time. But I sure wasn't going to just stand by and be the whipping boy for these two goons. No way. A little payback was in order for what they'd done to Vincent, not to mention me and my apartment. And also for thinking that I hadn't noticed they'd also taken my favorite *Road to Perdition* DVD.

Back on the Boulder Highway, heading south for what seemed like the 47th time that week, I decided that I was going to see this little adventure through to the end. I wanted to talk once more with Olivia Bonello and meet Stephano, the longtime man around the house.

The road was so straight and had become so familiar that the cruise control seemed to be able to handle the course by itself. I glanced up once in a while as I played around with the global positioning satellite. I was just getting the hang of how to enter an address to get directions and a street map display when the sign for Boulder City popped up, and I made a right onto Buchanan.

The gates were closed, as expected, so I buzzed in my name and intentions to a gruff male voice with a heavy accent. "Wait there" crackled out of the intercom.

A minute later I saw the large shape of a man come out from a stand of small trees. He gave my car the once-over, checked up and down the street, and pointed his left arm and aimed with what looked like a remote control at the metal barrier. I was relieved he pointed with that hand because he appeared to be holding a sawed-off shotgun down along his thigh with the other.

When the gates widened, he gave a jerk with his head that I took to mean I was to go up the driveway. I must have been right, because he didn't shoot me as I drove slowly by and nodded hello. He was too busy making sure no one followed before the gates clanged shut behind me.

Orsina was at the front door and welcomed me in. She said something to me in rapid Italian, gave both my arms a double pat, looked me up and down, and made the sign of the holy cross. She took me by the elbow. "Come, come."

I followed her out to the patio, where Olivia was sitting in a rocking chair with a blanket over her legs, lost in thought. Her reverie was broken by the sound of our footsteps on the cobbled brick flooring.

"Good morning, Jake," she said. "I am so glad to see you. Julius told me you were all right last night, but I wanted to see for myself."

"Morning Olivia, I appreciate your concern," I said. "Thanks for letting me come out to see you on such short notice."

"You are welcome here anytime."

Orsina poured each of us coffee from a silver thermal urn, and, with the polite chit-chat out of the way, Olivia asked me to go over last night for her. When I'd finished the recap, she seemed truly regretful that she or her past had caused me so much grief and genuinely remorseful that Vincent had lost his life.

"Please accept my sincerest apology for what has happened. In no way could anyone have foreseen that a 50-year-old rumor could escalate like this."

I assured her that I believed her, mostly because I knew I wouldn't have been the protector of choice if Big Julie had thought there would be any repercussions for or danger to Angelica. He had real security types with real hard muscles, real big guns, and real bad attitudes to deal with situations requiring force. I also told her I had a couple of ideas that I wanted to follow up on, and, if successful, perhaps I could shed some light on this whole affair.

"Jake, don't bother. You and Angelica are safe now, and I don't want anything else to happen. Besides," she said in a soft voice, "I don't have that much time, and all this will end when I am gone."

I wasn't totally convinced of that, but I didn't want her worrying over Angelica any more than she was.

"You know, Jake, I thought I had hit the bottom of despair when I lost my Carmine. I realized I hadn't when I watched my daughter Sofia's downward spiral and her eventual death. But if I was ever responsible for anything this evil happening to my Angelica . . . I could never forgive myself."

I assured her that everything was going to be okay and that Angelica's safety would never be compromised.

"Olivia, you mentioned the other day in the library about a picture of your husband. Would you mind if I took a look at it, just to get a feel for what the man looked like, you know, put a face to a name?"

"Of course you can," she answered and then with a grin said, "but don't be confused by the attractive woman standing beside him. That's me."

"Why would I?" I asked. "I'm not confused by the beautiful woman sitting beside me right now."

"You see?" she said with a laugh. "You broke our agreement. We said 'no more bullshitting' each other. Remember?"

"And I'm not," I said with conviction.

"Oh, Jake, please," she said, still smiling. "The photo is in Sofia's old room, up the stairs, second door on your left." She thought about something for a moment and then added, "You're welcome to have a look in the library for anything to do with Carmine if you think it will help. As for me, it was a late night. I'm going to try to catch up on my beauty sleep. Not that I need it, though, right?"

She said she'd let the staff know I might be wandering the house for a bit. Then we said our good-byes.

# Chapter

It was fully furnished and impeccably clean for a room that hadn't been used in over a decade. A double bed was laid out in soft-colored tones, with throw pillows and little stuffed animals at the headboard. A big bay window allowed plenty of light on a cradle inscribed with a large letter A. The dressers and makeup table were loaded with female trinkets and little bottles and tubes of this and that. A small white desk sat in a corner with bookshelves on both sides.

I went over to the desk and picked up a miniature telephone book and flipped through the names and numbers. Nothing rang a bell. I was nosy but not nosy enough to go through the drawers. After all, I didn't think there would be much that could help me learn what was going on in the daughter's room, except for the picture.

It was there on the bookshelf, a frameless black-and-white four-by-six leaning against an exquisite replica of the 1939 Bugatti Type 57 that sat parked in the garage next door. I took the photo from the shelf and examined it.

Carmine Bonello was dressed in a dark suit, tie, and fedora, and if someone had yelled "Say cheese!" when they'd taken the shot it hadn't worked. He seemed to look at not just the camera but through it, with dark, piercing eyes that had perhaps seen too much. He was about six feet tall, square jawed and clean cut, maybe 180 pounds with his shoulder holster and weapon.

Olivia was standing next to him, and she did look beautiful, dressed in a flower-patterned summer dress that fit her slim body perfectly. She had a thick head of hair that fell to her shoulders and a smile as wide as the Grand Canyon. In her arms, wrapped in a white blanket, was their daughter, Sofia.

They were standing by the front fender of the Bugatti, allowing the photographer to show his subjects clearly while also treating the vehicle as more than just background: it was all there, from grill to back bumper.

I flipped the photo over. In black ink the words "License to Love" and the date, June 9, 1958 were written. I put it back and picked up the clay sculpture of the Bugatti. It was a beautiful piece, carefully crafted, creating a perfect representation of the original. It even had license plates. Olivia had said her husband insisted on finishing the piece himself. Carmine had done a quality job, obviously using the best oils available back then, as the coloring had not worn or chipped after almost 50 years.

I poked around a little more and then put everything back. I left the room and went downstairs without encountering anyone. In the library, I sat down in the worn leather chair, leaned back, and tried to take myself back 50 years, to imagine what it must have been like to be a made man. Like the Godfather. *Don Morganelli* had a nice ring to it.

After a few minutes of role playing, I bent forward and began opening desk drawers. I started on the left side, working my way down three medium-sized drawers, then over to the right: one more medium and a large one. There was a bunch of old road maps, but none of them had anything like "OVER HERE! OVER HERE! TREASURE BURIED HERE!" written or circled in bright red ink. I'd already had a feeling this wasn't going to be that simple. It rarely is.

There were also quite a few old paperbacks, the 10 cent pulp fiction kind. They all had colorfully drawn front covers of sultry, half-naked damsels in distress and the tough-as-nails PI who was there to save them. I noticed most of them had titles with words like "mayhem," "dames," and "corpses" in them. There were Carter Brown novels: *Cutie Wins a Corpse* and *Madam Your Mayhem*. A couple of books by Richard S. Prather were called *Slab Happy* and *Strip for Murder*. And somebody named Evan Steele had one called *License to Murder/License to Love*. Sticking out of this one was an envelope containing more photos of the car shot from all angles. Perhaps these were the ones used by the sculptor.

I pulled open the wide, thin drawer just below the desktop. There was a bunch of old fountain pens and pencils and some stationery. Loose change, paperclips, erasers, and an old Zippo lighter lay scattered in the long, cylindrical tray that ran across the front. I checked the coins and their dates; all pre-1960. Very weird. Everything appeared to be as it had been left on the morning Carmine had disappeared, never to be seen again.

I closed the drawers and sat back again in the chair. I wasn't exactly disappointed in my lack of clues, because everything I'd seen had probably been gone over many times by the boys from Chi-Town. I shut my eyes for a few moments and enjoyed the quiet of the room. I went over all the things I'd seen so far and tried to see if there might be any pieces to the puzzle hidden among them. I even pulled out the maps and went over every square inch, but there wasn't a letter or number written anywhere.

After straining my eyes for another 20 minutes, I put everything back where I'd found it and left the library disappointed. I found my way to the front and let myself out. I stood on the porch and breathed in the fresh, if not warm, air. I decided that now was as good a time as any to meet with Stephano and tell him what I knew. I also had a feeling I could learn a lot more about the "old days" and how they had worked from this man.

I walked a little way down the drive and could see that the old man wasn't there. I made a left and walked over to the garage, under the portico, and out to the backyard. The patio and yard area were vacant. I traced my steps back and knocked on the side door of the garage. When no one answered, I figured Stephano must be in the apartment above and unable to hear me. Actually, I was surprised he hadn't seen me on one of the many monitors and come down.

I tried the door, and it opened. I walked through the three-stall garage and over to the stairway that led upstairs. Judging by the looks of the man, he didn't seem like the type who would appreciate someone sneaking up on him. Although, come to think of it, Stephano had to be close to 70, so maybe he was hard of hearing or the walk to the gate had tuckered the poor old guy out.

"Hello?" I called out cheerfully. "Anybody home?"

I took a moment to admire the vehicle Carmine had cherished as I leaned against a round wooden post that ran from floor to ceiling at the foot of the stairs. I didn't know a lot about vintage cars, but I knew the Type 57 was a rare bird and considered a classic. I'd heard the Bugatti family had stopped making commercial vehicles around the start of the Second World War, so Carmine had had himself a classic even back then.

As I was taking in the fine lines and the exquisite polish of the Bugatti, something swished around me from behind, and I was yanked back hard against the post. I found myself clawing at my throat for air, but there was some kind of thin wire cutting off my windpipe just below my Adam's apple. I felt nauseous almost immediately and wanted to throw up, but I quickly realized I'd choke on my own vomit. I tried to reach behind to find out how I was being pinned when the pressure eased up slightly.

"Who are you?"

It hurt to swallow, but I managed to call out hoarsely, "Jake. Jake Morgan."

More pressure eased, and air finally found its way down and into my starving lungs. I grabbed at my throat and brought out my hand to see if there was any blood. Luckily, there wasn't. I turned around to look at my assailant, and there was Stephano looking at me from under heavy, dark eyelids. He was holding a piece of wire about 18 inches long with a wooden handle at each end, and he was slowly coiling it into a spool.

I wanted to extend my hand as a gesture of good faith, but I was afraid he might take the forward movement as an act of aggression and cut off my hand at the wrist with some hidden machete.

"I am Stephano," he said. "Out of a corner of my eye, I saw somebody on the monitor enter the garage. Then, when I got down here, all I could see was shoulders and arms on the other side of that post. I thought you were still in the house. You should have told Mrs. B to tell me you were coming in here. It could have turned out very badly."

"For me," I said, still rubbing my throat. "But how did you get down here without me seeing you? I was standing right here by the stairs, and I know there are no other stairs inside or outside."

"I'll explain that later." He placed the spool in his back pocket and stretched his arm out to me. I took his hand, and it was like shaking an old baseball glove.

"If I had done that when I was your age and strong like a bull," he said, "the wire would have cut right through into the post."

I thought about that for a second. "Yeah, but that would mean. . . ." Staring into his eyes was like looking into a dark, bottomless well. "My head would. . . ."

"You get the picture."

"Jesus. . . ."

I fought the urge to gag again. "I'm glad you're older now, not as strong."

"That had nothing to do with it. The way the blood sprays out, you know, when the wire is going through the jugular. . . . I'd be okay standing back here behind the post, but with that car sitting right there in front of you? Uh-uh. Do you have any idea how many hours of waxing and polishing I've put into that car in 42 years? No way am I getting any blood on it now."

"I'm glad," I said, and I meant it.

He started up the steps. "Come on up. I wanna make you a big drink — see if you spring any leaks."

I stopped with one foot on the first step.

"Relax," he said, without even turning his head. "That's an inside joke, a trade thing. Don't worry; I'm just fuckin' with you."

Stephano led me to the main apartment and told me to have a seat. He did a quick security check of the monitors, went to the refrigerator, and pulled out two bottles of Peroni. He popped the caps with his key chain as if he'd been doing it all his life.

The place looked the same as it did the other day except for the five or six moving boxes that were probably Vincent's, piled on top of one another against the far wall.

"I suppose you'd like to hear about last night as well?" I asked, taking one of the beers and a long drink.

"Good idea."

I retold the story, reinserting the bullets, blood, and gore. It didn't seem to affect Stephano. He nodded here and there as if he was reminiscing about having been caught in cross fires of yore, and he seemed to especially like the part where Tony had gone to help Lip after I'd put a hole through his hand and I had snuck out to the hallway and nailed the other in the leg rather than hide in my room until the cavalry arrived.

"This one you call Lip, is he a big guy, kinda dumb?"

"That's him."

Stephano nodded again. "I think I know him. Maybe the other one, too."

"Tall, about six-four, mostly muscle. Black hair, combed back, and he likes to powder his nose."

"Sounds like a couple of guys I heard about. Used to do some collection work for a bookie named Jimmy the Weasel. Legs, arms, that kinda stuff. I think the one guy used to use some kind of steel pole or something."

I told him the story of Angelica being abducted at my place and how Tony had used a retractable metal baton on me.

He looked at my face and seemed to analyze the purple bruise and some of the minor bumps. "Didn't think you got all that from shaving."

I showed him the large bump under my hair and went on to tell him about the other night when the bad guys woke me up, tied me up, and slapped me around.

Stephano studied me for a moment. "So you can take a punch," he said. "You can think on your feet and under fire. Good. I like that. Even better, you haven't backed down from these clowns and seem to want to see the situation to the end."

I took another long pull of my beer and listened.

"I respect that." He pointed the opening of his bottle at me as a salute. "I will help you in any way that I can."

"Well, what I really need is more background on Carmine Bonello and what your relationship was with him. What was the guy like? What made him tick? Where were his loyalties? And I'd like to know more about the skimming operation they ran."

Stephano put his feet up on a wooden coffee table and crossed his ankles. "Mr. B was all right. I was just a kid off the boat in the Bronx back then. I'd come from Sicily and contacted a few names I had been given back home, and before I knew it I was doing muscle work for some of the New York people. When things started happening in Vegas, they shipped me down here. I did a lot of security work, played bodyguard for some of the big shots. Met a lot of people and got to know Carmine too.

"I wouldn't say we were best friends or nothin', but Mr. B got me off the hook once when I was in deep shit with some very ugly collection agency guys that would make your Lip and Tony look like Boy Scouts. They were disappointed when Mr. B came up with the cash because he had spoiled their fun. It wasn't the amount of the money really. They had the okay to whack me right there and then if I didn't have what I owed, and the fear that would have caused through the loan-sharking circles would have been worth more.

"He was extremely loyal to his family and friends. He was a stand-up guy who could be made happy just helping someone out. He was nowhere near a '*Don*,' but he acted like one. Don't get me wrong; he was no pushover. Uh-uh. When he had a tough decision to make, he'd make it, believe me. He was no choir boy, that's for sure."

"Was he the kind to leave his wife and child for some showgirl?"

"Nah, that's a lot of bullshit as far as I'm concerned. And I'm not saying he wasn't being offered some of the sweetest candy in the world, but I didn't ever see him tasting any goodies."

"What about the skimming?"

"What about it? Everybody was doing it. Chicago had it down to a science. A good chunk of their take was coming from the Desert Ranch, but Mr. B had a network filtering the skim from at least five or six joints that I knew of, and I wasn't in on much. The entire city seemed to be one big skim, but the casinos, my God, they must have been taking at least 30 percent off the top from the start. And they had other ways of cleaning out another 10 or 12 points if they needed it."

"Like paying off losing hands to house players, double billing, not reporting credit repayments. . . ."

"Yup. And lots more I don't even know about."

"How did they get rid of it?"

"Simple. They just filled suitcases full of cash and sent 'mules' back to Chicago, KC, or St. Louis by plane, train, or car. They never gave any one guy too much. They didn't want to tempt somebody into trying to make a run for it. But they had a string of guys and gals going seven days a week. Hell, for 20 years, every time I traveled I had it paid for by delivering a 'package' for the boys back east. No matter where I went, they always had somebody somewhere that they owed something to or could use a payoff."

"Tell me, Stephano. Could somebody skim from the skim?"

"I guess so, but why? Everybody involved was pretty well taken care of. And the risk wouldn't be worth it. You'd be dead before you could spend it."

"But it could be done?"

"Well, it would have to be somebody high up."

"Like Bonello?"

"Ah, now I see where you're going with this. It all ties in with the rumors and what these two goons have been asking about."

"Ever hear of any rumors of Bonello and a rainy day stash?"

"Yeah, I heard about them, but I don't know. Mr. B was in the power position, and it would've been a license to steal. But risking his life as well as his family? Gee, that's a hard one to accept."

"But. . . ."

"Yeah. . . ."

The two of us sat there pondering it all for a minute.

"Well, if Mr. B had anything to do with that, you'd think his bodyguard would have had to be in on it," Stephano said.

"Who was that?" I asked.

"Young kid. A real wannabe. His name was Massimo. Drove Mr. B everywhere."

"In the Bugatti?"

"Yeah, that's all he ever rode in. He called it his License to Love."

"I read that. And where's this Massimo?"

"Nobody knows for sure. He was last seen the same day Mr. Bonello was. But there were some whispers he wound up dead in Buffalo. But no money was mentioned."

"If you whacked him and found the cash, would you report it?"

"Probably not."

"Pretty big coincidence, though, don't you think?"

"The two of them missing?"

"Uh-huh."

"Yeah, you're probably right. But even if there was a hidden stash, you're never going to be able to find it. Chicago's been searching for it for 50 years. What makes you think you'll have better luck?"

"Don't know that I will. But it might help stop me from being knocked around and shot at if I found it. Although somehow I don't think Tony, Lip, and I are going to be socializing anytime soon."

"Next time you better see them before they see you. Or you'll be joining Vincent."

"You mean watch my back?"

"Yeah . . . maybe I'll have to give you a hand."

"You're going to have your hands full here. I'll let you know if I think I need any backup. For now, I'm just going to use the muscle in my head and try to figure a few items out. A couple of things are ringing bells, but I don't know what the tune is."

"I don't know what the hell you're talking about, but judging by that lump on your noggin maybe that ringing is from getting hit one time too many."

We both laughed. I got up to leave.

"Wait a minute," I said. "You were going to tell me how you flanked me after you saw me come into the garage. You didn't come down the stairs."

"No," he smiled. "Come with me."

We walked to the far corner of the room, just outside the bathroom. Stephano gave a light press to the corner paneling, and the wall swung outward like a door. Inside was a room no larger than an oversized shower stall, maybe four feet by four feet. A six-inch-wide pipe went from top to bottom. I leaned forward to get a better look.

"Be careful," warned Stephano. He reached in and turned a switch on the wall. A five- or 10-watt night-light came on and showed that the pipe did not end at the floor but ran through a three-foot wide hole and into the darkness below.

"It's a panic room?" I asked.

"More like a panic closet. You have to be careful, but there is enough flooring to be able to stand and a small bench built into the wall that comes down should one have to stay longer. There's an assortment of weapons and guns hanging on the far wall and a knot hole in the paneling that slides back to look into my room."

"Very clever," I admitted. "And when you slide down, there's no noise at the bottom?"

"Six inches of feathered mattress and a soundless, swing-away door built into the wall down there as well."

"Too bad there is no way to get up if needed."

"There is. The pole can be scaled, if you're strong enough, or there is a cord down there that when pulled will drop a rope ladder bolted into the rafters. I built it all myself. It was a hobby of mine over the years."

"I am totally impressed. And jealous," I said with a laugh. "I could have used one of these in my apartment the other night."

Then things turned serious again.

"I meant what I said, Morgan. Watch your back. Those guys won't take kindly to you putting holes in them. You're in a freezeout now with those assholes. Last man standing wins. If they catch you not looking, it's game over."

"I hear you loud and clear. I'll be careful. And I'll call you if I find out anything."

"Or if you need anything."

We shook hands, and I felt the beginning of a kinship.

I looked again at the hidden partition, back at Stephano, and raised my brows.

He said, "Yeah, go ahead."

"Thanks."

I stepped into the closet-sized room and wrapped my arms and ankles around the pole. Stephano was still smiling as I eased up on the arm pressure and slid slowly into the darkness below. I landed softly on the mattress and felt for the door handle. I pressed against a small metal bar, and light poured in as the door opened silently on some type of magnetic lock. I stepped out and closed the panel back against the wall, amazed that no lines could be detected. I put two fingers to the wood and pressed lightly and watched as the door once again popped open without a sound.

Before I left, I took a few minutes to look over the old Bugatti in all its beauty. Stephano had done a terrific job in maintaining the gloss of its metal and the shine of its chrome.

I walked around the vehicle, comparing it in my mind to the black-and-white photo, and then, especially, to the clay model. So much of the intricate detail had been captured in the sculpture: the funny-shaped trunk, the spoked spare, the headlights, and the larger space allowed for the Euro license plates.

It was then that something strange about the car started gnawing at me. I walked around it once more. I stopped and looked in the windows. I stepped back and tried to visualize it beside the model. Maybe Stephano was right. Maybe I'd had my bell rung too much lately. I gave the vehicle another once-over and left the garage.

I was just about to get into the Chrysler when that nagging feeling grew stronger. I went back to the front door, slipped inside, and tiptoed up the stairs. I quietly entered the daughter's old bedroom, closed the door, and went back to the bookshelf.

I took the sculpture down and studied it from all angles. It still looked correct in all aspects, including the scale. I tried to burn an image of the model into my brain; then I put the model back in its place and left the room, keeping my back to the walls all the way out the front door so Stephano couldn't sneak up from behind.

# Chapter

I decided to kill the rest of the afternoon in the Sports Book at the Oasis. I was still too wired from the events of the night before to even try to have a nap, and it was too early to round up Angelica for dinner. No, taking it easy and sipping suds while I watched dogs and horses run in circles was just fine by me.

I was nibbling on my second corned beef sandwich when something jumped out at me from the *Daily Racing Form*. The track was Santa Anita, and the race was the eighth, a one-mile, $25,000 claiming event. I wasn't even looking at the names of the nags, just penning circles around races of equal distances and training times when I came up with the one I was going to bet on. A mare with the name License to Love.

Now I may not be the quickest colt out of the stable, but even I was picking up on a trend here. Over the past couple of days, I'd run into way too many references to "license" and "love" to be normal. I started jotting them down on the paper. First, as far as I could remember, was the reference on the back of the black-and-white photo of the Bonello family beside the Bugatti. Then there was the dime novel that had some kind of title referring to a license and love as well as stealing. Even Stephano had made some kind of reference to skimming being a "license to steal." There weren't bells and whistles and sirens blaring, exactly, but I started hearing that little chime that goes off when you get an e-mail. I may believe in coincidences up to a point, but there comes a time when you have to come to grips with something that keeps slapping you in the face like it wants you to wake up and smell the espresso.

Okay, I decided, as if I needed an excuse to make a bet, if I wager on this horse and it wins, I'll pay attention to this sign as being more of an omen and follow it up. Besides, there was a horse in the next race named *BenJerry* that was making me crave a Karamel Sutra.

I went up to the counter with about a minute left to post and slapped a Franklin on License to Love to win at 7/2. There were two other horses being touted as stronger favorites, so I really should have bet License to Love to place. But what the hell? What good is an omen if it can't pick the winner out of a field of nine?

I settled back in my comfy chair and nursed the last of my beer when the track announcer said, "And they're off!" He never pointed out her name more than the cursory mention of her being in the back of the pack, but at a mile that's where the *Form* said she should be. Once they rounded the stretch, though, he almost tripped over the repetition of her name as she sprang to the outside and passed the speed horses with a precision late run that nipped the favorite by a neck.

That was good enough for me. I was convinced I had to pay a little more attention to the obvious premonition and thank the little mare for being the messenger. And the hell with *BenJerry*, I had enough now for a whole gallon if ice cream was what I wanted.

I went up to the counter, picked up my 450 smackers, and headed for my room and dinner with Angelica.

Just about every hotel in Vegas has a buffet of some kind. They are filled with a fabulous variety of foods at a fair price. Many of them are named after their establishments — the Mirage Buffet, the Monte Carlo Buffet — but some have more intriguing names, such as the Ports o' Call Buffet, the Palatium Buffet, the Emperor's Buffet, or the Pharaoh's Pheast. We were at the magnificent Bellagio Hotel, where Vegas's most sumptuous food fantasy was understatedly, yet appropriately, named The Buffet.

And it was. Continuous brass and glass sneeze guards protecting row after row of spectacular culinary choices: a seafood section second to none, serving everything from fat cleaned shrimp, cracked crab legs, scallops, and squid to sea bass, fresh salmon, trout, and shark; stations featuring lamb, pork, poultry, beef, game bird, rabbit, and even wild boar ribs. And for those true gamblers who'd risk tapeworms or intestinal bacteria, there was dim sum and a sushi bar where you could watch your favorite foods rolled and wrapped right before your eyes.

The only downside was that it was Friday night; the room was packed and a little understaffed. Our waiter was busy enough refilling our drinks and had lapsed a bit on clearing off the table. That was okay with me. After the night before, and lots of reflecting on existence that day, I had realized how fleeting life could be and planned to try not to sweat the little things. I would leave my worrying for the big stuff, like Tony and Lip, and what I was going to do to put them away. I'd just returned from surveying the desserts and felt like I had gained five pounds from just looking. Instead, I let my belt out another notch and had a bowl filled with fruit and watermelon.

I had told Angelica about my good fortune at the Sports Book and mentioned the eerie way in which "license" was appearing in my life the past few days. I went through all the examples.

"That's so stupid," she said when I finished. "A license to steal, okay, but a license to love? What the hell does that mean?"

"Beats me," I said.

At that precise moment, Jimmy Buffett came on over the house speakers. Now my paranoia was working overtime. Eating at a buffet while listening to Buffett was one thing, but when the song turned out to be "License to Chill," well, that was just too much.

"Jesus," I said loudly, shoving my dish on top of the others. "This is unbelievable!"

Angelica asked, "The license or plates?"

"No, the stupid . . . what did you just say?"

"The license or plates?"

After five seconds, it hit me. The *license* plates. *Yes!* The thing going around and around in my brain and eating at my stomach since investigating the photo, library, and garage was the license plates! Something was wrong with the plates on the Bugatti. I still didn't know what, but I was hell bent on finding out.

"Drink up, Angelica. We're outta here."

"Where we going?"

"To your grandmother's house."

"No way," she protested. "There's still a couple of clubs I want to hit."

I gave her a look meant to make her cower.

She sneered and made a face at me. "I'll tell Uncle Julius you were mean to me."

I wiped my mouth with the red cloth napkin, left a nice-sized tip for the overworked waiter, and started to walk away through the busy dining area.

"Jake!" Angelica shouted. "Don't you dare leave me here!"

Heads turned, eyes watched, and mouths kept chewing away.

I kept working my way through the tables.

"Don't you dare," she warned, standing up. "I mean it!"

The female diners looked at me as if I might be some kind of monster.

I marched on.

"Jake! Jake!" she pleaded loudly. "Wait for me."

The male diners looked at me as if I might be Svengali reincarnated as this vision of beauty dashed in and out of tables trying to catch up with me.

I was just entering the cavernous slot machine area on my way to Valet when I felt her arm encircle mine. Except for her "Hmmph!" no words were spoken.

# Chapter

After saying our hellos to everyone at the Bonello home, I asked Olivia if I could have another look at Sofia's room, as well as her husband's desk, and excused myself.

Upstairs I removed the sculpted model of the Bugatti and the black-and-white family photo from Sofia's shelf and took both down to the library. I placed the two objects on the desk, switched on the green banker's lamp, and studied the pieces. And there it was, clear as day. Just about every detail of the vehicle in the photograph was captured in the sculpture, except for the license plates.

First of all, the photo showed no plate on the front bumper, but the sculpture did. I dug into the drawer where I had previously seen other shots of the car alone and finally came to one taken of the rear bumper. It clearly showed a license plate with the letter C followed by the numbers 4435. I looked at the back of the model, and it read 11552 W. Maybe not a big difference to the casual observer, but it offered a wealth of information to someone like me. I jotted these details in a little notebook I borrowed from the desk and then took a look at the front of the model. It read 3655 N.

What the hell? How could a guy as meticulous as Carmine Bonello make such a mistake? And not even the same ones! I shook my head and jotted down that plate as well. Could they have been from a previous year?

I sat back in the leather recliner with my feet up on the open drawer, tapping the pen against my teeth. When my mind got around to the license to love connections, I opened the drawer on the other side of the desk and brought out all the old pulp and mystery novels I'd seen there earlier.

I flipped through each book, hoping for the kind of clue you see in the movies: an address written inside the front cover, a slip of paper with a combination for a locker at the bus station, a hand-drawn map of some ghost town with a big black X. Nope. Nothing like that.

The last novel was the Steele one I'd seen earlier, the one titled *License to Murder/License to Love*. I sat there staring at the title and the red-headed, sex-starved harlot locked in chains waiting to be saved and serviced. I started flipping through the yellowed, musty pages and noticed something different. Where the others were in perfect condition, this book had a number of pages where corners had been turned back. I counted and found that there were a total of seven pages affected. Four pages were turned up about two and a half inches, precisely in the middle of the centered page number. The other three were turned up half an inch only. I also noticed that all the pages up to 31 had been folded slightly at one time or another and then pressed back flat.

I sat there for a couple of minutes wondering if this could possibly mean anything. There were no markings on any of the pages, and, since I couldn't process any logical reason at the time, I took out the notebook and jotted down the first and last words of each page. That gave me a total of 14 words to work with. Maybe I was on to something. The words, in order, were *look thing women on than brown that better furry Barlow's the could pants mustache.*

All right. I was good at word puzzles. Hopefully, by rearranging these words in a specific pattern, I could learn Carmine's secret code: one that would lead to a vast fortune hidden all these years and change my life forever.

After struggling for 15 minutes, the best I could come up with was *that furry thing could look better on the women mustache than Barlow's brown pants*. Oakley would have had me committed if I took it in.

I looked at the novel again. Seven pages with the corners precisely turned up, three just a bit, and four halfway across the page. I jotted down all the page numbers and got 2, 10, 36, 52, 55, 59, and 115. I stared at the numbers for about five minutes and couldn't make heads or tails of any kind of code. I wrote the alphabet across one of the pages in my notebook; then I gave each letter a number, *a* being 1, *b* being 2, et cetera. For the numbers above 26, such as 36, I subtracted the two, got 10, and treated that as a *j*. All I ended up with after figuring out all that was b, j, j, z, c, g, k. I tried putting vowels in between, but it still came out sounding like Russian.

I wondered if the pages turned up differently meant anything. The ones turned up wide were 36, 52, 55, and 115. The ones turned only slightly were 2, 10, and 59. I wrote those down as well and scratched my head for a few more minutes. None of the numbers meant a damn thing to me, although now that I had broken them into two groups something seemed suspiciously familiar. I played around with the group of three because it was smaller and after about 10 minutes determined that 2, 10, and 59 could have been a date, except February 10, 1959, meant absolutely nothing to me.

There was a soft knock at the door, and Orsina came in with a tray containing coffee, cookies, and fruit.

"Thank you," I told her.

"You are very welcome," she said. "You look like you could use something stronger than coffee, perhaps?"

"No," I said with a laugh. "I may look rough, but I'm okay. Just a little confused."

"If you need anything, just use the intercom."

"I will, Orsina, thank you."

As she approached the door, I suddenly thought of something. "Excuse me, Orsina?"

She stopped before the door and turned around.

"I haven't worked out all the math and dates of the Bonello family tree, but," I picked up the notebook and read, "does February 10, 1959, have any significance to the family?"

"I don't think so. A few days before Saint Valentine's I would remember."

"Okay, thanks again."

Orsina had reached the door and turned the handle.

"What about October 2, 1959? Does that ring a bell?"

Apparently, it did. She released the handle, turned around, and then walked back to the desk and looked at the numbers my finger was pointing at. "The Bonellos always wrote their dates with the day first." She crossed herself, pulled a rosary from her apron pocket, and kissed the figure of Jesus.

"What's the matter?" I asked.

"2, 10, 59," she spoke solemnly. "That was the day Mr. Bonello disappeared."

The effect of the words struck me full force in my chest. If true, this book might hold the answer to everyone's questions.

"You weren't working for the Bonellos at the time. Are you sure?"

"Since I started here in 1960, every second day of October Mrs. B and I make the exact dinner that she prepared for Mr. B on the evening he didn't come home. Later, she lights a candle, places it in the front window, and waits for her husband to return. I wait until her tears wash away her memories, and then I help her to her room. We went through this ritual only two weeks ago."

Orsina became sullen in reminiscence. I told her I appreciated her help, and maybe together we could put Carmine Bonello's disappearance to rest. She said I was to ask her for help anytime and left me alone in the library as I tried to absorb the impact of this new revelation.

I wrote the date over the numbers in my notebook, proud at the success, and studied the other numbers for another 15 minutes to no avail. My brain needed a break, so I sat back and flipped through the copyright and dedication pages. *License to Murder/License to Love* was printed by New World Publishing out of New York in March 1956. The book was dedicated to Jean. Evidently, the author had written a previous novel, because at the top of the copyright page an underlined headline read *"Also by Evan Steele"* and underneath that the title *Attitudes and Latitudes.*

I sat there flipping through the book for another 15 minutes or so, but nothing got any clearer. I was still ecstatic that, because of the date discovery, apparently the book did hold some information. It just had to be deciphered.

I tidied up the desk, returned the sculpture and photo, and located Mrs. Bonello in the kitchen with Orsina. I thanked them both and asked Olivia if I could borrow the Steele novel.

"But of course you can, Jake," she replied. "If there's anything I can do to help you figure out what's going on, you just ask. That goes for the staff as well."

"Thank you, Olivia. I make no promises, except that I'll do everything I can."

"I know you will, Jake. I saw that in you from our first meeting."

I didn't do a "Well, golly gee, ma'am" routine. I just said, "I better be going."

"Aren't we forgetting something?" came the harsh-sounding words from behind me. "Or some*one!*"

I turned around, and there was Angelica standing in the doorway, arms crossed, lips pursed, and the right toe of her shoe tap-tap-tapping on the granite tiles.

"As I was saying," I said, "I better be going, as soon as I round up wonderful and beautiful Angelica Bonello."

"Yeah, right, cowboy," she said and then smiled. "It's Friday night. In Vegas! There's one more club I want to see before I go." She pushed out her bottom lip into a pout. "You promised me."

"Angelica," said Olivia. "Leave the poor man be. He's been through so much recently. I don't think he wants to do more dancing."

"I'm still pretty limber from dodging all that lead last night," I said with a laugh. "And what I do isn't exactly dancing. It's called sitting at the bar, sipping a drink, and watching Angelica enjoying herself on the dance floor. Really, I don't mind celebrating my survival a little more."

"Well," the older lady said. "Take it easy on Jake anyway. Now come and give your *nonna* a great big hug."

Angelica went over and put her arms around her grandmother and said, "I'll see you before I go back home." She gave Olivia a kiss on the cheek and skipped out of the room. From the hallway, you could hear her shout out, "I love you, *nonna!*"

I laughed and said my good-byes to the two women again. I made it down the hallway and out the front door without skipping once.

# Chapter

It was just after 11 p.m. when we arrived back at the Oasis to change clothes. In the hallway, Angelica insisted upon entering my room and using the connecting door to get to hers, something about not being able to find her key. Right. We agreed to be ready by midnight. When she left, I waited a moment, then quietly engaged the lock and took one of the dining room chairs and propped it against the handle to the connecting door. Why take chances?

I normally wouldn't turn away a hot number from a hotel suite, but I still valued my life, and I didn't need the overhanging cloud of Julius Contini threatening my psyche or my most valuable body organ. And besides, she was only a kid.

♦

At about five minutes before midnight, I quietly unlocked the connecting door and replaced the chair. Angelica came barging in 30 seconds later.

"Your door was stuck," she said.

"I don't remember locking it."

"I unlocked it, but there was something jamming it."

"Must have been stuck."

"Yeah, right."

"Maybe it's the humidity," I surmised. "You know, swells the door jambs. Gets a little tight."

"Gimme a break. What humidity? It's a desert, for God's sake!"

She had me there. "You look great," I told her. And she did.

Suddenly, the door was forgotten, and Angelica spun around a couple of times so I could appreciate the full view. She was wearing a pair of low-cut, hip-hugging, champagne-colored pants with wide flares and no panty lines. Her top was a white halter with thin sparkled fringes, made to help promote and enhance a woman's attributes on the dance floor. A pair of black-and-silver stiletto heels made her long legs invitingly longer. Her blond locks were subtly curled at the tips and fell to her shoulders.

"You think so?"

With her knowing full well there wasn't a man alive who could *not* think so, I told her, "I guess you'll do as my date for the first part of the night. . . ."

By the time the implication of the statement hit her, I was halfway out the door and ready to run.

"Why, you . . . ," she shouted and picked up an orange from the fruit bowl and fired it my way.

I stepped out of the doorway and into the hall and heard a thud on the inside wall.

"Make sure the door locks on your way out," I called out good naturedly and let go of the door.

"I'll get you for that!"

"Not in those shoes, you won't," I replied as the door closed and shut out what had started to sound like a very disparaging remark.

I was three or four rooms down in the long corridor when I heard my door open again and then close. I glanced over my shoulder to see if she was still mad. Apparently, she was. She had taken off her shoes and had one held up in the air with the sharp stiletto heel pointed in my direction. And then she started to run.

I shifted from first gear to second, unable to burn rubber on the thick carpet, and was in third by the time I had passed two more rooms. I chanced a peek behind me to see if she had quit. Nope.

My body had not been built with an overdrive, but I slid into fourth and had a comfortable lead turning the corner for the bank of elevators. An elderly couple must have come from the other wing as the doors on one of the elevator cars were just beginning to close. I managed to get my wrist between the doors as they shut. The startled couple slipped back into the corner, and the man unconsciously patted his inside jacket pocket.

Now that I knew where he kept all his money, I said, "It's okay, it's okay," and punched the black button with the two sideways arrows pointing at each other.

The doors began to close once again, and, before they did, we all heard "Don't you dare, Jake!" coming from around the corner.

The doors closed, a little chime started to count off the floors as we descended, and I slicked back my misplaced hair. The elderly couple still cowered in the corner.

"Everything's okay," I assured them. "It's my wife. She has a severe gambling problem. I'm trying to get our cash and jewelry into a safe deposit box before she pawns it all."

They looked at each other and then back to me, and both nodded sympathetically as if they understood.

"It's a sickness," I explained.

The doors opened to the sounds of casino gambling: hoots and hollers and bells and whistles all clamoring for your attention. I held the door for the couple. "After you," I insisted.

As they exited the car, the woman patted my arm and looked up at me. "You poor thing," she said.

"Pardon me?"

She pointed at my face. "They may be fading, but I can still see the bruises on your face in this light. If she beats you, there are places for battered husbands, too."

I kept a stiff upper lip. "I'll be fine, ma'am," I said. "And, by the way, you should tell your husband not to keep all his money in his upper left jacket pocket. Spread it around so he doesn't pat it for reassurance. It's a bad 'tell,' and the pickpockets in this city will pick it up."

Her husband came back to retrieve her, and they were quickly swallowed up by the gaping mouth of the slot machine area.

I stood there waiting for the inevitable. When the inevitable showed up, she had her heels back on and her chin held high. And for the second time in one night, she entered a casino with the word *Hmmph!* This time, however, it was me calling out "Wait up!" as I slipped my arm through hers.

♠

The Rio is a massive hotel complex on Flamingo Road far behind Caesars Palace on what was once referred to as the "wrong" side of I-15. In the past, all of the so-called four- and five-star hotels were on the Strip. The Rio was one of the first that took advantage of the cheaper land deeds on the other side of the interstate, where motels and strip malls flourished. The Rio featured 2,500 rooms, all considered luxury suites, at the regular Strip room prices, with a minimum of 600 square feet. In the past year, it had been voted Las Vegas's Most Romantic Hotel and was known by all fraternities in North America as having the sexiest cocktail waitresses with the most revealing costumes.

And Club Rio didn't do anything to hurt its image as the Scinta Showroom had been named Vegas's best dance club nine years running. It was 30,000 square feet of meet-and-greet space, with 12 virtual video walls and interactive 3-D laser lights. The top DJs from across the country spun hip hop and house on Fridays and Saturdays. Lucky me.

It was a quarter after two, now early Saturday morning, and the jam-packed room was on the verge of breaking fire code restrictions. Angelica was on the dance floor, where I caught occasional glimpses of her doing the Salsa and Meringue with a different male or female partner each time. Once she was just dancing by herself, but no matter with whom or where most of the male eyes followed her every move.

I was sitting at the bar sipping my second piña colada, donating $20 bills to the built-in video poker machine in the bar top. Angelica would stop by every other song or so to taste her wine and catch her breath. After a few minutes, the wolves would start lining up, licking their chops at a chance to give her their best line. When she was ready, she'd turn around and survey the collection of admirers; then she'd point a long, painted fingernail at her selection and tell him to follow her to the dance floor.

I was especially impressed with her most recent choice: a below-average-looking, bespectacled computer type, far too shy to compete with his *Gentleman's Quarterly* buddies. They stood there scratching their gelled haircuts while their geeky friend took Angelica's hand, looked back over his shoulder, and gave them the thumbs-up.

My time wasn't being totally wasted sitting alone at the bar. I knew I was definitely onto something with the book and the discovery of the hidden date code. I could almost taste it. All that had to be deciphered was the other cluster of four numbers and why the license plates didn't match between the model and the original. I was sure that if I could crack this riddle I'd be on my way to solving at least one of the mysteries. I might not find buried treasure, but perhaps I could put Olivia Bonello's mind to rest regarding the enigma of her missing husband.

What if Carmine Bonello *had* been skimming, and what if the strange numbers would somehow lead me to his hidden cache? Who knew how long he had been planning his escape from the mob with his family and what the sum of that nest egg could be? Hundreds of thousands? Probably, at the least. And if the boys from Chi-Town had been so alarmed for so long, it could be in the millions!

With visions of me discovering a hidden room or burial site on the Bonello property, I pulled out my notebook to once again peruse the numbers. I went over everything I'd written. I checked off the four numbers from the novel: 36, 52, 55, and 115. Two odd numbers and two even didn't seem significant. Neither did the amount of missing digits between each: 36, 3, 10, and 60. I put those numbers through the alphabet test again and still didn't come up with anything intelligible.

I caught the eye of the bartender and ordered a cappuccino and went back to my notes. The coffee came before the revelation. I sat there sipping on the hot drink, licking milk foam from my upper lip, and staring at the figures, knowing I was one brainstorm away from crying out "Eureka!"

I went back to the license plate numbers and stared them down for a minute or so, but none of them gave anything up. I copied the numbers from that page over to the one with the four numbers from the novel. Now I had 11552W from the rear plate of the model, 3655N from the front plate of the model, c4435 from the rear plate of the photo, and 36, 52, 55, and 115 from the page numbers in the book. After a few minutes of turning them upside down and sideways, I was about to call it quits for the evening when my eye caught the simplest of corresponding digits; 3 and 6 from the front plate matched the page number 36. That left two 5s, or a 55, also in the page numbers.

My breath caught for a second or two, and I could feel my heart quicken its pace. It didn't take a rocket scientist to figure out that the rear plate digits 11552 could be read as the last of the two page numbers, 52 and 115, reversed.

I wanted to shout "Bingo!" but swallowed back the word when I realized that still left the 4435 from the original plate. Then again, so what? Those numbers on the photo would have been the actual plate, and Carmine wouldn't have been able to manipulate it at all. So that *did* leave me with a bunch of page numbers that coincided with numbers drawn on a model car. Now I just had to figure out what the correlation meant. The hell with it, this was definitely a big break, and a celebration was called for.

"Yes!" I shouted, not that anybody could hear me over the reverberating bass the DJ was throwing out. I punched the air with a fist and slapped the bar top; then I heard somebody yelling in my ear.

"You okay, Jake?" Angelica had snuck up from behind.

"Yeah, sure," I yelled back. "Couldn't be better."

She took a sip of her wine. "Well, you looked kinda weird sitting there by yourself yelling and punching the air. You looked like a spaz."

"Never mind. I think I came up with something that might explain why those two goons have been harassing us."

"Really? Cool!" She looked around the room. "Let's go find the lounge. It'll be a lot quieter."

"And leave all this noise and attention?"

"Yes! I need a rest and a fresh drink." She glanced behind her and saw that a line was already starting to form. "And I could use 10 minutes with somebody who won't be drooling and pawing my ass."

I jumped off my bar stool and told her, "Well, I'm your man. I promise not to slobber."

"Yeah, well, I could make an exception. Come on, party pooper, follow me."

Angelica found an empty sofa in the lounge area, and the two of us both ordered a glass of dry California white. I showed her the notes and numbers and how they formed the date her grandfather had disappeared and matched the license plate numbers on the model car.

"So that's why the license reference was bugging you so much?" she said.

"Yeah, and it paid off. When I saw the title of the book, *License to Murder/License to Love*, it became too much of a coincidence."

Angelica frowned and bit lightly at her bottom lip. "But we don't know what the numbers on the front and rear license plates mean."

"No, but I'm really close. I can feel it. By the page numbers in the book backing up the plate numbers, I know we're just one clue away."

She took a sip of her wine and looked at me. "You love this kind of thing, don't you?"

"Sure, I like figuring out puzzles, little mysteries, and righting things that are wrong. That's probably why I spent so many years as a cop," I admitted. "But I especially like putting closure to things that really need it."

"Like my grandmother missing my grandfather. . . ."

"Exactly."

Angelica was quiet for a moment; then she looked me in the eye and asked, "But what drives you? Besides your piece-of-crap Vega."

I smiled and drank some wine and thought about her question. "First of all, the cuts and bruises I see every time I look in the mirror."

She laughed at that. "You're healing nicely, though. And the bruises are yellow instead of purple."

I laughed with her but soon became serious again. "The two goons taking you in front of my place, slapping you around, and throwing you in the bushes: that drives me. Why they would snoop around your family's property: that drives me. Breaking into and tossing my home, tying me up, and busting my chops: that drives me, too. Coming back and shooting up my entire apartment and killing Vincent: that drives me. And making me pick up a gun after all these years and putting two bullets into a human being again: that drives me."

Angelica's eyes had become misty. I leaned forward, and with a thumb wiped a tear off each of her cheeks.

"Forcing me to look over my shoulder every minute of the day so I don't get shot in the back of the head drives me, too."

She wiped at the corner of her eye and said, "If anything was to happen to you. . . ."

"Nothing's going to happen to me, Angelica, except that I'm going to decipher your grandfather's codes and try to put an end to all of this."

"Promise me you'll be extra careful."

"I promise."

We both sipped at our drinks.

Angelica asked, "So, by *nonno* having the date of his disappearance in the book, he must have been keeping some kind of calendar."

"It looks that way. Seeing as all of the first 31 pages were bent meant he had been doing it for a while. It was probably a ritual he did every morning in his office before going to work. He wanted us to know that there was an even bigger message in the novel by discovering the simple calendar code. I'm sure of it."

"And these notes over here?" she said, pointing to my scribbling at the top of one of the pages.

"Those are the titles of the books your grandfather had in his desk, but none of them had as much as a pencil mark on them, much less a turned-up page. They were in pristine condition. It was almost as if he was pointing out *License to Murder/License to Love* by it having flaws."

"What about this one over here?" she asked.

"Oh, that's the title of the only other book the author wrote. It was called Attitudes and Latitudes."

Angelica repeated the title out loud. "*Attitudes and Latitudes.* . . . That doesn't make any sense at all to me."

"Me either."

Angelica got a distant look in her eyes, as if she were taxing her memory. "That's weird. . . ."

"What's that?"

"You know how you were getting paranoid about all the references to licenses and love and all that stuff?"

"I wouldn't call it paranoia. . . ."

"Well, you know what I mean. The unusual way that those words were creeping into your daily life."

"Okay, so what?"

"I don't know why I thought of it, but do you remember the drink that cross-dresser Darling ordered at the bar?"

I thought back. "No, not really. Was it a slippery something or other?"

"No, not the Slippery Dick. The first one, when she/he came up to the bar. I think it was an Attitude Adjustment."

"Oh, right. I told her I could use one, too."

"Well, I just remembered that, after seeing *Attitudes and Latitudes* written there."

"I don't know, that could be stretching it. I'm not one to believe in the paranormal or ghosts and whatnot. Those clues by your grandfather were put there for a purpose. The references made by Stephano, or Darling, they were just coincidences."

"And the horse's name you won on, the song at the buffet. . . ."

"Jesus, Angelica. What are you saying? That external forces, ghosts and goblins, are somehow slipping these songs and drinks and horses on me to lead me down the right path?"

"If not, it's pretty goddamn weird, that's all I can say."

"Well, if Casper or Carmine are out there giving me a hand, I appreciate it, but right now I'm going to stick with good old-fashioned logic and deduction. The rest I'll write off as good luck."

"I still think it's spooky," she said. "And I still think *Attitudes and Latitudes* is a stupid name for a book. It doesn't make any sense. The two things don't have anything to do with each other, do they? One means 'the way you're feeling' or whatever, and the other is some geography thing, isn't it?"

I was looking at the enciphered numbers while she was talking, and something she had said was piquing some lonely beta wave nerve cell buried deep in my brain, and it was shouting out for attention. I was being pushed from inside.

Angelica kept her soliloquy going. "I mean think about it, wouldn't *Attitude and Behavior* have made more sense? Sheesh! Even *Latitude and Longitude* is more logical." She went back to her wine. "Mmm. Yum, yum."

A gong went off in my head. I looked at the notebook, I put two and two together, and it came out to four. I even double-checked my addition.

"Son of a bitch!" I yelled.

"What?" asked Angelica.

"I could give you a big kiss!"

Her eyes opened wide, and she smiled coquettishly. "Of course you can."

I grabbed her by the shoulders, and she closed her eyes readying herself.

"No, Angelica, I don't mean it like that! I mean I think you just solved the last piece of the puzzle."

She opened her eyes. "I did? What did I say? What did I say?"

"Latitude and longitude."

"Yeah. So?"

"Well, I know absolutely nothing about either one of them, but I'm willing to bet my next month's pay that the two groups of numbers represent some kind of measurement in latitude and longitude." I poked a finger at the notebook. "I mean, look, there's even a W and an N after the plate numbers."

And there it was, clear as day: 3655N on the front and 11552W on the back.

"Wow," Angelica beamed. "I can't believe I helped you. That is so 'out of the frame'!"

I gave her a big smile back. "I haven't a friggin' clue what that means, but I know I couldn't have figured out that last set of numbers right now without you."

She seemed so excited to have played such an important part that she practically glowed.

I was almost giddy myself. I took Angelica's shoulders once again and planted a big kiss on her lips. "Thank you."

She gave me a dreamy look. "Maybe we should go back to the hotel and celebrate?"

*Uh-oh.*

"Umm, I don't think so. I've still got some figuring out to do on these numbers and how I'm going to use them."

"But, Jakey," she said with a sexy leer. "I'm *really* in the mood to celebrate."

"I thought we already were celebrating. Look, shouts, drinks, a kiss; that's celebrating, right?"

"Ooh, sometimes you make me so mad. Do you have to be so damn moral . . . you know . . . like you're afraid you'll have to go to confession?"

I gave her a friendly smile to keep her on my side. "I'm not even a practicing Catholic. I converted to Frisbeetarianism about three years ago."

Her face scrunched up. "To what?"

"As a Frisbeetarian," I said sincerely, "we have only one belief: that when you die your soul goes up on the roof and gets stuck."

Angelica looked at me with glazed eyes. "I haven't a clue what you're talking about, but, seriously, I am really, really, really in the mood."

I was beginning to realize the true meaning of being caught between a rock and a hard place. "Look, its 3:30 in the morning. This joint is open until 5 a.m., so why don't you dance with the boys and have some more fun here, and we'll talk about celebrating the rest later, okay?"

"Promise?" she said with a pout.

"Sure."

"Okay," she said, jumping up, ready to go. "But I needs me another *vino*, please."

Good. The three or four wines she'd had were already working on her grammar. Another hour and a half of dancing and drinking and she'd probably forget all about celebrating. And just to be sure I protected myself, I left the rest of my wine and decided to switch back to coffee for the remainder of the morning. I also realized how close I was to cracking this case and remembered Tony and Lip and their promise.

Instead of taking my old seat at the middle of the bar, where I was fully exposed, I walked over to where it curved and ended and took a stool where I could sit with my back to the wall.

# Chapter

I awoke to the shrill 9 a.m. wake-up call after only a few hours of sleep, remarkably glad to find the other half of my bed empty and exceptionally eager to get this Saturday started.

After some toast and coffee, I wrote a note for Angelica. I told her that I was going to follow up on what we had discovered last night and that she was to stay around the Oasis; then I slid the sheet of paper beneath the connecting door. Just in case, and to cover my ass, I left a message with Julius Contini's office saying I had some important Bonello business to take care of and, if Angelica required company, he should use hotel security until I returned.

The Clark County Library is one of the larger suburban research facilities and is located on East Flamingo. It was just after 10 a.m., and the library was quite busy, with mothers and daughters returning and taking out their weekly supply of books and a number of old-timers who probably came in every week to discuss the news and events in the heavy, weekend editions of the newspapers.

I looked out the door of the library to the parking lot. The only disconcerting part of my trip out here was that I had an uneasy feeling that I may have been watched. I stood for a full five minutes and monitored every vehicle and person that moved in the lot until I got bored.

I went to the information desk, and the nice lady there directed me to an area with a number of computers. I wasn't a geek, but I followed a few gambling forums and played on-line poker, so I could handle the basic moves of the Internet. I also would have preferred to use my PC at home, but the cops had said I wouldn't be able to enter my apartment until some time the next week. I took out my notebook and pen and placed them by the keyboard; then I Googled my way to "geography latitude," and the very first heading to come up was "Latitude and Longitude" at geography.about.com.

An article defining latitude and longitude caught my eye, and I clicked on it first. It was a terrific explanation for the layman as to how these two things worked. The lines that you see on a map are like a grid system of the Earth, with the horizontal lines called latitude and the vertical lines called longitude.

The degrees latitude are numbered 0-90 degrees starting at the equator and going north as well as south. Numbers north of the equator are designated with an N and those numbers south with an S. Zero degrees longitude is located at Greenwich, England, and runs 180 degrees east and 180 degrees west, meeting and forming the International Date Line over the Pacific. The article added that there are 60 minutes in each degree and that each minute is divided into 60 seconds.

So far, so good.

I opened the notebook to the page with the license plate numbers from the model car, both front and rear: 3655N and 11552W. The article went on to say that the U.S. Capitol building was precisely located at 38°53'23"N, 77°00'27", which meant the license plates were lacking a few numbers.

I started breaking the plate numbers down. If the N stood for north, as in latitude, then the 36 on the front plate should stand for degrees. It made sense seeing as how Washington was listed and defined as a 38, and it was farther north than Vegas. *Okay*, it was good for a start. But it was becoming evident that I was going to have to call on parts of the old noggin that had done me so well through the Boston Police exams but hadn't been used much since.

The next number for the Capitol was 53 and marked with an accent, which I assumed meant minutes. The rear plate numbers, or the longitude, could be analyzed the same way. Since Washington was way over in the east, and the degree number for the Capitol showed as 77 degrees, it again stood to reason that the 115 and the W on the plate stood for degrees west. If all that was true, then the 52 should be the minutes.

As I was perusing the rest of the site, I noticed a link to MapQuest and wondered what the hell that would be doing here. I had used the MapQuest service on my drive from Boston to Las Vegas and found it very helpful. I gave it a click of the cursor, and, sure enough, there I was on a MapQuest page asking for latitude and longitude input so it could help find my location. Very impressive.

The first highlighted box had a line titled "Latitude" with three blank boxes to the right with the headings "Degrees," "Minutes," and "Seconds." Seemed pretty simple to me. I typed 36 in the degrees box and 55 in the minutes box. That left me with an empty seconds box as I had no more numbers left to use. I typed in 00 to fulfill the field requirement.

The second box was titled "Longitude," and I typed in 115, 52, and again 00. It looked okay to me, so I hit the Get Map button, and before you could say Rand McNally the map appeared on my screen.

"All right!" I called out.

Realizing where I was, I stole a glance around my monitor. To my chagrin, seven or eight faces were turned around or looking over book covers in my direction. I knew I should have excused or explained myself, but I had better things to do, such as maybe finding a treasure chest full of mob money!

The map was there in all its glory, sparse as expected because of the desert nature. A bright red star marked my coordinates. The "red" star should have been an omen. Only two towns were shown, about 20 miles apart. The closest town was named Linqinq and the other Qinghe, but neither one looked familiar. I clicked on the Zoom-Out button, and the map expanded a few times. All I got were more towns with even more confusing names. I zoomed out all the way and sat there staring at the screen when I finally realized where I was.

If the treasure was buried at these coordinates, I was in big trouble. How the hell was I going to get in and get out of Communist China? That's where it had me: 400 or 500 miles south of Beijing and just in from the East China Sea.

*Son of a bitch!* And here I thought I was doing so well. This was practically on the other side of the world.

*Hold the phone!* It *was* on the other side of the world. The latitude seemed to be in order as to how far north Las Vegas would be of the equator. Then I remembered the article said the longitudinal lines started at Greenwich and went 180 degrees both east and west, meeting over the Pacific.

I looked at the MapQuest boxes again. If 115 degrees brought me to China going east, then I figured going west must be like subtracting, so I punched in a minus sign before the 115, clicked on Get Map, and held my breath.

Now a bright red star showed up just off Interstate 95, about five miles before Indian Springs, Nevada, and no more than a 45-minute drive northwest of Las Vegas. A coincidence? No way!

I was giddy, and almost yelled to the bartender for another; then I realized where I was. Instead, I relaxed, smug, for a few minutes. I thought I'd earned that at least.

I went to the librarian and asked for her assistance in printing off the page. Back at my computer, she typed something.

"It comes out on my printer, and it costs 25 cents per page," she advised in a quiet tone. "Seventy-five cents if you want color."

"What the heck," I whispered. "I'm celebrating. Give me one of each."

"Big spender," she said, then typed something else and pressed Enter. "I'll be back in a couple of minutes."

Happy with myself, I thought maybe, just maybe, this whole thing was starting to unravel. A few painted numbers matching a bunch of folded pages in a book did not a mystery break, but I was pretty sure I'd gotten further than anyone else up to this point. And then the bubble burst.

I was daydreaming, basking in my achievement, when a face flashed from between two bookcases and caused the hairs on the back of my neck to rise. The face just as quickly disappeared, but I could have sworn it was Tony from the Mob Squad. I was sitting with my back to a wall of books and glanced around to see if I was being flanked by Lip. The big lug was nowhere to be seen. Good for me.

I double-checked the distance to the fire exit door to my left in the near corner. It led to a staircase with another door leading to the outside. I looked back to the main library. Other than the keyboard I was using, I had nothing to fight with if they came in firing, so escape would be the logical route to take. I glanced back to the stairwell. It looked like I could probably block the exit if I took two chairs with me and wedged them behind the door and against the railing. That would give me at least a 30-second lead on them to get out of the library and circle the building.

I watched for a couple more minutes and decided: the hell with it.

They wouldn't be walking around with their guns at the ready. If I could get the jump on them, I wouldn't have to run. I had a pretty good idea where both had been hit, and those would be my first points of contact.

I got up and walked nonchalantly to the main room of the library, stopping occasionally to flip absently through pages of books. I went up and down various aisles, and, except for an elderly woman who crunched my toe with her walker, no one attacked me.

Relieved, I walked around the main room and stopped at the front door and peered out. I couldn't swear on it, but it looked like a tall man with a visible limp had just gotten into a silver, newer model, luxury car in the parking lot. The vehicle didn't move. It was facing the library, but the windows were so heavily tinted I couldn't see in. It was also parked next to my Chrysler.

I passed by a librarian's desk and took inventory. There were no scissors and no letter-openers, so I picked up the longest pencil I could find. I stepped over to a gray filing cabinet and used the electric sharpener until the pencil came out to a long, fine point. Not much of a weapon if they jumped me with a gun, I admit, but it would do just fine in an eye or a neck. I slipped the pencil under my watchband on the inside of my wrist for easy access and took my seat in front of the computer again.

The elderly librarian returned and, as she handed me the copies, asked, "Planning on doing a little hiking, are you?"

"I'm sorry?"

"The maps," she pointed out. "Not much else to do out there . . . except maybe hunting snakes to make some boots."

*Oh, I'll be hunting all right. Treasure hunting!*

"No," I said with a laugh. "Nothing like that. A buddy and I are thinking of doing some metal detecting, looking for old Indian arrowheads, guns, stuff like that."

"Well, be careful where you boys wander."

"Why's that?"

She was pointing to a large shaded area just north of Interstate 95. "You don't want to be going too far in there, that's for sure."

I peered more closely at the faint type. "What's an AFB? Or an NTG?"

"One doesn't want you near," she said, laughing. "The other you don't want to be near." She saw the confusion on my face. "That there is the Nellis Air Force Base."

"Pretty big."

"Yes. It's about the size of Rhode Island."

"And just inside their grounds — what's that?"

"NTG stands for Nuclear Testing Ground."

"Ah" was all I could think of to say. To me, it was starting to look like *Not too Good.*

"Henry says they had more than 150 aerial tests, until the effects of radiation started to come forth. Of course, this was in the '50s, early '60s. Then they went underground."

*Right around my treasure time. . . .* "Henry?"

The older woman looked around the building. "Henry's a bit of a state history buff," she said proudly. "He had an older brother in the army who worked the tests. Cost him his life, Henry says." She stopped searching for him. "He must be downstairs cataloging. He volunteers here on weekends. He's retired, but he likes to keep busy."

I had a feeling she'd like to keep the old boy even busier.

If Henry was that knowledgeable about the history I was interested in, it could be beneficial to meet him. "Sounds like a wonderful fellow," I told her.

"Oh, he is," she said, her eyes sparkling. "Henry's a sweetheart."

I got directions on how best to find our boy Henry and an overly biased description of the handsome man I'd be looking for. I hoped Cary Grant wasn't nearby as I'd have a tough time telling them apart. I was told to tell Henry "Louise" had sent me.

·

"Good old Louise," Henry said when I'd finally found him. "She's a nice lady."

I concurred. "She tells me that you're sort of an expert on Nevada back in the 1950s."

"I know a bit. Why?"

"I came across some information of my grandfather's," I told him. "In an old journal. It seems he was trying to buy some land way back when. Found some old survey maps. Some coordinates. It's up 95 somewhere, near Indian Springs. We don't know if he was losing it or not, but some people say he was going to try to start a 'new' Las Vegas up that way." I showed him my map.

Henry looked at it and then at me as if both my grandpappy and I were crazy. "Well, first off, if you're talking the '50s, the old guy would have had a bit of a zoning problem, most likely."

"How's that?"

"See that star there?"

"Yeah."

"Well, back then that land would have been owned by the government."

"For the AFB and NTG?" I asked, as if I knew what I was talking about.

"Exactly. Nellis was one big son-of-a-bitch piece of land for an air force base. It still is. But after the Cold War and Nam, they started cutting back on their property. The base was so big they were probably having a hard time keeping it safe and sound with personnel and expensive, high-end security equipment." He looked at the map again. "Yeah," he said. "I think this land is maybe just out of protected jurisdiction now. And if it is, it's barely. But don't be surprised if you find one of those dunes is an old military bunker covered up by half a century of sand."

*Hmm*, I thought, *an abandoned bunker would be a terrific place to store a couple of million dollars.*

"They still keep that monstrosity that well guarded?"

Henry dropped his head slightly and looked at me from beneath lifted brows. "Son, there was strange shit going down there 50 years ago, and it'll still be going on 50 years from now. You do not want to be trying to breach the perimeter of Nellis or the testing grounds at any point."

He watched me taking it all in.

"They got security out there that the world ain't even thought of yet. Why do you think all the bullshit about UFOs and aliens and all that crap ends up out here? This whole complex is one big Area 51, with more secrets than J. Edgar Hoover. Where do you think things like the atomic bomb were conceived and built? We used to have T-shirts with a falling bomb on them that read "Built in America, Tested in Japan." Sure, the place is filled with secrets. And why? Because no one can breach the place. Christ, they got noise sensors, motion detectors, and infrared cameras that are hooked up to automatic weapons, death ray lasers, and chemical grenades that will take you out without a human having to fire them. Go out to the brink of the fences some day after some poor deer or coyote or lost transient passes the no-cross line and see what's left. It won't be much."

"Surely not today. . . ."

"Today more than ever. There's such high classification shit going on there even the scientists working on it don't know what they're working on."

"But the government wouldn't —"

Henry held his hand up and took a large breath.

"Son," he said softly. "The government don't know shit. Back in the '50s, when they were testing nuclear bombs with aerial and above-ground explosions, it was a publicized media event. People would gather a few miles from ground zero to watch the so-called fireworks with the mushroom cloud. Now, I'm talking families, son: parents with their kids, mayors and public figures with their wives and families, government and military personnel, Las Vegas celebrities, out there in the rocky desert with their lounge chairs and umbrellas and beach balls. And no knowledge. Totally unaware. Not just the horrific implications of what they were witnessing, but of the dust that fell on their skin and was breathed in by their children. They didn't even know the meaning of the word *radioactive.* . . ."

"Jesus."

"Not even he could help them. This went on, week after week, month after month, until the early '60s, when the ugly truth and buried lies were too large to ignore or hide any longer."

"What would have been the first sign?" I asked, totally intrigued.

"Well, the first signs *publicly* were probably all the babies and children getting sick and dying from leukemia. Remember, many of these tests were bombs that were held in place on tall towers when set off. Unfortunately, and inexcusably, these great minds, the men who could put together these marvels of mass destruction, had not taken into consideration that this leftover residue, ash, dust, whatever, was deadly. As implausible as it may be, these geniuses failed to realize that winds move across the United States from west to east and that this lethal radioactivity would be airborne. It was years before medical records showed a 100-mile-wide path of thousands of sick babies, genetic mutations, and dead children — from Utah to New York state."

"You can't be serious?" I said, appalled.

"As a heart attack. You see, these little particles of death floated east until they fell. Much of it on neighboring Utah, on grass being grazed by cows. For years, farmers wondered why so many of their sheep and cows were dying or their offspring were stillborn. Unfortunately, the dairy cows were digesting this grass and producing milk. Babies and children drink milk. They die."

"But surely the public would have been on this sooner than that?"

"Sure they were. But you know what our good old government did? First, when their own scientists and doctors refused to lie about the effects of radiation, they brought in hired guns to soothe the public, out-of-state specialists with arguing proof. When that no longer worked, they reluctantly admitted there might have been some implications because of the fallout. Then they played upon the patriotic nature of the good people of Utah and asked them to affirm their love for America and help with the fight against Communism."

"This is almost too hard to believe."

"Oh, it's all true. It's one of the biggest lies the American public was ever asked to swallow. Look up St. George, Cedar City, and the other sacrificed places along that path. These people were referred to as the 'downwinders.' Look up *Allen* v. *The United States of America*. It's all been hidden, but you can scratch the surface."

"What about the people in Nevada? And the ones who worked on these things?"

"Most of the spectators got ill with something or other, but as I said, the majority of the fallout landed east of here. As for the ones who worked on the projects, like my brother, well, they didn't last.

"You have to understand, the people who were running things were really flying by the seat of their pants. Unbelievable, considering the ramifications. These bombs were being built to keep a free America and fight possible Japanese or Russian oppression. Nuclear warfare was a new toy, and they really didn't know how it worked. The army would build little villages of bamboo huts, wooden shacks, and brick buildings. They would put bicycles, cars, trucks, food, and sometimes animals there to evaluate what the detonation would do to them.

"My brother Mike was a 20 year old in one of the early crews they sent in to photograph and record the destruction at ground zero. Which of the buildings, if not all, were blown down by the blast? Were the vehicles overturned? Did their tires melt? Did the chickens die? If the cows died, was the hide burned? And on and on and on. Mike went in too many times. He was getting sick, often, and he started losing hair and teeth. He was pulled off for good one day when he came back from a study and said he was finished. He told me, if they sent him in again, he'd go to the newspapers with what he knew."

"Which was what?"

"The last time, Mike went out and was doing what he was supposed to do when he saw something new was being tested. Humans."

"Cadavers?"

"Some were. The ones on stretchers. But those had been used before. No, this time there were a number of metal posts cemented into the ground with a burnt body attached by handcuffs and chains. Some of them looked like they had tried to bite through the flesh at their wrists."

"That can't be. . . ."

"Yes, it can. I've seen the pictures. When a group of soldiers threatened to go public, the government explained that the bodies were lifers from Carson City Penitentiary who wanted to do some good for their country and volunteered. Of course, no paperwork was ever found confirming the prisoners' wishes."

"And your brother?"

"Ah, Mike. Poor bastard. Married to the army at 20, and he never saw 30."

"Because of the job?"

"More than 300 people worked on the project, close to the effects at some time or another. Not one lived another 12 years. You tell me. . . ."

"That's quite a story," I told him. "So this area on the map here should be pretty safe now?"

"Yeah, I think so. But I wouldn't go traipsing about much farther than around here," Henry said, drawing a line on the map with his thumbnail.

"That shouldn't be a problem."

"One piece of advice, though. I'd get me a better map."

"I wasn't sure where to look."

"Hmm," he said, scratching his chin. "I think we've got some down here waiting to be repaired."

Henry went off and in less than a minute came back with a large leather-bound book with a missing back cover. He went over to an ancient photocopier, placed the book facedown, and pressed a button. A moment later two crisp and clean ledger-size sheets slid out, and Henry brought them over to me.

I was about to give him two quarters, but he waved me off. "They're on me," he said. "Just don't go telling Louise."

"Well, thanks for the copies. And especially for the history lesson. I have a whole new appreciation for what went on back then."

"Then it was well worth it, son."

When I left the building, the silver car next to mine was gone.

**Chapter** 🂭🂭

"What now, Morgan?" Lieutenant Oakley was leaning against the door-frame of his office with his arms crossed, his body language screaming *Look, I've got better things to do.*

"I just need a couple of minutes."

He lifted an eyebrow. "Okay, okay, you've got 10, max." He looked down to his thick sports watch and pressed a small button as if setting a time. "What's up?"

I gave Oakley a capsulated version of everything that had happened since picking up Angelica at the airport and the discovery of the coordinates on the map that morning. He sat there in his chair, leaning back, not saying a word until I was finished.

"And exactly why are you telling me all this?" he asked.

"I thought maybe something in all this might tie in these two goons who have been causing me so much grief. Not to mention that I might be onto solving a 50-year-old murder case."

"Don't flatter yourself, Morgan. You've got some silly assumptions and a MapQuest star in the middle of a landscape that might have been used to televise the lunar landing. And as far as solving some ancient murder, we don't even have a case file on Bonello. The feds have one, but they believe he's missing, probably with a bundle of loot he took from his employers." He let his large body slip forward with the chair as it rolled up to his desk. "Now give me some info on your buddy Vincent's shooters, and I'll be interested."

"I think in the end it'll all tie in together."

"Come on, Morgan! Do you really think there's some kind of buried treasure out there? What have you been doing, reading old Hardy Boys mysteries? Or maybe Nancy Drew? Get with it! There's no way one guy could have skimmed that much from the mob. A couple thousand bucks, maybe. What do you think is out there? Millions? Shake your head. There's no way anybody could have ripped off the mob for so much that they'd still be looking for it 50 years later. Cripes, even if he did, he'd be long gone and spending it somewhere in Mexico."

"But what if he got knocked off before he could leave?"

"Right. All that money and only one guy would know about it? And if he got knocked off, whoever did it would have taken the dough and either returned it or run like hell. Nah, there's gotta be some other reason you're telling me all this." A small beep sounded, and Oakley pressed a button on his watch. "You know, every time I run into you, you're trying to get some babe out of trouble. It's like you've got some kind of guilt complex, like you need to be the avenging hero, helping the poor, distraught damsel in distress. Maybe it's that 'wounded bird' syndrome, and you feel you have to be their savior."

I got up and made my way to the door. "Or," I said, turning the knob, "maybe I'm getting a little nervous that I might be closing in on something very big and that, if I succeed, something very bad could happen to me."

Oakley nodded his head. "That makes more sense. So why not just leave it alone?"

I opened the door wide and turned back to the lieutenant. "There's more to it than just discovering the money or helping out some girl. I know Mrs. Bonello is looking for some closure before she leaves us, and I

don't think anybody else is going to go to the trouble of finding it for her."
I started through the door, stopped, and looked at him over my shoulder.
"And just in case something does happen to me, the envelope on your
desk has a copy of everything I know: the maps and numbers and stuff."

Oakley was studying me as I turned to leave. "Watch your back, Jake. . . ."

"Stephano, it's Jake."

It was just after noon, and the streets were busy with Saturday action.
The intercom on the security panel outside the iron gates of the Bonello
estate crackled with a couple of beats of static, and then I heard, "Come
up to the garage."

I pulled up to the covered walkway that led to the main house, and
Stephano stepped through the side door of the garage.

"What is it?" he asked.

"We need to talk."

Stephano surveyed the yard and beyond the fence to the golf course.
"Let's talk out here," he said. "I found fresh footprints in the flowerbed
this morning. Something's not right."

I looked out over the front grounds. "I know what you mean. I'm getting that feeling, too. Like somebody's watching me, getting ready to
pounce."

Stephano studied my face. "In my line of business, we learn to trust
those instincts."

I nodded. "I used to be in the other end of the business, and we trusted
them, too."

I took a few minutes and gave him a recap of the past 24 hours and
explained what I thought I had discovered.

"And you think you can find that red mark on the map?" he asked.

"I think so," I told him. "With your help and maybe a stop on the way."

Stephano looked at the watch on his wrist. "It's just after noon. I drove Mrs. B and Orsina out to the Contini home late this morning, and they're going to be there most of the day. I'm supposed to pick them up around nightfall."

"No problem. That still gives us at least eight hours of light. Can we pick up some tools from here, or do you want to stop and rent some?"

"Nah, I got plenty. Follow me."

We went around the back of the garage and came upon a large metal utility shack. Stephano flipped through his keys and eventually clicked open the lock. He stepped inside and flicked on an uncovered bulb.

"Okay," he said. "Name your pleasure."

The shack was well stocked with lawnmowers, chainsaws, hedge clippers, and an assortment of garden tools, extension cords, and ladders.

"Let's start with a couple of shovels," I told him. "Maybe a steel rake, some garden bags, gloves — what the hell's that?"

Stephano turned to see what I was pointing at. "Oh, that," he said. "That's a metal detector."

"What are you doing with one of those?"

He looked at me sheepishly. "Well, I'd heard the stories of a possible pile of hidden money, too, you know. . . ."

I gave him a smile. "You old pirate. So you did a bit of digging yourself?"

"Well, yeah . . . who wouldn't? What the hell, if Mr. B had stashed some cash, it could have just as easily been buried here on the property."

"So the grounds have been covered?"

"Yeah, unfortunately, every square inch. Last time I used it was yesterday when I heard you and Vincent thought we had intruders out back. I ran it over the grass at the back fence to see if they'd dropped anything. All I found was a couple of beer cans and a golf ball."

"Well, let's take it."

Ten minutes later we were packed and ready to go. Stephano told me to wait and went into the garage. A minute later he came out with an ankle holster and a small pistol. He opened the passenger door of the Chrysler and put his foot on the seat as he tightened the Velcro binding of the holster around his ankle. He looked up at me and said, "You never know."

I wasn't about to argue. "Come to think of it," I said, "maybe we should take two cars."

"Why's that?"

"I don't know this area on the map at all and don't know what the conditions might be. Having a second vehicle for insurance couldn't hurt."

"You got a point, Jake. I'll take the suv. Four-wheel drive can't hurt either."

"You follow me. I've got a stop to make on Boulder Highway. At a car dealership." Something twigged in my brain. "Stephano, just in case, stay back from me as far as you can and check for anything suspicious."

"Like what?"

"Like a silver four-door Benz or Acura, something like that. I noticed one at the library this morning, and it gave me very bad vibes."

"Don't worry. I've got your back."

"Good. Don't do anything if you see them. Just observe."

"You got a cell phone?"

"Yeah."

"The Explorer's got one inside. We'll keep in contact that way."

We exchanged numbers, he backed the big black suv out of the garage, and we headed down Buchanan in tandem.

Ten minutes later I turned into a Chrysler dealership, and Stephano pulled in about 20 seconds later and parked beside me. He signaled me to roll down my window.

"You picked up two sleaze balls in a silver Lexus about a minute from the house."

"Son of a bitch." I glanced over my shoulder and down the lot.

"They didn't turn in," Stephano stated. "They pulled over on the shoulder about 50 yards before the dealership. They're sitting there waiting."

"Okay, here's what I want you to do. Drive over to the Rio and park on the north side of Flamingo. I'm going to take them to the Oasis parking lot and enter through Security with my employee pass. There's no way they'll be allowed in. I've got three other exits I can use to get out, and they can't cover them all. Wait for me to come by. I'll honk, and you follow and make sure I lost them."

"Sounds like a plan."

Stephano rolled out of the lot, and I went in and asked for a technician who could run through the instructions and use of the global positioning satellite, especially regarding the plotting of latitude and longitude coordinates. Within 15 minutes, and with the help of a Benjamin Franklin, I had all I needed to know about GPS and the application of coordinates. I jotted down the expense in my notebook as I pulled out of the dealership.

Sure enough, as I hit the maximum speed limit of the road, I spotted a silver streak as it tried to catch up.

**Chapter** ♠ Q ♠ Q ♠ ♣

By one o'clock, we were back in tandem and doing a swift 75 miles per hour up I-95, with nary a soul reflected in our rearviews and visions of buried treasure steaming up our minds. Well, at least mine.

Indian Springs was a town of 1,200 situated on I-95 about 40 miles northwest of Las Vegas as the vulture flies. But we wouldn't be going that far. I'd been playing with the coordinates on the onboard GPS system, zooming in and out on the newly installed Nevada topographical maps that the $100 had bought me back at the dealership and found that we would be turning off, east, about five miles before town.

The special program was keeping abreast of the latitude and longitude as we were moving, and just before we hit the 36°55' north position I noticed a heavier sanded area of the shoulder that would allow us an easier ramp off the highway and into the rock and sagebrush. I pumped my brakes a couple of times to warn Stephano and slowed down to take the exit. We moved gingerly over the hard-packed dirt, apparently on some kind of slight trail — one that may have been used years ago.

We dipped over a few small inclines, dodging various types of cacti, Mojave yucca, and creosote bush. I aimed the nose of the Chrysler 300 in the direction that I hoped would intersect the coordinates I'd uncovered. I checked behind and saw that Stephano was having no difficulties whatsoever in handling the terrain.

As I rounded a small rocky dune, I had to swerve wide to avoid the wooden remains of what looked like a tower. The numbers on the GPS screen began to slowly flash, and as I crawled ahead at about five miles per hour the numbers flashed more frequently and held fast at the sound of a low, resonating beep. I stopped the car, put it into park, and turned off the ignition.

Stephano did the same, and a few moments later the two of us stood there stretching.

"Jesus Christ," he said, lifting his sunglasses and doing a 360-degree turn. "This is like the middle of nowhere. . . ."

He was right. The land was a dried-out basin of lava rock and cracked potash soil. Sprigs of various vegetation fought for survival, and it seemed as if nothing in the way of wildlife could exist in the environment. One of the most dramatic discoveries was the absence of sound. For someone used to hearing bells and whistles and coins dropping into buckets all day, the impact was eerie.

"You hear that?" I asked.

"Yeah," Stephano replied. "Absolutely nothing."

The afternoon sun was beating down, but thankfully it was October and not July. Nevertheless, as the two of us pulled the shovels and equipment from the Chrysler's trunk, we donned a couple of Oasis Hotel baseball caps that had been left in the car.

"So this is it?"

"That's what the GPS says. Or thereabouts. Don't forget, without the accuracy of the full coordinates, it could be anywhere a football field from here," I said, jabbing the business end of a long spade into the caked earth.

"What's that out there?" Stephano asked, looking off to the north.

I did the same. "Don't know. But it could be the fence for Nellis or the testing grounds. Either way, we don't want to go too far in that direction."

Stephano put the shoulder strap of his metal detector around himself and flipped one of the switches. Immediately, the machine gave off a collection of clicks and clacks, which he silenced by resetting the oscillator measurement dials. He gave me a thumbs-up and started to search, throwing a couple of coins a few feet in front of himself for testing.

I took a box of wooden stakes Orsina had used for her tomato plants and laid it on the ground where Stephano had begun his sweep. I took out one stake and hammered it into hard soil. This would be our "ground zero." For a point of reference, I took a spool of string and another stake and walked 20 paces south. I tied the string from one post to the other, marking our western boundary. I did the same to the north and the east, and in a few minutes we had our first quadrant. I attached a red rag to the string so Stephano could slide it along and mark his progress as he made six-foot swaths with his detector.

While he combed the surface, I took a shovel and pick and started digging away at some of the rises of dirt: dunes that might be old army bunkers. The two of us took a break every half hour or so in the shade of the Explorer's rear door and drank from a six-pack of water I'd stopped for while getting gas before meeting up with Stephano in front of the Rio. At around five o'clock, after seven or eight dunes and into our fifth 360-square-foot quadrant, we switched tasks.

The picking and shoveling had been hard, sweaty work, where the combing and sweeping of the metal detector was monotonous and boring. I had to throw the hammer out in front of me every once in a while just to give me a thrill and make sure the machine was working.

At around 6 p.m., while we were into our eighth quadrant and 12th dune, I realized the excitement of the hunt had all but withered, and I was now beginning to have second thoughts about whether we were on the right track. What if the coordinates were off? What if our calculation was off? Christ, what if the numbers had not been to identify a location for a map but for a Swiss bank account? Or, as many believed, what if Carmine Bonello had taken the money as well as some floozy and shacked up in Cuba? Hell, we could spend six months looking for something that wasn't even there.

These pessimistic doubts echoed so loudly in my head I almost missed the sudden clickety-clack of the detector. It vanished as I completed my sweeping arc and returned when I swept back. I looked down to make sure I hadn't thrown the hammer; then I called out excitedly for Stephano to bring a shovel.

He double-checked the reading without saying a word, but I could tell by the sparkle in his eye that he liked what he saw. He drew a spot with the toe of his shoe and motioned for me to start to dig.

The earth was caked and crusted, but no match for my enthusiasm. Within four or five shovelfuls, I hit something firm yet pliable. Stephano took another shovel, and we started going sideways, clearing out a two-foot by one-foot strip.

A minute later we found that what we had hit was black and thicker than cardboard. We cleaned a little more and found what had set the detector off: a big copper clasp and a metal handle. Stephano and I looked at each other; then I shrugged and started digging out more.

Five minutes later we had what looked like a big guitar case. Stephano leaned over and opened it up. Nothing. "What the hell?" he said.

Okay, I thought to myself, let's look at this logically. Here we are, in the middle of absolutely nowhere, and we find a musician's instrument case. That's strange in itself, but where the hell was the instrument? Surely one wasn't so despondent about one's musical ability that one would drive out here and leave the case by itself. Christ, that would be like a car mechanic not being able to fix a car and dropping his empty tool box in the middle of a lake!

"There has to be an explanation. . . . "

"You're damn right!" Stephano started digging and said, "Why would anybody bring out an empty case? The instrument probably won't have enough metal on it to register, but, still, it's got to be somewhere around here."

I started combing the area once more, and in two or three more steps the detector went off like a knight's armor through an airport detector. Even Stephano looked up at the noise. We didn't bother marking any spots with our shoes; we just started digging like two crazy men on Treasure Island.

Stephano hit something, and it made a light clinking sound. He widened his cut, and when the earth was loose he went to his knees and started scraping away the dirt with his hands. "Yes!" he shouted.

"What is it?"

He yanked on a piece of tied-up cloth, and a canvas bag popped out of the ground like a rabbit out of a hat. It appeared heavy, and as Stephano worked the opening wider the bag gave way, and the contents spilled out through his dirt-covered hands. Silver coins. And lots of them. Hundreds of quarters and half-dollars.

A few inches down my shovel hit and broke through what sounded like a bunch of branches. I cleared away a three-foot circle and discovered that they weren't branches at all; they were bones. I had pierced a ribcage with my shovel. There was no trace of internal organs or body matter evident, most of which would have been lost to the desert carnivores, the rest to time.

"Uh, Stephano. . . . "

By this time, he had uncovered two more bags, both full. He looked up from his silver coins with a big grin on his face. "Yeah?"

"I think you might want to have a look at this."

"You found another case?"

"Uh, no. But I might have solved one."

He crawled the short distance on his hands and knees. "What is it?"

I reached down and picked up two of the severed ribs.

Stephano whistled through his teeth. "Are you thinking what I'm thinking?"

"Probably," I said. "Can you clear out more of this? Try down the left side. See if you can find a hand."

"Why? You think you're going to find fingerprints or something?"

"No, but we might find a ring. Or a watch."

Stephano realized my train of thought. "Good idea," he said, already clearing away the dirt with his hands.

I picked up the metal detector and ran it around the immediate area. It didn't take long. About three feet to the right of the skeletal remains I got another hot hit. I went down five or six inches and felt a piece of thick metal. I then used my hands and finally came up with the result of my search: a first-generation Smith & Wesson nine millimeter.

Parts of the Bonello puzzle were starting to fit together. The safety was off. I popped the clip and found it full. That told me a whole lot more.

"You were right," Stephano called out. "I've found something. A watch, a wedding band, and a key on a chain."

I brought the pistol over and showed it to him. "Nice piece. Brings back a lot of old memories. Had one of those before I had my first bicycle."

I reached down into the excavation and pulled the ring along the spindle of bone. I didn't want to break any more bones than I had to, so I fiddled around with the leather strap of the watch until I got it off.

"Try the skull area."

Stephano looked at me. "I think I know what you're after."

I nodded and went back to the jewelry.

The watch was a Rolex "Oyster," a fine piece for its time. The wedding band was 24-karat gold, unadorned, and carried the inscription "August 21, 1954, *Forever.*" I put the two pieces in my pocket with the key and chain, clicked on the safety on the S&W, and tucked it in the back of my waistband.

"Hey, Jake. Have a look." Stephano had cleared away most of the dirt from the skull. "This what you're looking for?" He had a finger in each of the two holes spaced about three inches apart in the forehead.

I pursed my lips and nodded. "Classic hit."

"Yeah. You want me to dig for the slugs?"

"Nah, I don't think it'll do us much good," I replied. "Let's leave that for the body boys at the coroner's office. We've got all we need for an ID, I think."

The two of us went over to the Explorer and drained the last of the water.

"Well, you wanna keep digging today?" Stephano asked.

I looked at the western sky. "It's getting late. Let's call it a day. Why don't we mark the area and come back tomorrow?"

"Sure. It'll give us a fresh shot at it."

"Well, keep in mind there might not be anything out there. If that's Carmine Bonello lying in that hole, there's a good chance the rest of the money is gone."

"You think so? What if the shooter just took what he could, except for the heavy coins, and took off? Maybe he didn't even know about the rest of it."

"Maybe. Let's not draw any conclusions yet. Right now I want to show what we found to Mrs. Bonello and see if she can identify the jewelry. If it's him, we should probably see what she wants us to do about it."

"You're right. She might not want us to do anything."

"We'll have to keep our eyes open for those bozos in the Lexus. I think they've got the treasure scent and aren't going to give up without a fight."

"Maybe we should let them follow us out here," suggested Stephano. "We could do a little one on one with them. You know, end your freeze-out. Last team alive gets the prize."

"I don't know. Let's sleep on it."

We packed up our gear, left our markings, and placed a number of stakes well into the ground on our way out to make sure we could find our way back the next day with the boys in blue.

# Chapter

I told Stephano to head back to the Bonello estate. Covered in dirt and in dire need of a good cleansing, I told him I would come by around nine that evening to talk to Mrs. Bonello. He told me that would be fine, and in case he was busy washing or tasting Orsina's tomato sauce he gave me the security code for the gate in the drive.

Judging by the expressions I got while walking through the lobby of the Oasis, I must have looked like a homeless person ready to gamble his can collection. I made it to my room after convincing Security I was who I said I was.

I finished up in the bathroom, threw on a hotel bathrobe, and sat in a comfortable leather recliner. I sipped a cold Corona and watched the blank, dark television screen, deep in thought.

Reflecting on our discovery, I was coming to the conclusion that things did not look good for finding either Carmine alive or unearthing his cache. I didn't know what DNA forensics could find at the Bonello residence after all this time in order to identify the body officially, but the watch, ring, and gun were good enough for me. I called Oakley to tell him what I'd found, but he was out of the office.

The hot desert sand combined with the hard work and warm shower had done me in. The clock read 8:14 when I awoke with a start. It was Angelica, knocking.

"Well, Mr. Sleepy Head, it's time to get up." She scampered through the doorway and into my suite. The heady scent of lavender followed behind her, awakening my senses. She was wearing tight, low-cut, black jeans and a copper-colored knit sweater that fit her perfectly, everywhere. Her thick hair was loose and fell naturally to her shoulders. It was an outfit that would succeed in meeting her grandmother's standards and please most of mankind at the same time.

I ruffled my unkempt hair and yawned. "I could sleep for a week."

"You can sleep when you're dead. Get your ass in gear. I was talking to *nonna* about an hour ago, and she told me Stephano said you were coming over and that I should drive with you. She said for us not to eat too much because Orsina was making spaghetti and meatballs for dinner. *Nonna* seemed real eager to see you. Have you come up with anything?"

I held back a yawn with my fist. "Some. It's a long, complicated story. I'll tell it to everyone when we get there."

"Well, hurry up. I'm starved." She turned into the kitchenette and broke a finger from a hand of bananas. She plopped herself into a deep loveseat with her legs over the arm and pulled the first piece of skin back off the fruit. "You know this is my second-to-last night in Vegas, don't you?" she said in a soft voice.

I cleared my throat. "Um, no. Really? Time flies."

She was on her second piece of skin, but she was looking steadily at me. "Uh-huh."

"You've had a pretty exciting time, I bet," I said with a chuckle and then turned serious. "Although I'm real sorry about those guys attacking you and everything."

"I hadn't planned on that kind of excitement," she admitted as she finished with the peel. "But, you know, under the right circumstances, and with the right guy, being attacked —"

Before she could finish her sentence or start to eat her banana, I turned and went to my bedroom. I put on jeans and a light pullover sweater and threw on a sports jacket. After I put the watch, ring, and gun into an inside pocket, I looked at myself in the mirror.

If I didn't look like a million bucks, I could at least look like a guy who was trying to find it. I took a deep breath and reminded myself that I had to put up with Angelica for only another 24 hours, and then I could get my social life back on track.

**Chapter**

We arrived at the Bonello estate just after nine. Dusk had fallen, and the streets were quiet and empty as I turned the Chrysler into the drive. I stopped before I punched in the security code and sat there for a moment.

"Well?" asked Angelica. "Are we going in or not?"

I dropped the transmission back into reverse and moved us back onto the street. "In a second. I just want to check something out."

I cruised the nearby streets for a couple of minutes.

"What are you looking for?" asked Angelica.

"Either the two guys who jumped us at my place during the week or a silver Lexus."

"Cool," she said, lighting up a cigarette.

We drove past the house in the other direction when suddenly Angelica called out, "Hang on. What's that?" She was pointing across the street at what looked to be a two-story professional building with a small parking lot in front. In one of the spaces, and all alone, was what appeared to be a new silver Lexus. I slowed down and scanned the windows of the building.

"There's no lights on in the building," said Angelica.

"That's what I was thinking, too."

I turned the car across the street and entered the parking lot with my high beams on the Lexus. It was empty. I jotted down the plate number and returned to the gate.

The security code worked, and the gates parted to allow us through. Since the driveway up to the house was lit with garden lights, I turned off the headlamps and nosed the Chrysler toward the house in stealth mode. I wasn't sure why, and it was probably all for nothing, but something in my gut just didn't sit right. Either that or I was really looking forward to Orsina's spaghetti and meatballs.

I pulled up in front and parked there. The house was brightly lit, as if company was expected. I turned and looked to the second floor of the garage, but Stephano's apartment was dark — one place inviting and the other not.

"Stay here for a minute and wait, Angelica."

"Where are you going?"

"I'm going to look around first. Something isn't right."

"And you think that silver car has something to do with it?"

"It might or might not. But it's worth being sure. Have you got your cell phone?"

She nodded and pulled it from a burgundy suede purse.

"Okay, call your grandmother's number. If they're making dinner, they'll be in the kitchen, at the back of the house."

"What do you want me to say?"

"No matter who answers, tell them I slept in and that we're just leaving the Oasis and should arrive within the hour. But be yourself, Angelica."

She seemed confused, but she dialed anyway and a moment later mouthed the words *it's ringing.*

I nodded, and we waited. Her eyebrows furrowed, and she hunched her shoulders. "There's no answer."

"Okay, look. Wait a minute and try it again. Tell whoever answers what

I told you; we'll be an hour. Do not get into any kind of conversation. Just keep it short and hang up. And stay in the car."

"You're scaring me, Jake. Where are you going?"

I turned to her and took her hand. "Don't be scared. I'm just going to check things out."

"If anything happens to you. . . ."

I patted her hand. "Nothing's going to happen to me. I'm on a roll."

Even in the darkness of the car's interior, I could see her eyes were moist.

"Here," I said. "Take my seat. If anything goes wrong, take off. The gates will open automatically. Get out to the street and call 911. You understand?"

Angelica nodded. She crawled over the console between us, wrapped her arms around my neck, and hugged me as tight as she could. Words were not required. Her trembling body spoke volumes.

A minute later I was going around the main house with my back to the ivied walls, skirting in and out of bushes. I'd taken out the old gun that I'd found that afternoon and was holding it in the aimed and armed position. I wasn't about to try the pistol: it was caked with sand, and I was afraid of being hit in the face with a back flash. I was simply using it as a prop for a stalemate — or as a hammer for knocking someone out cold.

I had worked my way around to the back of the house when I heard the phone ring. I went up to one of the open kitchen windows, where the aroma of garlic and tomato attacked my olfactory system. My stomach began to make noises, but the gurgling was caused by the distasteful sight of Tony and Lip standing in the middle of the Bonello kitchen. Even worse, Olivia and Orsina were both tied to kitchen chairs. Orsina was disheveled, with her eyes closed and her chin on her chest. One of Olivia's eyes was slightly discolored and closed, but she sat defiantly.

Tony was speaking, telling Angelica that he was Stephano and that everyone was waiting for her arrival. I was glad to see him limping and pacing in pain. When the call was disconnected, Tony said, "They'll be here in less than an hour."

Lip's face was crestfallen. "Jeez, I don't think I can wait that long."

I was also glad to see him wearing a huge gauze pad wrapped around his left hand, almost the size of a boxing glove.

I tried to get a full look at the interior of the kitchen and noticed Stephano was missing. I glanced over to the side door of the garage and realized the light over the door was also dark, and I knew it was on a timer. Turning quietly from the window, I ran across the walkway. As I approached the garage door, my shoes stepped on pieces of glass, and they broke into even smaller pieces. I looked up at the light and saw that it had been smashed. I turned the door handle and went in.

The interior of the large garage was dark, for the most part, but down at the end, near the Bugatti, the area was lit up by a bank of long fluorescent lightbulbs. Sitting at the bottom of the stairs was Stephano. I approached him slowly.

"Stephano," I called out, "it's Jake."

His head jerked slightly but never really came up off his chest. I got up beside him and involuntarily sucked in my breath. His hands hung limply in his lap, and his back was to the thick wooden pole I'd been held against earlier. His arms and torso were tied tightly to the post with rope. There was blood all around him. The evidence of torture was everywhere. He had been cut and sliced in numerous places, and a box of kitchen salt told me they had taken their time to inflict as much pain as possible. I noticed a bolt cutter lying on the cement floor and was about to try to use it to cut through his binding when I saw the blood on the blades. I looked over to Stephano and down to his lap and noticed the fingers and thumb had been severed from his left hand. I lifted his chin to check his vitals, and my hand came away from his throat coated with warm blood. His throat had been cut — but only enough that he would suffer a slow death.

"Jake. . . ."

I almost jumped at the mention of my name, but I was relieved to see he was still alive.

"It's me, Stephano. Save your breath. I'm going to call for help."

I put the useless handgun down, felt in my pockets for my cell phone, and realized I had left it in the car. But then it dawned on me: what would happen to the ladies in the house if Tony heard sirens coming up the drive?

"Shit!" I hissed.

Stephano must have read my mind. "Ms. B. . . ."

I touched him on the shoulder. "I'll be back in a minute."

There was no way I could call in the local cops on something like this. They'd come in blaring and blasting, and there would be at least two more dead: Olivia and Orsina. And what about Angelica?

"Damn!" I had to warn Angelica not to call in right now either.

I went to the door, peeked out, and sprinted down the drive to the front door. She was still there. I ran over to the driver side and slid to a stop when I saw that the driver's door was open.

"What the. . . ?"

I looked over the roof and noticed the front door of the house ajar.

"Jesus Christ. . . ."

I ran back around the house and crept up to the same kitchen window and found Angelica. Unfortunately, she was being held from behind by Lip, who had one thick arm around her and the other hand holding onto the back of her hair. He had a wide smile on his stupid face, and it grew bigger each time he yanked her head. Tony was slapping her in the face with the back of his hand every time he asked her a question. He might have smiled too except for the fact that he looked like he was "powdered" up to the gills and probably fantasizing about her instead.

I was extremely worried about Orsina; she hadn't moved a muscle since I'd seen her last. Olivia was alive and well and spewing all kinds of venomous threats and curses in Italian at the two enforcers.

Tony hit Angelica with another shot. "Whatta you mean he didn't come with ya? I know he's here. What did he tell you about the money?"

She mumbled something, and he leaned over.

"What didja say?"

Angelica looked up. "I said. . . ." Then she spat a mixture of saliva and blood and caught Tony right in the face. When he brought his hands up to wipe it off, she flicked out a leg in one quick motion and nailed him square in the sac. Tony's eyes went wide, and he fought for his breath. Lip yanked harder on her hair.

"You bastards!" yelled Olivia. "I pray you rot in hell."

"Put her out," Tony coughed.

"For how long, Tone?"

"Twenty, thirty minutes should do it."

Lip used two of his sausage fingers and squeezed a vertebra or nerve somewhere at the back of her neck, and Angelica fell to the floor like a sack of laundry.

Olivia cried out in Italian.

Tony gave her an evil grin. "Let's work the old lady over again."

There wasn't a whole lot I could do, so I did the first thing that came to mind. I put a fist through one of the windowpanes, stuck my face in the open window, and called out, "Aren't you two a couple of tough pussies. Why don't you take a shot at me, girls?"

And son of a bitch that's just what they did.

They both yanked out their guns and fired without even aiming. I jumped back, and every pane of glass blew out of the window. I rolled to the side, ran to the garage door, and entered it on the run. Two shots coughed out, and I heard both slugs hit the side of the wall.

I sprinted toward Stephano and turned to go up the stairs. I had taken my first two steps up when the side door flew open.

"There he is!" one of them shouted.

Two guns started firing, and hunks of the wooden steps and railing started breaking apart all around me. I was an open target. I jumped over the far railing and bounced off the side of the Bugatti and landed on the cement facing Stephano.

"Okay, we got him trapped."

"He gotta piece?"

"Don't know. Be cool. There's no hurry. He ain't going anywhere."

I took a quick look to see if the keys were in the ignition of the Bugatti. It cost the opposite front fender two bullets. I fell back to the cold ground, eyes wide, my mind working overtime.

Stephano was looking at me and trying to speak: "Aunka, aunka," was what I heard, but with the blood in his mouth and the air leaking out his throat I couldn't decipher what he was saying. He looked down at his foot and willed it to move an inch. I tried to get closer to him, and another round fired. This one caught Stephano in the left shoulder, and he winced and yelled out at me, "Uncle!"

Now it dawned on me what he was saying.

I crawled to the bottom riser of the stairs and reached toward Stephano's outstretched leg. I was only partially in the shadows, whereas Stephano was not. I could hear them whispering to each other from beyond the Explorer. I didn't have much more time.

"Morgan," Tony yelled out. "You got nowhere to go. You don't even got a gun."

"Okay, Kreskin! Why don't you step out into the light and find out if you're right?"

I crawled another few inches toward Stephano.

"Big deal! So what? There's two of us and only one of you. Oh, sorry," he corrected himself and started to laugh. "Two of us and one and a quarter of you!"

I could feel the tip of Stephano's work boot and pulled his leg toward me another couple of inches.

"Tony," Lip whispered, but it still came out clearly across the garage. "Lemme take this fuggin' prick!"

"Shut up!"

"But you promised me, Tone. . . ."

"Just tell us what you found out about the money. We're not stupid, you know. We saw you guys gathering equipment to go off into the desert. And we saw the dirt on the Explorer out here when you got back."

"Well, genius, it's the part in between that's important."

"And that's the part you're gonna tell us, if you wanna live, 'cause we also found the bags of coins you brought back, so we know you found the missing money. You got one minute to think about it."

I had worked a finger into a lace and pulled Stephano's leg as far as it would reach, but I was still short. I'd have to crawl out into the open. I got up on my knees with my ass still covered by the rise of the stairs and pushed myself out as quietly as I could. One of them caught the action as I slid Stephano's pant leg up, and a bullet caught him in the left thigh.

"Go, go," coughed Stephano as I unclasped the thumb break ankle holster and tugged out the Beretta Cheetah. I slid back and got to my feet.

A couple more shots came: one into the railing, about four inches from my head, and the other into the beautiful Bugatti. The Beretta was a .32 caliber and only had a clip of seven, so I'd have to fire sparingly.

"Your minute's up, Morgan! Tell us where the money is."

"Let me draw you a map, and I'll mail it to you."

I could just make out Lip's big dark shadow at the far corner of the workshop and could hear the two of them conferring across the garage.

"Don't be stupid. He won't *really* mail it, you moron."

I tried to formulate my next few moves while the two of them bickered.

"Hey, Morgan. Lip said he got all hot and bothered holding that young piece of ass against him in the kitchen." I had Tony placed somewhere just past the van and over the hood of the Explorer. "He wants me to let him bring her back in here and have you watch him finish the job, so to speak."

"Lip likes girls?" I asked, trying to pinpoint both their positions. "Who would have guessed? I figured the two of you were into each other. Are you the pitcher or the catcher, Lip?" The more I could get them to talk, the closer I could home in on them.

"Fug you, Morgan."

"How's the nose, Lip? Still breathing through your mouth, I hear. Or is that just a family trait?"

"You a fuggin' dead man. . . ."

I just about had him in my sights.

"I hear you've now got a hole in your hand for when you play with yourself."

"Okay, that's it. . . ."

I fired off a shot at Lip and heard it hit some glass near him.

"Jesus!" he shouted, flailing about and knocking cans and jars everywhere and falling to the floor. He knocked over a bunch of tools as he got up again.

"Lip, you okay?"

"Christ, Tony! He winged me!"

"That just leaves you to chase me, Gimp!" I swung around the thick newel post of the staircase and fired off a shot where I thought Tony might be. I caught his attention, because a track of bullets followed me all the way up the stairs.

"Lip, you stay down here," I heard him yell as I turned right at the top of the stairs, ran to Stephano's room, and locked the door behind me.

I ran to the far corner and pushed open the magnetic lock of the panic closet. It wasn't long after I'd closed the closet that I heard the splinter of wood and the apartment door being kicked open. Tony wasn't rushing into any shootout, so I collected myself and switched on the little night-light. An array of weapons adorned the wall, and I selected a spare clip for the Beretta and a Remington double-barrel, hammer-cocked, 12 gauge shotgun, an oldie but goodie. I picked up a Velcro wristband that held six more shells and placed it around my wrist. Glancing through the little peephole, I saw Tony looking through the doorway in every direction, trying to decide where I might be.

I held onto the Beretta and tucked the Remington under my arm. At the last second, I grabbed a machete off the wall and clipped it to my belt; then I took a deep breath, grabbed the pole with my free arm, and slid silently into the darkness below.

I hit the bottom with absolutely no noise. I squinted through a small peephole and saw Lip standing over Stephano, glancing now and again up the stairs.

The closet door opened without a sound. I stepped out into the garage, just a few feet behind the Explorer and 15 or so feet from the two men. As I tried to lower my heart rate to an acceptable level, Lip began to kick Stephano in the ribs, apparently just for the hell of it.

I moved the shotgun to my left hand, not wanting to risk hitting Stephano. I held the Beretta in my outstretched right, aimed at Lip's back, and was pleased to note that there was no tremble.

"Hey, do you only beat up girls, old ladies, and invalids, tough guy?"

Lip's entire body froze, and his arms came out to his sides. The right still held his gun. "How da fug?"

"Why don't you drop that piece and try beating me up, you pussy?"

His right arm twitched in anticipation, and I had a bad feeling.

"Drop it, you dumb shit. Last warning."

And it was.

Lip swung around in a blur, and we both fired at the same time. His bullet caught me in the left thigh, but my aim had been steadier and fixed on his chest, and that's exactly where I hit him. He fell against the post Stephano was tied to and then over on his side with a thud.

My leg was burning like hell, but I knew Tony would have heard the shots and was probably wondering what the hell Lip was doing. I limped over to Stephano, withdrew the machete, and cut the bindings in three hacks with the razor-sharp weapon. Not that it would matter much right now; Stephano wasn't going anywhere. He was able to move his arms and hands slightly, and that was a good sign, but the blood covering him was thick. I feared the worst.

"Gnn," he said hoarsely, pointing a finger at the 12 gauge. I wasn't sure if he wanted to back me up or put himself out of misery, but I held the rifle out in front of him, careful to watch which way he was going to point it. I noticed he still had fire in his eyes and was glad to see him flick off the safety, aim the gun up the stairs, and place the twin barrels on his raised knee.

"That's right, Stephano. Cover me," I told him, knowing it would help fuel his pride.

I turned and limped up the steps, then suddenly stopped. I'd forgotten how many shots I had fired from the seven-bullet clip and decided I'd better reload. I popped the clip from the Beretta and tossed it into my left jacket pocket.

As I was about to reach in my right pocket for the other clip, Tony called out from upstairs: "Lip, quit fuckin' around down there and give me a hand. That asshole Morgan disappeared."

I was on the fourth step, in no-man's land, railings on both sides and nowhere to go. I fumbled for the clip and found it, and just as I brought it out Tony's voice called out again from just around the corner. "Lip, didja hear me?"

My hands started to shake as violently as my leg, and I had a problem getting the clip to go in. Just as I was about to slap it home, a voice right above me said, "Well, what do we have here?" Tony was four steps above me, with his gun pointing at my head. I held the Beretta out over the railing. "Good idea, Houdini. Drop it over the side."

I know when I'm up the creek without a paddle. I did as I was told.

Tony noticed the blood on my pants and me favoring my left leg. "You don't look so good, Morgan."

"Oh, yeah? You should see the other guy. . . ."

His eyes scanned the garage for his cohort. "Well, his nine lives were almost used up anyway. Now, Morgan, I'm only going to ask you once more. Where's the money?"

I heard a click from behind me, and then another. Then, a loud gurgling sound.

Tony heard the gurgle, too. "Is that old wop still alive?" he asked, trying to see around me. "I tried to make it last, but I never thought he'd fight this long."

That's when it dawned on me; Tony was on the landing and couldn't see Stephano at the bottom of the stairs because I was blocking his view. Now the significance of the two clicks grew louder, and I quickly improvised a routine.

"Please, Tony," I begged. "I'll do whatever you say. Just don't hurt me." I concentrated on the burn growing in my thigh, and tears began to well up.

Tony cocked his head, and then he grew a great big smile. "I knew it! I knew it!" he chimed. "I always knew you were a momma's boy."

"I'll take you to the money," I cried. "There's millions out there, Tony." I clasped my hands together in prayer and slowly lowered myself to my knees. "Millions, Tony. . . . More money than you'll ever be able to spend in a lifetime. . . ." He was mesmerized by the sensuous references to money that were coming from my mouth. "Just don't hurt me." I flattened myself on the steps and started crying out softly. "Please, I'm begging you."

"Holy shit," he said. "More money than I could spend in a lifetime? Really?"

I lifted my head. "Sure, unless you don't have much time left." I placed both my hands behind my head.

He blinked a couple of times. My last words didn't fit with all the other wonderful things I'd been saying. I buried my head into the stairs and tensed.

"What do you mean I don't have much —" He suddenly became aware of his tortured victim at the bottom of the stairs. "Oh, shit —"

The first barrel caught Tony in the chest and straightened him up. The second threw him back against the wall. He flattened there for a second or two and then slowly slid to a sitting position on the landing. Tracks of blood trailed his way down. I looked behind me and saw that Stephano had dropped the shotgun to his side. He fought to keep his eyes open. A smile had formed on his lips.

I limped up the remaining stairs to the landing, kicked down Tony's gun, and stared at his lifeless form. "What's wrong with being a momma's boy, tough guy?"

# Chapter

As I slowly made it down the steps, the shock of being shot overcame the adrenalin rush, and I began to feel like I was going to pass out. I held onto the railing tightly as I reached the bottom; the sounds of sirens could be heard in the distance.

Stephano said "Gnn" again and pointed to the Beretta lying on the cement between the staircase and the Bugatti.

I did as I thought I was being told, picked up the pistol, and took it to him. His right hand was shaking, but he managed to pop the full clip and hand it to me. He motioned to my left pocket, and I took out the half-used clip, which he inserted into the Beretta and pushed it closed. He looked up at me, took a piece of his shirt, and wiped down the metal; then he put the pistol in his hand with his finger on the trigger.

I was amazed at the man's stamina. Here he was with five missing digits, a couple dozen knife wounds, two bullets in his side, a slit throat, and his mind was still able to comprehend the implications — self-defense or not.

I had one leg wound and felt like I was falling apart. I slid down and rested against the newel post of the staircase looking at my friend. "You don't have to do this, Stephano."

The blare of sirens could be heard coming up the drive, as could the chirping of rubber as the emergency vehicles came to a stop.

He nodded and smiled.

I sat back and closed my eyes and let the light-headedness take over.

I came to sometime later, overwhelmed by the sounds of official voices and the sense of hands working on my legs. I was on my back, on the garage floor, and people were milling about above me. My eyes focused on a familiar face.

"So, what do we have here?" asked a solemn Lieutenant Oakley to a young Boulder City cop.

"Well, at first it looked like some kind of home invasion with three women beat up in the house. Then it looked like the St. Valentine's Day Massacre with what looked like four dead guys in the garage. Turns out we got two dead, one on his way, and one with a superficial."

I sincerely hoped I was the superficial.

"If it means anything," said Oakley, "I can vouch for this guy."

He hadn't seen my eyes flutter open. "Gee, Lieutenant, I didn't think you cared. . . ."

Oakley was taken aback. "Get this joker up and on a stretcher, pronto. I wanna talk to him outside." With that, he stomped out of the garage.

About 10 minutes later, I was rolled out on a gurney to the covered walkway of the house. Oakley was talking to another guy in a suit.

"Thanks for helping us out, Lieutenant. It would have taken us a while to tie this in with the Vincent DeMarco shooting you had last week."

"No problem. I've helped out in Boulder before." He looked over at me as the paramedic applied the manual brake. "When I heard the Bonello name over the radio, I kind of had a feeling this guy would end up being involved anyway."

The other cop looked down at me and asked Oakley, "Is he a good guy or bad guy?"

Oakley thought about it for a second. "I can't decide."

"Well, thanks again, Lieutenant."

They shook hands, and the Boulder cop departed.

There had to be at least 15 cop cars and ambulances on the property. Their flashing lights and static radio messages gave an eerie look and feel to the backyard. Oakley unwrapped two sticks of chewing gum and handed me one.

"I came here expecting a spaghetti and meatball dinner," I told him.

"Well, too bad. Wrigley's will have to do." He crossed his big arms across his chest. "So what happened?"

I told him the part about finding what I thought were Carmine Bonello's remains and that I had left a message with him to tell him that earlier. He said he would confirm that later. He was more interested in what had happened here.

I figured he had already talked with Angelica, so I told him exactly what had happened at the house.

"You broke the window and challenged them to a fight?"

"What was I supposed to do?"

"Jesus. Go on. What about the garage?"

"What do *you* think happened there?"

"Look, Morgan, you can only push this buddy-buddy thing so far. Murder is still murder, and that's my job."

"So tell me what you think," I told him. "Otherwise, I'm getting very sleepy. . . ."

"You know, you're the only meatball out here," he sighed. "Okay, this is what the locals think happened."

I lay back on my pillow and listened. I was a sucker for a happy ending.

"They say it looks like you and the old man were cornered in the back after he was tortured and you came upon him. Because of the gun placement and initial prints, they put you around that old car taking one in the leg from the big guy with the pea shooter."

"It was a lot bigger —"

"You managed to cut free the old guy, and he was able to retrieve his ankle gun, even with all his wounds, and unload on the big guy, center bull's-eye. One down."

I nodded my head for him to go on. "Somehow the old guy got his shotgun, and when the other bad guy came down the steps he let him have both barrels. Two down."

"He's a friggin' hero," I admitted.

"Was."

I lifted my head from the pillow. "*Was?*"

Oakley nodded. "He didn't make it. But he managed to sign an affidavit of the cop's findings."

"Then that's my story, too, Lieutenant. It happened just like Stephano said."

Oakley looked like he had a bad taste in his mouth. He removed the gum, rolled it up in the original wrapper, and stuffed it in his jacket pocket. Then he leaned over and said softly so only I could hear, "I don't think that's exactly the way it went down, Morgan. Not by a long shot. But there are two less scumbags on my streets and a murder back at your apartment I can tie them to. Whatever happened, you and the old guy did good. Maybe you'll tell me about it some day."

**Chapter** KING QUEEN JACK

Oakley and I still haven't had that conversation. Oh, sure, I had to fill out all kinds of reports and statements, both that night and through Sunday morning, but the exact details of how the shotgun got into Stephano's lap and where the extra clip for the Beretta came from never materialized.

It turned out the bullet I'd taken had actually left the leg. The slug had entered the tissue on the side and gone right through without hitting anything vital. It still hurt like hell, though, and I didn't get as much sympathy as I thought I should have. Hell, after another 20 minutes on the stretcher resting and letting the painkillers do their thing, I got up from the gurney and limped into the house.

The ladies, Olivia and Orsina, fussed and fretted over me with food and drink as if I was Indiana Jones and had just saved their homestead from the evil masses. Angelica was appreciative as well, but she had a different kind of look in her eyes, as if she had a totally different kind of reward in mind.

After I refused hospitalization and signed numerous release forms, the paramedics gave me a handful of free woozy pills, and Olivia and I spent some time in the library. The gun had been lost somewhere outside, but I showed her the key and chain, the watch, and the wedding band. She took the ring and stared at it for a long time, wiping a tear away each time a distant memory came forward; then she examined the inscription inside. "Yes," she said softly. "That was our wedding day."

She took the watch next and smiled as she held it against the palm of her hand. "I bought this for him for Christmas the year Sofia was born. He wore it every day."

I could see this was an extremely personal moment for her, and I began to excuse myself.

"Wait, Jake," she requested as she collected her thoughts. "I want you to know how much this means to me. The knowledge that my husband did not leave me." She began to weep, and I passed her a tissue. When she composed herself, she said, "People have no idea of the pain and suffering I have lived with for the past 50 years — the stories, the rumors, the snickering behind my back. Carmine was the love of my life, and I knew in my heart that he would never abandon Sofia or me. As lonely as each night has been without him, a part of him was always with me.

"And now, with my final days approaching, you have made me whole again. I will pass from this life knowing Carmine is waiting for me, with our Sofia, and for that, Jake Morgan, I will never be able to repay you."

We talked about the hidden money, and Olivia decided that for now we would leave it. She explained to me that, if we continued to locate the cache, our lives, but mostly mine, would never again be the same. First, what if the money had not held up to the extreme conditions? Then it would all be for nothing. Not only that, but the original owners would still hold us responsible, and with the demise of two of their people my life would be highly expendable. Their pursuit would be relentless.

Olivia explained that she had another idea and for me to leave her the exact location; then she told me to forget everything I had ever learned about a hidden treasure in the desert just outside Las Vegas. I had to promise her. And I did.

Angelica and I stayed overnight at the Bonello estate, and I made sure my room had a lock. In the morning, after a delicious breakfast of thick bacon, fresh bread, and pampered affection, Angelica and I said our good-byes.

For Angelica, saying good-bye was even harder; she was leaving for New York that night and was worried about her grandmother's health. The two of them spent some special time together alone on the patio that ended with a long hug and a kiss on each other's cheek.

When we got out to the Chrysler, I found a message on my cell phone. Oakley had asked that I meet him at Indian Springs around 10:30 that morning so he and a coroner's rep could exhume what we believed to be Carmine Bonello's remains.

I didn't feel like driving that far with my leg in the shape it was in, and I wasn't sure if operating a vehicle while taking painkillers that would drop a giraffe was against the law.

"I'll drive," Angelica said as she assisted me into the back seat, where I could sit comfortably with my legs up on the bench seat. I was apprehensive. She started the car like a pro, and we moved down the driveway. At the gate, she came to a complete stop and looked in both directions, just the way she was supposed to. I sat back, more reassured, but kept an eye on her.

"I didn't even know for sure if you had a driver's license," I said with a chuckle.

She switched her left signal indicator on and turned right. "I don't," she giggled.

# Chapter

That last ride into the desert seemed ages ago, but it had just been that morning. Now it was three in the afternoon, and I was taking it easy watching my Patriots beat up on the Cowboys. And it wasn't just any old taking it easy like it would have been in my recliner back home. I still had the suite at the Oasis, and I was enjoying a thick bubble bath in the Jacuzzi, watching the built-in color TV, and sipping on a rum punch the size of the Heisman trophy through a curly straw as thick as my baby finger. I couldn't think of anything else I'd rather be doing.

After all, it had been a rough week. I'd been beat up, hit on the head with a metal rod, thrown into fences, dunked in a pool, tossed out of bed, tied up, slapped around until my eyes looked like two rolling dice, shot at multiple times, and hit in the leg — even if the bullet had gone right through!

"Damn it, Jake," I said, toasting myself in the mirrored tile. "You deserve it."

Looking at my reflection, the bubble bath seemed kind of effeminate; but, what the hell, it felt great, it smelled terrific, and no one was around to tell. My aches and pains seemed to melt away.

My reverie was broken by the soft ring of the telephone beside the tub. I pressed the speaker button.

"Hello?"

"Hi, Jake. It's me."

"Hey, Angelica. What's happening?"

"Not much. I just woke up. What are you doing?"

"Me? I'm enjoying a nice manly whirlpool and watching football. You know, guy stuff. We're still on for dinner before I take you to the airport, right?"

"Sure," she said. "But that tub thing sounds like a good idea."

"Go ahead, enjoy yourself. We'll get together around six. Okay?"

She must have clicked off — there was no answer.

I was almost finished with my drink and starting to feel its effect when I thought I heard a noise. I punched down the volume on the keypad on the wall and listened again. Nothing. I turned the game back up, placed a wet wash cloth over my face, and lay back against the head rest. I had just decided to fire up the water jets when I heard someone speak.

"Room service."

I froze. I was afraid to take off the wash cloth because I was sure I recognized the voice.

"Uh, I don't think I ordered —"

"Let's just say I read your mind. Ooh, and I love the bubbles. Are those rose petals?"

"Uh, lilac, actually. Okay, just put it on the table, then. There's money on the kitchen counter. Help yourself."

"I won't fit on the table, silly!"

The cloth was lifted from my face.

"Angelica! What the hell are you doing here?"

Her hair was pulled up, and she was wearing an oversized, thick white bathrobe with the colorful Oasis logo.

"Surprise," she said in a sultry voice.

"I've had enough surprises to last me a lifetime. You have to go."

"But, Jake. I'm leaving tonight. And this is a surprise you'll never forget."

"Angelica, please. . . ."

She smiled and started playing with the knot in her robe. "Does no mean yes?"

"Jesus, Angelica! No means no!"

Her head dropped, and she pouted. "You may have saved my life, Jake. I want to show you my appreciation before I leave."

"Buy me some candy," I stammered. "I like those little Pez things."

"I can be sweeter than any candy. . . ." She had one loop of the belt undone. "What's that smell?" she asked, sniffing.

"Incense."

"Ooh, I love that smell," she cooed. "It really turns me on."

I flicked some water with my foot and tried to put out the fragrant burning stick at the end of the tub.

"Look, Angelica. This isn't right."

There was no denying her. She had the belt completely undone and was about to lower the robe from her shoulders.

And then a buzzer sounded.

Angelica was oblivious. One shoulder was now bare.

The buzzer sounded again.

"The intercom!" I yelped.

Maybe it really was room service. I checked the little keypad, found what I was looking for, and pressed Door Monitor. The Patriots clicked off, and Julius Contini filled the screen.

My life flashed before my eyes. If Big Julie caught a near-naked Angelica in my suite, I might as well fill out the donor card on my driver's license. Maybe he'd just go away if I didn't answer.

Big Julie stuck a thick thumb to the intercom. "Hey, Jake," he yelled, in a metallic voice. "It's me, Contini. Open up. I gotta talk to you." He pressed again. "I know you're in there. Room service said they brought you a

Hurricane Honduras." He laughed. "You pass out already, Ace?"

I pressed the intercom. "Hey, Mr. Contini. Sorry I didn't hear you. I'm in the tub. You want to make it later?"

"No, I gotta talk to you now."

If I hurried, I could probably grab Angelica and throw her back into her room before he was the wiser. I decided that was my best plan.

"Hang on, Mr. C. I'll be right out."

"Okay," I waved to Angelica. "Let's go!"

She must have thought I said "let go," because her bathrobe was sliding from her shoulders and headed for the floor. A couple of seconds later, she stood in all her splendor.

"Don't worry, Ace. I got a master key. I'll let myself in and wait."

I sprang from the tub and grabbed my bathrobe and tried to put hers back on as I put on mine. "Hurry, Angelica. It's your uncle. Into your room!" I gathered her and her robe and ran for the open bathroom door, ignoring the sudden fire shooting through the bandage on my thigh. Just as I was preparing to carry her through the room to her connecting door, the door to my suite started to open.

I spun around and slid back into the bathroom, gently clicking the door closed. I put her robe around her, took her chin in my hand, and forced her to look me in the eye. "Angelica. That is your uncle out there. He is a very powerful man who thinks of you as a child. A child he has to protect. Do you have any idea what will happen to me if he finds you in my room?"

She dropped her eyes and sniffled. "I probably don't want to know, right?"

"That's right, Angelica. I have to go out there and talk to your uncle. Right now he is a very happy man. Let's not make him angry. You stay in here and don't make a sound. I'll come get you as soon as he leaves."

"Okay, Jake," she said softly. "I'm sorry. . . ."

I patted her on the head. "Just remember what I said."

I tied up my robe, left the bathroom, and limped over to my guest.

"Hey, Ace, there you are!"

Julius Contini, of all people, gave me a warm hug. "I want to thank you for everything. You did an outstanding job. Outstanding. I spoke with Olivia this morning, and she told me the whole story. She thinks of you as family, you know. She was heartbroken when she heard about Stephano, but she was really afraid she had lost you in that garage as well. Stephano understood his role as family protector and had accepted the downside. But you, hell, you were virtually an innocent bystander who was doing me a favor."

"She's a wonderful woman. A special friend. I was glad to help both of you."

"Thank you, Jake."

*Goddamn!* As far as I could recall, that was the only time he had called me by name.

"You're welcome, Mr. C. Truly. But right now I think I better get some rest."

"Of course, of course," he said and gave me a slap on the upper arm. "Just let me use the can. I gotta piss like a race horse."

I could see over Contini's shoulder that the bathroom door was open a crack, and I could see a flurry of movement at Big Julie's words. He turned and walked that way.

I didn't know what good it would do to slow him down, but I blurted out, "I hope you don't mind me staying here another couple days. My place should be ready by the middle of the week."

"No problem, Ace, stay as long as you need." He stopped just outside the bathroom door. "Oh, and before I forget, make sure you fill out all the expense forms for the money you spent. I told you I'd take care of all that." He turned again and opened the door to the bathroom and walked in.

I didn't know whether to run down the hall or jump through the window. I probably wouldn't get far either way. Security would grab me before I even stepped into the casino, and I heard the windows of the Oasis were unbreakable. It didn't matter. I was a dead man. I walked over to the window, put my forehead against the glass, and watched the Strip down below. I wondered if this was the last time I'd have this view. There was nothing I could do but wait for the blood-curdling scream that any second would be coming from the bathroom.

I heard the toilet flush, the sink spray, and a whistling tune.

Contini came out into the living room. "A bubble bath? Huh, you never struck me as that type."

He wasn't screaming, and that caught me off guard. "Oh, that. I was so tired I thought it was shampoo." I let out a fake laugh.

"Ah," he said and then smiled. "I guess you thought the incense stick was a cigar?"

I looked down at the carpet with a sheepish grin on my face. "You got me. . . ."

Contini let out a hearty laugh and headed for the exit. "Don't worry, Ace," he said as he opened the door. "Your secret is safe with me." With that he was gone.

I limped away from the window, and Angelica came walking out of the bathroom, dripping and wrapped in her robe. "Is he gone?" she whispered.

I looked at her in astonishment. "How did you do that? There's not even a closet or vanity cupboard in there. Even the shower stall is right across from the toilet."

"Well, when I heard him say he was coming in, I saw there was only one place I could hide."

I raised my brows. "Where?"

She gave me a smile. "In the Jacuzzi. Under all the bubbles."

"But he was in there a couple of minutes. How did you know you could hold your breath that long? You were taking a big chance."

"Not really," she laughed. "You know that big drink you had?"

I nodded for her to go on.

"Well, I jumped in the tub and grabbed the funny straw; then I lay back under the bubbles and used it like a snorkel."

I shook my head back and forth. "Brilliant," I admitted. "Absolutely brilliant."

"Then everything is cool?"

"As a cucumber."

"That reminds me," she said. "Where were we when we were so rudely interrupted?" She began playing with the belt of my robe.

"Ah, that's right," I said. "I almost forgot."

She had an expectant look on her face.

"I'll take care of my robe, Sweetheart," I told her. "You bend over that counter."

"Oh, Jake." Her eyes lit up, and she did as she was told. "You are so nasty!"

"Extremely. Now be quiet and close your eyes." I moved to her side.

"I love it when you order me around!"

"Good. Now pull up the back of your robe."

"I've never done it like this before," she admitted, but she had her robe hiked just above her butt in about two seconds.

"This'll be my first time, too. Now keep your eyes closed."

"They are . . . ooh, Jake."

I raised my open hand above my shoulder and slapped her as hard on the ass as I could. My hand stung, and a red imprint welted up on her tender, nontanned skin.

She yelped, and her eyes went wide. "Why the hell didja do that for? That really hurt!"

I pulled her bathrobe down to her knees. "You asked me where we were when we were so rudely interrupted? Well, you were about to get your ass spanked and sent to your room for sneaking in on me the way you did."

I gently walked her toward her room, opened the connecting door, and guided her inside.

She turned and shot fireballs at me from her eyes. "I hate you, Jake Morgan!"

I gave her a stern look. "Well, if you stop hating me by six o'clock, I'll be waiting for you in the Pyramid Room. A special table for two."

"Yeah, right. Like you can afford the Pyramid!"

"I can't." I smiled, reached for my comp card lying on the table, and waved the piece of plastic in the air. "But Uncle Julie can."

"I'll hate you way past six o'clock."

"We'll have a nice dinner, a couple of drinks, and then I'll drive you to the airport."

She pouted, shot me another look, and closed her side of the connecting door.

"And I hope your stupid Patriots lose, too!" she yelled through the thin door.

"By the way, Angelica," I called back.

"What?"

"I know where you put the other tattoo."

I shut my door quickly. Angelica flung her door open and started hammering with her fists on mine, yelling, "I hate you, I hate you, I hate you!" After she stopped her antics, I put an ear to the thin door and listened. I could have sworn I heard her giggle to herself and say, "Just you wait, Jake Morgan."

# Epilogue

*December 8th*
*2:33 p.m.*
*Somewhere on Las Vegas Boulevard South*

I was driving back from the memorial for Olivia Bonello in Boulder City. Her body had been interred with her husband's, as well as Stephano's, in a private cemetery after her funeral in New Jersey. She had died in her sleep about a month after I last saw her, when she had summoned me to her home for something she wanted me to have.

We had talked prior to that, and she had told me she had decided to give the location of the cache to the family organization back east. They would, in turn, contact the original family in Chicago and offer them the location, on the sworn condition that no retaliation would ever be ordered against any of her family, or associates, over any matter pertaining to the money. I understood that included Angelica, Orsina, and myself. It also seemed that the loss of Stephano and Vincent, and the two goons, was being considered a "wash."

That's how things worked in their world. Chicago accepted the deal and must have found what they were looking for, because Contini said there were a lot of grateful faces and expensive floral wreaths from the Midwest at her funeral.

Right after the shootout in the garage, I was a little disappointed that I wasn't going to end up with anything to offset my nifty code deduction, my desert effort, or the fact that I'd been shot at a couple of hundred times. Hell, I didn't even get the tomato stakes back! Well, at least I wouldn't have to look over my shoulder when I walked down the street.

Still, things had worked out okay.

Angelica showed up in the Pyramid Room around 6:15, just late enough to make her point. She tried to be aloof and distant through the early part of dinner, but she was too young to pull it off. By dessert, we were laughing at the whole Jacuzzi and Julius situation; she even admitted my spank stung so much she thought my hand imprint might end up as a third tattoo. The ride to the airport was quiet for the most part, and the good-bye consisted of a warm hug and a kiss on her forehead.

Angelica later wrote to tell me about her grandmother's funeral and what had been going on with her and her work. I learned that she had quit smoking and was considering getting a real tattoo, maybe when she came out to Las Vegas next September for her birthday.

As I stopped at the busy intersection at Flamingo Road, I couldn't help but be grateful for what Olivia Bonello had done for me. Not only was the Type 57, 1939 Bugatti a reliable and comfortable ride, but it got a lot of attention from people on the Strip. And I loved to show it off. I couldn't even remember where I'd left the Vega.

I'd kept the bullet holes — they gave me a great opening with the girls who wanted to know more about me and my historic vehicle. Oh, sure, sometimes the previous owner's name changed from Dillinger to Siegel, depending on my mood, but everybody enjoyed the stories. I even got a date out of it a couple weeks back from a girl who said she was a distant relative to Bonnie Parker.

And Mrs. Bonello surprised me even more. Just that morning a package came by courier from a law firm in New York to my newly renovated apartment. Inside was $20,000 in $100 bills and a simple thank-you. It was signed "Olivia."

I had to find a seat.

The things I could do with that kind of money fought for my attention all day. I could put a small down payment on a new condo, pay off my credit cards, or get that plasma big-screen television I had seen at the mall. I could even put it in a bank, saving for a rainy day at minimal interest and hoping the bank wouldn't go under.

Or I could do just what I was doing now: pulling into the Bellagio to play $100-$200 Texas Hold 'Em with the big boys!